THE ARTIFACT ENIGMA

THE DANIEL CODEX™ BOOK ONE

JUDITH BERENS MARTHA CARR MICHAEL ANDERLE

The Artifact Enigma (this book) is a work of fiction.

All of the characters, organizations, and events portrayed in this novel are either products of the author's imagination or are used fictitiously. Sometimes both.

A Michael Anderle Production

LMBPN Publishing
PMB 196, 2540 South Maryland Pkwy
Las Vegas, NV 89109

First US edition, October 2018
Version 1.03, January 2019

THE ARTIFACT ENIGMA TEAM

Thanks to Early Readers

Debi Sateren, Michael Robbins, Kathleen Fettig, Terry Hicks Bennett, Bep Hvilsted-Koopman, Mary Morris, John Ashmore, James Caplan, Peter Manis, Angel LaVey, Kelly ODonnell

Thanks to the JIT Readers

James Caplan
Daniel Weigert
Danika Fedeli
Nicole Emens
Peter Manis
Misty Roa
Mary Morris
Keith Verret
Mickey Cocker
Paul Westman

If we've missed anyone, please let us know!

Editor Lynne Stiegler

DEDICATIONS

From Martha

To everyone who still believes in magic
and all the possibilities that holds.
To all the readers who make this
entire ride so much fun.
And to my son, Louie and so many wonderful friends who
remind me all the time of what
really matters and how wonderful
life can be in any given moment.

From Michael

To Family, Friends and
Those Who Love
To Read.
May We All Enjoy Grace
To Live The Life We Are
Called.

CHAPTER ONE

Daniel glanced over his shoulder as he made his way through the dense Parisian crowds. A tall, leggy blonde in a gravity-defying dress gave him a lingering glance as she passed him, but he didn't have time to stop and make something of it. *Next trip.*

He'd hoped the two humans and the tall elf dressed as if he'd stepped out of the *Matrix* would have given up by now, but the bastards had proven damned stubborn. They had tracked him since he'd recovered the amulet, despite the press of people along the sidewalk who separated them. It didn't help that he was tall enough to be seen over most of the crowd.

They'll take away my Spy of the Month badge if I can't lose these amateurs. A glance to his right as he passed a large plate-glass window showed them moving into view.

I'm tired, assholes, and I just want to catch my flight back home.

Daniel frowned and quickened his pace. For a moment,

he considered calling his support for access to drone recon but decided against it. The three idiots following him weren't exactly practicing anything approaching stealth.

He wouldn't need Company resources to handle these fools.

After all, the CIA had enough confidence in him at only thirty years old to send him across the globe without handlers—ever. The occasional researcher or hacker on the Company's payroll as backup was more a bonus than a requirement.

Besides, contacting them might result in them forcing him to stay in France another day.

If I take too long, Pops will start bitching when I get home about how I didn't buy enough Fresca to hold him over.

He jogged away from the stream of people into a nearby alley and reached into one of the many pockets lining the inside of his specially-made dark-navy suit. It was breathable, fashionable, and functional.

Instead of his weapon, he retrieved a small silver disk—a short-range broad-spectrum jammer. It would cause a little inconvenience for the locals, but he needed to make sure his newfound buddies didn't nail him with a rocket drone.

He hurried away from the street as the trio entered the alley and gave an aggravated sigh.

If he killed them there, it would raise too many questions. There was also not enough certainty that a cleanup crew would arrive in time to take care of them.

Daniel took a deep breath and stopped fleeing. He turned and waited with his hands in his pockets. One rested atop a dark-blue cylinder, a nice little prototype toy the Special Assistance Division researchers had recently cooked up.

Nessie wanted me to test this thing anyway.

When his pursuers turned the corner, he took a step forward to greet them. "Can I help you, gentlemen?" he asked in fluent French, his trademark smile firmly in place.

The elf looked at the two men beside him before responding in French, "You'll need to come with us, sir."

Daniel shook his head. "Sorry, no can do unless you've got candy or need to find your lost puppy. I was always told I shouldn't go anywhere with strangers, and you three are very strange."

"Just kill him already," the elf snarled, exposing a gold front tooth.

Great, I got the rapper elf.

The two men drew pistols from their jackets, apparently keen to follow orders. Daniel pressed a small button on the edge of the cylinder and threw it in front of him. Arcs of electricity crackled as it hovered momentarily in the space between them.

Loud gunshots echoed in the alley as both men fired. The bullets impacted an invisible field emitted by the experimental active deflector, producing a spark with each hit. The rounds hit the ground at Daniel's sides.

Nice, Nessie. It works better than you said.

He resumed running as the deflector hit the ground, blocking further bullets. With a grin, he yanked out a sonic grenade and twisted, whipping the device in their direction.

The elf responded with a fireball that destroyed the deflector and shoved Daniel forward. It took his breath away, and he gasped for air. He knew enough to not try to gulp oxygen in and instead, inhaled slowly as his feet kept moving. His head swam, but the sensation cleared quickly as his lungs filled to capacity again.

Thick smoke shrouded the alley behind him. Blackened scorch marks marred the asphalt road and the brick of the nearby buildings.

Small fragments of the deflector lay strewn about the alley. It was good at deflecting bullets, but fireballs? Not so much.

Need a generic force field, already. I have to make sure I note that in my report. Sorry I broke your shiny new toy, Nessie.

"Be careful," one of the men yelled from behind the smoke. "We make too much trouble and the Anti-Magic Gendarmerie will come."

The elf snorted. "He dies. We run. They can clean it up. This is easy."

Daniel checked their positions behind him quickly but could only see the outlines of their forms as they moved toward him through the smoke. He stayed low and ran as bullets whizzed down the alley, missing him by inches.

"You guys are making it really hard for me not to kill you."

He yanked out another sonic grenade, and this time he lobbed it high. People in firefights tended to look forward, not up. The telltale whine was swallowed by more gunshots, and a second later the two humans fell to the ground, groaning.

The elf snorted and walked closer. A glyph glowed in the center of his forehead, and a red aura surrounded his body. He raised his hands and made intricate movements.

The sound of distant sirens cut through the air. Daniel didn't have time to have a chat with the local authorities. Even if the U.S. government secured his eventual release, he doubted the powerful tracking amulet he'd retrieved from the gang at the hotel would end up back at Langley.

He snatched a grapple gun from inside his jacket and fired toward the roof edge of a tall building. The line retracted and pulled him up as another fireball ripped through the alley. The heat washed over him, but his black Oxfords remained unburned.

Daniel liked those shoes, and these were fresh out of the box that morning.

With practiced ease, he reached the roof and pulled the hook away from the edge. Any sense of satisfaction vanished as the elf rocketed to the same roof on a stream of concentrated fire beneath his arms and legs.

"Great, a real-life Firestorm. He's not burning? Damn magical. No one has the decency to hide their hocus-pocus anymore and cause mayhem the old-fashioned way. Let's show 'im how it's done."

The agent pulled his gun and opened fire. The bullets melted a yard away from the elf, who jumped to the side to avoid the molten metal.

"On second thought..." he muttered. He holstered his pistol and shook his head, pulling out his grapple gun. Time for a little test.

The elf gave him a grin, the gold tooth glinting in the sun. "You can't run forever. You realize that now, I hope."

"Not running, merely evaluating tactical possibilities." He fired the gun directly at the elf. The hook and the line melted at the same distance as the bullets, but none of the molten metal reached the target.

It was worth a shot.

He sighed and tossed it to the ground. There went more of the American taxpayers' money.

The elf chuckled. "Give me the amulet."

"I don't feel like it."

The sirens grew in volume. A black dot trailed by gray grew in the distance in the sky.

What the hell is that?

The elf frowned. "Give me the amulet or die."

Daniel shook his head. "Not only don't I feel like it, but I also can't let you keep it. My bosses would get pissed, and I could lose my pension. If your stupid little gang had minded their own business, they probably wouldn't have attracted the attention of my employers, and we wouldn't be having this conversation."

The dot grew closer. It was now clearly revealed as a man hurtling through the sky and leaving a trail of smoke behind him.

Not something you see every day.

His adversary raised his hands. "Last chance before you die."

A light rumble now heralded the imminent arrival of the flying man, but the elf kept his attention on Daniel.

The agent backed toward the edge of the roof and grabbed a small tube from his pants pocket. "Maybe I'd rather take my chances on the ground."

"Go ahead and jump. I'll simply take it from your dead body."

Daniel shook his head. "I think you'll have someone else to worry about soon enough."

"Who? The police?" The elf scoffed.

"Well, okay, them too."

The light rumble became a roar as a helmeted man wearing a pair of jet wings screamed toward the roof. He pressed a button on a joystick in his hand, and his flying device released him while he was still high overhead. The jet wings circled the area.

The elf blinked and stared at the falling man. A parachute deployed, and the new arrival glided down to the roof. A large, clear crystal on a necklace hung around his neck, an anti-magic deflector.

Oh, this is perfect.

Daniel laughed. "Oh, someone from the Sky Jagers. Didn't even know they were in town."

The helmeted bounty hunter released his parachute and pulled his gun on the elf. "You're a level-four bounty, and you're coming with me," he rattled off in German-accented French.

Daniel waved at his adversary. "Sorry, but I think he's earned his bounty after that little stunt. See you around." He dropped the tube he'd held and fell backward over the side of the building.

Loud gunfire ripped from the top of the roof.

The tube struck the ground first, and the foam cushion that spread instantly from it broke his fall.

He smiled and hopped to his feet. "Like landing in pillows. I don't get why they are so inconsistent with these things, but this one worked out okay."

The foam was already dissolving with a hiss. A massive

explosion rocked the top of the building, followed by another burst of gunfire.

Loud sirens filled the air. Between the police and the bounty hunter, the elf was no longer in any position to come after Daniel.

The two human men he'd left out cold in the alley moaned and sat up. He rushed toward them, slamming his foot into one man's head, snapping it back and knocking him out. Two quick punches restored the other man's unconsciousness.

He adjusted his tie and sprinted for the road. The amulet was safe, and he had left no dead bodies to explain. Time for him to make his exit.

"That went well, if I ignore the property damage." He shrugged. They were probably all insured.

CHAPTER TWO

The agent smiled as he stood in front of the checkers set that occupied one of the unassuming wooden shelves of the shop. He absently scratched the long, thin scar that ran down the side of his face. The narrow mark was a familiar part of him now and only added to his charm.

It was a remnant from a long-ago mission that had come dangerously close to going wrong. Now it served as a reminder to him to be careful whom he trusted—as few as possible, and only for short periods of time when absolutely necessary. Working for the CIA meant friendships would always be tenuous, especially in an age filled with magic.

"Yeah, you think you're going to beat me, but you're not that good."

He reached down and moved a black checker. A few seconds later a red checker moved by itself, threatening his piece. He almost expected the board to start taunting him.

Daniel chuckled and stepped away, running his hand through his sandy brown hair. "Okay, maybe you're better than I thought, but don't get too much of a big head."

Twenty years ago that would have been impressive, and now it's merely another toy. Guess that's what the return of open magic and portals to a fantasy world will do.

Rooney's Antiquities and Oddities. That's what the outside sign proclaimed, and that's what he offered for sale —everything from self-playing checkerboards to rare action figures, and all manner of unusual items in between. Nothing too impressive, but nothing too normal either.

He maneuvered over to the front door and unlocked it, not sure if his grandfather was even up yet. He'd not heard him come down from the apartment upstairs.

Daniel stepped outside, stifling a yawn with his hand. Too damned early to get up, plus a late night made for fatigue.

A quick movement out of the corner of his eye made him step back and raise his hands, ready to defend himself. He lowered them when he recognized it wasn't a thug, merely a long-haired teenager with slightly pointed ears. He had one gray eye, the other a bright blue.

Huh. With that long, brown hair, Tommy looks a little like I did as a teen when I think about it—if I ignore the half-elf thing and heterochromia.

"Hey, Tommy." Daniel smiled. "Glad you're here. I'm running on fumes."

The boy lifted a large black mug with a picture of the Green Lantern on the side, Kyle Rayner version. "Here you go, dude. Your little pick-me-up, as ordered."

The man grabbed the mug and eyed the boy. "And this

is the good stuff? Not some crap from a chain?"

Tommy rolled his eyes and adjusted the straps of his backpack. "Yeah. I got it from Killer ESP on King street. What? Do I need to start bringing you receipts now? I thought we had a trust thing going."

Killer ESP coffee wasn't only good for Old Town Alexandria. Daniel had traveled all over the world, and he believed the place had some of the best coffee he'd ever tasted. There was simply something about the way they handled their beans. For all he knew, they secretly used magic. Or maybe the secret ingredient was well-paid employees giving a damn.

Daniel opened the door and nodded toward the inside of the shop. He didn't share his philosophy on trust with Tommy.

"Trust? We *did* have that unfortunate incident last week. I'm still trying to get the taste of that nasty coffee out of my mouth." He made a face.

The boy laughed and entered the shop. "All coffee tastes like ass to me, dude."

"You merely need to develop a more sophisticated palate. Like many good things, it's an acquired taste."

Tommy made his way to the front counter, his gaze locked on one of Daniel's hand-painted Dungeons & Dragons minotaur miniatures. "'Acquired taste' is something adults say when something tastes like ass. I mean it doesn't even make sense. Nature lets you know when something tastes good, right? Why go out of your way to drink something like coffee that tastes nasty?"

"Blasphemy from a heretic." Daniel made his way behind the counter and took a large gulp, the hot Stumptown coffee sliding down his throat. The warm brew made its way to his stomach, his fatigue already lifting from the simple idea of the coffee. The caffeine would follow up in a few minutes.

The boy shook his head. "You should just do what everybody else does and go to Starbucks." He laughed. "A lot of coffee snobs go there, right? And there's one right around the corner, dude. You don't have to send me to go grab your coffee then."

Daniel snorted. "Yeah, there's one right around *every* corner, and that's the problem. You know exactly why I don't want to go there."

Tommy looked around for a second then leaned closer. "I don't see why it bothers you so much."

"The fact that every Starbucks has a secret entrance to a magical underground rail system?"

His companion nodded. "Yeah. Most humans don't even know about it, so I'd think *you* would think it'd be cool or something, knowing their little secret. It's not like you're down on magical stuff. It's why I like hanging around you."

Daniel smirked. "Maybe to me it's merely like going to a place with too many people in a hurry, and the whole secret magical train station thing only makes that worse."

He couldn't help it. It wasn't that he had a problem with magicals, but going to a place where there were so many felt too much like work—at least work for his *other* job, the one he couldn't tell Tommy about. Human undercover agent for the CIA, special missions.

It was hard to go to a place where there'd be so many possible threats and not find himself scanning for dangerous magical thugs passing through the neighborhood on their way to some other city or country.

You can take the man out of the office, but not the office out of the man.

Daniel shrugged as a follow-up in the silence. "Besides, shouldn't you always support the local place over a chain?"

Tommy furrowed his brow. "I don't know. Jobs are jobs, right?"

Daniel smiled. "Don't worry about it. Just grab the coffee I want, and as always, you can keep the change."

"You sure? I mean, I'm not complaining. I buy lunch with this money, but you could just give me a smaller bill when I grab your coffee."

"Nah. It's worth the convenience." A small smile appeared on the man's face, and he waved a hand.

A good man helps those around him when he can, even if they don't notice. It's even better when they don't notice.

Daniel's grandfather had told him that almost daily growing up. Even now, despite everything he had seen, he didn't think it was a bad way to live. If anything, it was what led him into his day job and why he stuck with it on the days he came limping home or found it hard to forget what he saw.

At this point, I wouldn't be satisfied with only running the shop.

Tommy stuffed the money in his pocket, then his smile vanished and he rubbed the back of his neck. "You think I could maybe crash in the back of the store tonight?"

Daniel frowned. "You should try going home some nights. This isn't about those bullies calling you a half-Ori again, is it?"

"Nah. They haven't said anything to me in a while. Something spooked them. I don't know, maybe someone told them that I'd curse them or something."

The man nodded. He hoped they *were* spooked. A few well-placed punches had helped him make it clear to the boys that they should leave Tommy alone unless they wanted real trouble. The real trouble came with small weapons, or maybe an IRS audit for their parents. Daniel shuddered. *Nah, that'd be going too far.*

He crossed his arms. "What's the problem, then? You've asked to stay here a lot lately. Pops whines about your snoring."

"That dude snores louder than me."

"Yeah, can't argue with that." Daniel chuckled. "But seriously, what's the deal?"

Tommy sighed. "My dad doesn't get me. He wants me to be a musician like him." The boy held up his index finger and pinkie to make horns and thrashed his head back and forth. "But I'm not interested in that kind of thing."

"What are you interested in, then?"

The boy pulled out a small black metal cube from his backpack. "I'm thinking cooler tech. Maybe biorobots."

Daniel narrowed his eyes as the youngster worked the cube in his hand. It opened with a loud click and shot a thin strand to the ceiling.

The boy tugged on it and jumped up, swinging in an arc for a few feet. A higher ceiling might have allowed for more fun.

I don't know if it's a good thing or bad one that he can't go full Spiderman in here.

He held out his hand. "I see you've been in my secret

stash again. Careful there, Peter Parker. Wouldn't want you to hurt anything."

Tommy smirked and pressed on the cube. The webbing sizzled from the base and fell to the ground, where it disappeared in a pungent vapor. He stuck the cube in his pocket.

Daniel chuckled. "It's not a toy, you know."

The boy shrugged. "Nah. Way cooler than a toy."

"You've got a point there. Now come with me. You know the deal." He waved over his shoulder, walking toward a large door in the back. Tommy followed close behind.

Each step moved them past different antiquities and artifacts. One shelf contained hundred-year-old candlesticks and a set of equally old silverware in a wooden box. On the opposite shelf sat the self-playing hand-carved checkers set, still waiting patiently for Daniel to make his next move.

A little farther on was a shelf filled with small figurines, sculptures, and paintings that depicted several different races on Oriceran, Earth's magical sister planet from another dimension. Oriceran had always influenced Earth, but it had been a secret from most of humanity until recent decades.

Some of the races depicted looked enough like humans and were more easily accepted, such as elves and dwarves. But others were a bit more of a challenge, like the insectoid species and living rocks.

The average visitor to the shop would think it was a section containing Oriceran artwork, but every single piece of art on the shelf was at least fifty years old, if not older. All were made long before the truth of Earth's magical sibling had surfaced.

Daniel opened a door at the back of the room. "You know my rule. We hang with the heroes when you're here."

Shelves and racks filled with comic books in plastic sleeves surrounded a large table in the center of the room, mostly DC, Marvel, and Dark Horse. A careful check of the room by an alert fan would have revealed a distinct pattern —every book was a hero title, with not even a single questionable antihero in the mix.

A smaller table with framed pictures stood in the corner. All the picture frames lay face-down. The door to the basement was in the center of the back wall.

Tommy pointed to an old toolbox on the table. "That new? What does it do, repair things on its own?"

"Those are Pops' tools." Daniel chuckled. "And they're normal. He was fixing a vent last night. Must have forgotten them."

He performed a quick scan of the room and frowned. *What the...* He marched over to a rack in the corner. "Something's missing. What did you take? Give it back."

Tommy laughed. "Dude, sorry. I only borrowed it. It's at home."

Daniel winced. "Tell me you didn't bend the pages or anything like that."

The boy held up three fingers, giving him the Boy Scout sign. "Never," he replied solemnly. He shot another web to the ceiling and hung upside down, his oversized black-and-white Converse high-tops above his head. "Heroes don't bend pages."

The comment pulled a smile out of the man. "Don't

hang upside down in here and risk getting dust in my coffee or on my comics there, Peter Parker."

He laughed and flipped right-side up before dropping to the ground. "Your comics all have plastic covers, dude. What are you worried about?"

Daniel shook his mug in a menacing manner. "Dust is a determined enemy, much like a supervillain."

They both chuckled. Tommy vaporized the webbing before slipping the cube back into his pocket. He grabbed a couple of comic books and settled down on the wooden floor with his back to his companion. His movements were slow and deliberate, as if he wanted to be sure to prove to his host that he could be careful with his precious treasures.

The man watched him for a moment. "Any more postcards from your mom?"

The boy shook his head. "Not lately. She's pretty much MIA and hanging out with humans, the kind who don't care much for magicals. Not sure her half-Ori son would fit in too well with that crowd."

Daniel sighed. "Thought she said she missed you in the last one."

"Yeah, she said that, but it's not like we're living in ancient history like the year 2000. She could drop me an email if she really cared." He shrugged. "And she didn't say she was coming back. I know, I know, better than dead. At least your parents weren't trying to disappear on purpose."

"That's one way of putting it."

Tommy stood and made his way over to the table in the corner with the pictures. "You have more than a few ticks, dude." He picked up one of the framed pictures and looked at the smiling couple. “Your grandpa seems okay, though, even if he’s cranky and snores, but that’s all old people, right?” He shook his head. “I don’t get it. I mean, I know your parents kind of ditched you, too, but why keep their pictures out if you’re just gonna turn them over? I find them everywhere. Almost slept on one last week. You using my space for storage now?”

Daniel snorted. “Not your space, Tommy.”

The boy’s jaw tightened, and he looked down.

Damn. This is one of the few places he feels safe. I shouldn’t take that from him.

He sighed. “Fine. Don’t go looking all hurt. For now, it’s your space. And no, I don’t sleep in the shop. I have a bed upstairs.”

At least I do for when I need to stay here. For when I get *to stay here.*

Tommy looked up and shook his head. “Just saying, it's like some weird trail of breadcrumbs or something."

Daniel took the picture from the boy and stared down at it for a moment. His parents smiled at the camera, standing in front of a dig site close to Ankara, Turkey. He set the picture face-down on a nearby shelf with a sigh.

“It’s my idea of a compromise,” he explained. "I don't shut the door completely. They may still be alive out there somewhere. Being a tomb raider is a dangerous job, though, so probably not.” It still stung to say the words “probably not.” “But people who chase after artifacts, especially magical artifacts, can end up popping back up when you least expect them.”

The basement door creaked open, and a dapper, silver-haired man in a short-sleeved plaid shirt, khakis, suspenders, and a bow tie stepped through. Peter Rooney, Daniel's grandfather, carried a small engine in his thick, weathered hands.

Tommy eyed the basement door with a hungry gleam in his eyes. "When will you let me go into that basement, Pops? I bet you have some cool gadgets down there. Way cooler than the stuff I've seen."

Peter shot his grandson a stern look.

Daniel shook his head. "Never, Tommy. A man's got to have a private place."

The boy rolled his eyes. "That's boring, dude."

"Can't argue with you there." He smiled. "But it's time for you to pretend you're going to school. Go on, humor me in my denial or I'll feel obligated to drive you. Then, I'll have to walk you in, maybe meet some of your friends…"

Tommy sighed. "I'm going. I'm going. Don't have a stroke."

He stepped through the door, pulled out the cube, and shot a web to swing through the shop.

"Watch out for the tchotchkes," Daniel yelled. "You break it, you buy it."

The half-elf laughed, landed, and vaporized his web. With a quick, mocking salute, he was out the front door.

Peter pushed aside a few comic books on the table to set down the engine he carried.

Daniel waved a hand. "Whoa. Careful there, Pops."

His grandfather rolled his eyes. "Daniel, I remember how many times the basement was flooded when our old washing machine overflowed, and we lost piles of these things. I always bought you more. Get over it. They're picture books. These days, you can buy ones that move.

Hell, you can watch an entire movie in your hand. I don't even understand why you're wasting your space with all of these."

He shook his head. "Missing the point, Pops. It's art."

"It's men in spandex costumes." The old man shrugged. "But whatever. Your money. You're doing a good job of running my shop, so I can't complain too much. It means I can have something resembling a retirement."

Daniel chuckled. "You'd prefer to take a cruise to exotic places?"

"I've had enough exotic nonsense to last me five lifetimes." He glanced toward the main shop. "Speaking of exotic, that kid's taken a shine to you."

"I can relate to him. I think that helps." He shrugged.

His grandfather gave him a sly smile. "You going to show him your D&D setup? Not like it'd shock him. He already knows about the comic books."

He shook his head. "What's the point? Tommy's already living the game."

The older man snorted. "We're all living the game now. Your friends are coming over later this week to play, right?"

"Yeah."

Peter frowned. "Tell Connor to stay out of my Fresca stash." He grabbed a hammer from his toolbox and waved it menacingly. "I know he was sneaking cans out last time."

Daniel laughed. "No one wants your Fresca, Pops. Last-century soda. Put your hammer down and lower your eyebrows. I'll tell him."

"You better. That stuff is hard to get. Have to go to the big store across town, and they don't deliver. Who doesn't deliver in this day and age?" Peter nodded toward the basement door. "I've got a job I want you to hit while you're in Munich for the agency. It might be a shop find, or it might need to be put in the vault."

The agent frowned. The vault was where his parents had stored all their tomb raiding treasures prior to their disappearance.

Too many memories down there. Too many that didn't involve him.

His grandfather snorted. "Don't think I can't see the look on your face. I know what you're thinking. Let it go. I need you to read the file for the side job. It's time to get to work and save the world again. You can do that while helping out in this shop as much as you can during your day job."

Daniel sighed and ran a hand through his thick hair—his tell when he was frustrated. His grandfather ignored it. He nodded quickly. "Yeah, I know."

Peter walked toward the door. "If you don't like the stress, you can always quit the CIA, you know. Not that I think this shop needs somebody here fulltime. I like the idea of it having erratic hours. It adds to the mystique and that kind of garbage. Helps me raise the prices." He shrugged. "Or you could run around as a tomb raider. Just as dangerous, and fewer bureaucrats."

"The Company needs me, and the country needs me." He shook his head. "Besides, I do it for one simple reason, Pops."

"What's that?"

Daniel locked eyes with his grandfather. "I'm one of the best there is." He shrugged. "I'm going to finish my coffee. Bring me the file, and I'll check it out if I have time."

Peter muttered something under this breath and headed downstairs while his grandson returned to the main shop with his now-lukewarm brew. Once finished, he set the mug on the counter. Tommy would be able to find it there later.

A couple of minutes passed before the old man stepped back into the main room of the shop with a folder in his hand.

Daniel chuckled from the counter. He pulled a small silver mirrored cube out of his pocket and set it on the counter and tapped the sides in a precise order.

His grandfather snorted. "Not like there is anyone here to overhear us."

"Never hurts to be careful."

"Besides, should you even have that when you're not on the job?"

He nodded. "The Company wants me to be able to talk without risk no matter where I am. It's one of the few things they let me sign out permanently for general use."

Peter handed him the folder. "I should have asked you this before, but you *are* still going to Munich, right? This is pointless if you're not going."

"Yes, I am."

His grandfather looked to the side for a moment before nodding as if making up his mind. "This one was sent to us by your buddy Rolf. He called your second phone."

Daniel chuckled. "He's not my buddy, he's a contractor. The guy's pretty damned shady, but he does have a nose for artifacts. What's the overview?"

"A shotgun."

Daniel arched a brow. "A *shotgun?*"

The old man nodded. "A shotgun that allegedly has strange powers, which in this day and age is saying something. Some sort of artifact. They've been blabbing about it on the internet. The current owner has made it clear that he wants the right person to take it away for the right price."

"I'm assuming the right price is very high, but who's the right person?"

"Someone who isn't crazy or evil." Peter shrugged. "Doing this helps you with your cover for your other job anyway, *and* it benefits the store. Even if we never sell the thing, it might improve our reputation."

Daniel frowned. "You said they were talking about this on the internet, Pops?"

"Yeah, on the dark web. At least, that's what Rolf's message said."

"I'm surprised the Company doesn't know about it yet. Even if they don't go after every artifact out there, they usually are at least aware of them, especially if it's a hot subject of discussion."

The older man furrowed his brow. "Well, maybe my German is off, but it won't hurt to go check it out since you'll already be over there."

Daniel laughed. "It won't hurt? With artifacts, I don't know if you can ever say that." He ran a finger down the thin line on his face again.

CHAPTER THREE

A few hours later and wearing a nice blue suit, Daniel made his way to the King Street-Old Town Metro station, his hands in his pockets. Nothing like a nice walk in Old Town Alexandria when the weather was beautiful.

He smiled at a sight in the distance—a row of trees that grew on the other side of the tracks and the tower of the George Washington Masonic National Memorial rising above them. He wondered if Tommy had visited the place and checked out the museum. Sometimes, it was nice to remind a boy that not all heroes wore spandex and were in comic books.

Daniel chuckled at the mental image of George Washington, powdered wig and all, wearing spandex. The boy liked the never-ending rumor that the founding father was really a Light Elf.

It would be a few more blocks until he arrived at the station. His immediate task was crossing the street and surveying the neighborhood without letting on to anyone watching from a window. He glanced back and forth, his attention lingering on a corner grocery store.

He narrowed his eyes. Numerous liquor and lottery signs covered most of the large front window, making it hard to see inside, and a huge ESTABLISHED 2001 sign didn't help. A sliver of open window allowed him to check the interior. A large man in jeans and a white t-shirt leaned across the counter, shaking his finger. His mouth was curled into a menacing sneer.

Haven't seen him around before, and I don't like that look.

Daniel pivoted in a neat turn and hurried toward the grocery store. He opened the door, only to be greeted by furious barking. After poking his head in, he spotted the owner's golden retriever behind a baby gate in the corner near the front of the store.

He ignored the bunches of bananas on the counter that were crowding the take-a-penny saucer. In Alexandria, every corner grocery store had bananas. It was almost like it was part of the license.

I hope some things never change.

The man leaning over the counter murmured something. The owner swallowed and went pale.

What's going on, Charlie? Shakedown?

Daniel sauntered forward, keeping a light smile on his face. Time to engage in a little local civic education.

The stranger pointed to the candy rack in front. "Laffy Taffy? Charleston Chew? What's this shit? It's last-century crap. Your sign says this place was started in 2001. It's been almost forty years, and you're still selling shit like it's the Great Recession?"

Charlie swallowed, holding his hands up in front of his

chest. "You'd be surprised. I sell what people buy. That's all. If no one bought them, I'd replace them."

The rude man slammed the palm of his hand down on the counter. "You trying to piss me off, asshole?"

Okay, I've heard enough.

Daniel cleared his throat. "Excuse me, sir."

The stranger spun around. He was a good head taller than Daniel and more than a few pounds heavier. All muscle and no fat from the looks of it, but that didn't do much to intimidate the CIA agent.

The thug sneered. "You're gonna have to wait, pal. I'm having a conversation here with Mr. Recession Candy. He thinks he can mouth off to me. Can you believe that shit?"

He clucked his tongue and took a step forward. "You see, there's an issue here. This is *my* neighborhood, and you know, there are certain basic rules of etiquette—social norms, if you will—that should be observed. I'd almost go so far to say they *have* to be observed."

The other man's face scrunched in confusion. His front teeth were stained brown from tobacco. "What the fuck are you talking about?"

The agent took another step forward, keeping a smile on his face. He held up a hand. "Look, I get it. I don't recognize you, and I come to this store a lot, so I'm guessing you're new. And since you're new, you wouldn't know about all those social norms I just mentioned. That would be the most likely and only valid excuse for your behavior."

The man reddened, and his watery eyes narrowed. A mix of anger, frustration, and confusion painted his face. Charlie backed up against the wall as the dog continued to bark.

The stranger glared at him. "What the fuck are you talking about? Who the fuck are you to mouth off to me like that? You think you're a hero?"

"No, I think I'm Daniel."

A flicker of recognition passed over the man's face, but it vanished quickly.

"Never heard of you," the thug growled. "Now get the fuck out of here unless you want me to smash your face into some Charleston Chews."

Daniel shrugged and shifted into a better position, just in case. "You still don't get it. I live around here. Like I said, *my* neighborhood. You can think of me as the kind of man who takes a vested interest in ensuring that people are polite to one another around here. This seems to be an argument about something that really doesn't matter, so maybe it'd be better if we went on our merry ways and forgot about our issues with candy before we all do something we regret over something so stupid."

The thug's face tightened, and he glanced at the door.

This is working. He is frustrated and pissed, but his little brain must be telling him that it's not worth it to escalate the trouble with someone he doesn't even know.

"Daniel, huh?" the man asked, that look of recognition returning.

"Yeah. Why? You heard of me?"

"Maybe."

Daniel nodded toward the door. "Then this should be easier for you to figure out. Please leave."

The dog continued barking even louder, occasionally letting out a low growl.

The thug shook his head and glared at the dog. "If you

don't shut that fucking mutt up, maybe I'll shove a bunch of Charleston Chews down its throat until it chokes."

Oh, pal. I was really trying to give you an out here. Pops would say you made your own bed, and now it's time to lie in it.

Daniel's smile vanished and he adjusted his stance, spreading his feet. His hands curled into fists at his sides. "What did you say?"

The man shrugged. "You got a problem with me shutting that yapping piece of shit up, Daniel?"

He spat the name.

Okay. Got to do this the smart way. Can't show too much. Plus, don't want to rip my suit. I like this suit.

"Okay, I see how it is."

The man grinned. "Yeah, glad you see it my w—"

Daniel slammed a fist into the man's face.

The thug stumbled back, holding his face as blood trickled out of his nose. "You motherfucker. I will fucking kill you for that."

Without hesitation, the thug charged him, but he took an easy sidestep that had the dog-hater almost slam into the wall.

Daniel spun and kicked his foot, planted it squarely against the man's ass, and helped him complete his journey to the bricks.

With a growl, his opponent pushed off the wall and turned. He wiped blood off his face. "You think you're a big man, fucker? I'm gonna break every bone in your body."

The thug threw several quick punches. The agent blocked them, fighting against his instincts as opening after opening presented itself—an obvious arm lock here and there, or a good throat strike.

It's been a while since I fought a good old-fashioned regular goon. I forgot how pathetic they are. This is like watching a kid come at me.

He dodged a wide swing and followed up with two quick jabs of his own. His opponent grunted and took a few steps back. At least the man didn't go for a weapon. That was one of the few things that kept the CIA agent from risking showing even half his true skill.

It was time to end things. If the situation continued, the asshole might damage something in Charlie's store.

Daniel waited for his opponent to charge him again, then smashed a fist into the top of his head. The dog-hater dropped to the ground, his head thudding on the hard tile floor.

He let out a long, pained groan. The dog stopped barking and wagged his tail.

Charlie leaned over the counter. "Do yourself a favor, pal, and just stay down."

The agent leaned to whisper menacingly into the man's ear. "Like I said. Social norms and etiquette, but if that's too much for you, I've got a really, really simple rule you can follow. Don't ever threaten a fuckin' dog when I'm around."

He pushed a sensitive nerve just under the man's clavicle. The thug groaned and twitched in pain.

The CIA agent yanked his opponent up by his collar and dragged his heavy frame to the door. He flung it open and literally kicked the man's ass again, this time out onto the sidewalk.

"Consider your passport to this neighborhood revoked. If I see you around here again, we'll have a longer and more private sit-down, and I doubt you'll walk away so easily."

The dog-hater stumbled to his feet, holding his swelling jaw. He jogged down the street in a wide gait, alternately holding his ass and then his jaw.

Ten yards down the road, he turned around. "I'm only the messenger. You don't know it, but you're not the damned mayor here anymore. You got in a few lucky licks today, but you'll see. Next time, I'll break your fucking face."

That was why he knew my name. Someone sent him. Daniel took a single step in the man's direction. His target's eyes widened, and he spun and sprinted away.

What the hell was that threat about? What trash is trying to move in now? Time for a few more questions and some pest control soon. Maintenance spraying makes for a clean garden.

The CIA agent shook his head and stepped back into the store. "You okay, Charlie?"

The other man nodded and pressed his hand against his chest. "I'm okay. Just a little rattled."

"Is that the first time they've tried to pressure you?"

The old man hesitated and looked down. "No, shady guys have dropped in a couple of times, but this was the first time they got so rough."

Daniel gritted his teeth but forced himself to smile. "Next time, you call me sooner. Can't help you work on a solution if I don't know about it."

Charlie laughed. "Guess that's why we all call you the mayor. You're more a mayor than the real mayor."

"I'm merely a man who likes a peaceful and quiet neighborhood."

"Nah, you say that, but I've lived here longer than you've been alive. Too many people don't want to get involved when they see something bad going on. It's even worse nowadays because you don't know if it'll be some strange magic nonsense. But you don't walk away, ever."

Daniel shrugged.

Charlie looked him up and down. "Nice suit. You heading out on a buying trip for the shop?"

Not like I can tell him I only wear a suit when I'm on CIA business.

"Yeah," he answered. "I'll only be gone for a few days at most, but if you have trouble, I can come right back. You have the number, right?"

The shopkeeper pulled a phone out of a drawer. "Yeah, it's still programmed in the phone that you gave me. I keep it handy, just like everyone in the neighborhood does."

Daniel could only hope no one ever started thinking too deeply as to why he'd given them all burner phones instead of a simple phone number. From what he'd heard, a few people sensed that he was more than a simple shop owner, but they didn't want to risk knowing more. Many of them assumed that he had access to dangerous magic because of the shop, but they didn't care as long as he defended the neighborhood from thuggish dog-haters and the like.

"If you're okay, Charlie, I'll head out."

The store owner shook his head and pointed to his dog. "I'm fine, and he's not barking anymore. That means the danger's gone."

Daniel waved. "See you in a few days."

He stepped out of the shop and took a moment to

survey the area, looking for anyone out of place or packing weapons. A light stream of pedestrians strolled around, but no one looked dangerous. Normal-looking cars drove up and down the street.

The agent continued toward the Metro station. When he'd confronted the man, he'd assumed the idiot was simply a clueless outsider, but the final threat made it clear that something far more targeted was happening.

Gang? Organized crime? Far too sloppy to be related to anything with the Company, but they won't appreciate it if I get wrapped up in something strange.

Daniel shook his head. He would have to worry about it later. Time for the day job.

CHAPTER FOUR

He emerged from the Metro station and glanced around. In Old Town, he might only be worried about local pests infiltrating his neighborhood, but now that he was out of his neighborhood, he couldn't count on the support of the locals. A spy who made it to old age was a spy who paid attention to his environment.

No one's ever gone after me in Alexandria, but it's not like it would be impossible to track me down.

No one more dangerous or obvious than a surly businessman presented themselves as he made his way down the street for several blocks to a private parking garage. He approached a locked front door and ran a keycard over it. With a beep, it opened, and he stepped into a lobby connected to an elevator.

The small black elevator again required his keycard, along with a destination code. It made a low hum as it took him to his floor. He stepped into a well-lit underground parking garage, and a narrow road led toward a closed metal gate at the end.

Not sure if it's worth it to rent a spot here—good comic books money—but it's better than having to go all the way to the Company to get my wheels.

Daniel pulled out his phone and opened the garage app. He tapped in the code, and a loud, echoing grinding filled the air. A moment, later, the center of the road opened, the concrete pulling apart, and a silver Jaguar G-Type rose on its own personal elevator.

It's almost worth it simply to see that awesome sight every time. Besides, it's not like I'm paying for the car.

He marched toward the vehicle and slipped into the driver's seat, the quality leather molding itself to his body.

"Damn, that's comfortable."

It was almost hard to drive his own car at times when he knew this beauty sat in a garage waiting for him.

Daniel smiled. There were more than a few nice toys built into the car, but he wouldn't need them driving to the office. At least he—almost—hoped not.

He entered a few commands on his car's touchscreen, and the garage door rose. He revved the engine a few times, letting it purr before zooming out of the garage and onto the street.

Wonder what everyone back in Old Town would think if they saw me in this thing. Too bad I can't let them, even if it's annoying having to take the Metro to get to the car.

Until he left the CIA, he needed to maintain his cover, and he doubted the Company would let him keep the car after he resigned from their employ. He liked this ride far better than some of the other enhanced vehicles the agency had loaned him.

He sighed. Bureaucracy. His grandfather had mentioned it, and the old man wasn't wrong.

Daniel was proud to serve his country in the CIA, but his division was still new. It focused on protecting the country against foreign magic, particularly Oriceran, and that was a good thing.

He knew they were playing catch up, but it shouldn't have taken the government almost two decades to start adapting to the threat. Chaos had reigned in the early years, but the whole point of the CIA was to anticipate foreign threats so the country wouldn't have to deal with that kind of mess.

The agent didn't care that there were existing organizations tasked with that mission within the government. They had participated in covering up the truth about magic, and, in a sense, had left the world and the country less prepared. Oriceran aligned magically with Earth over thousands of years, allowing magic to seep back to the planet. Even if true magic had never completely disappeared, the energy flowing now made things like half-elves and gnomes a daily reality.

Unfortunately, magic was no guarantee of morality, any more than wealth, technology, or any other tool available on Earth had been since the dawn of civilization.

Magical criminals were enough of a threat in many cities that specially-licensed bounty hunters now supplemented the police force, and in addition to SWAT teams, larger cities maintained special Anti-Enhanced Threat forces.

Regular people shouldn't have to live with that kind of uncertainty and fear.

If we're doing our job at the Company, at least we can help cut down on the amount of crap the locals have to deal with.

He shook his head as he switched lanes, enjoying the smooth handling of the car. Magic had its place, but precision engineering was a type of magic all its own.

Can't complain too much. The past is the past, and now we've got everyone focused on the same thing—protecting the country from all threats, foreign and domestic. So what if a few of those foreign threats come from a little farther away?

"Please lean forward, sir," the security guard asked with a bored expression.

Daniel complied, sticking his eye against the retinal scanner.

The guard's computer beeped, and he nodded. "Thank you. Badge, please."

The CIA agent pulled out his badge and handed it over. The other man waved a scanner across it and tapped a few commands into his computer, then moved it over the badge again.

"Confirmed." The guard handed the badge back. "Have a good day, sir. Oh, just so you know, Nessie is looking for you."

"Thanks." Daniel clipped the badge on his suit jacket and gave the man a polite nod. "Have a good day yourself."

As much as it would have amused him, the Company didn't have the Loch Ness Monster in a secret pool at the bottom of Langley. In fact, despite the return of magic, no one was even sure the monster existed. There would always be a few mysteries left in the world.

In this case, Nessie was the current head of the Special Assistance Division, which no one dared call SAD. In other words, she was the Queen of Gadgets, among other things. Not the first one he'd worked with at the CIA. Most were a little afraid of her and only whispered her nickname, but he had no problems with the woman.

Daniel continued past the checkpoint and down the hall toward the express elevator. With a ding, the elevator doors opened, and he stepped inside. He entered a code on a keypad, then placed his thumb against a small silver panel. The familiar slight burn of a DNA scan followed.

"Verified, Daniel Winters," the elevator reported in a soft feminine voice.

Why is every fake voice in this place female?

The corners of his mouth quirked up in a smile. The shop was named after his grandfather, so people rarely used Daniel's actual last name around him. To protect the store, he never used his real name when he was on jobs for the agency, not to mention that he often dyed his hair or changed his appearance.

The CIA agent had been everyone from the dark-haired Daniel Goldstein to the redheaded, green-eyed Daniel Travers. Disguises and aliases weren't always necessary, but they were damned fun—another fringe benefit of working for the Company. A few fake cute jokes about his childhood here and there and no one ever suspected he was lying through his teeth about his background, even if they already knew he was a CIA agent. It was almost like people wanted to be lied to. Maybe they merely enjoyed the fantasy.

The elevator lurched and zoomed down. He watched the display as the numbers and letters changed. B1. B2. Soon, he'd hit B10.

The doors separated, and Daniel stepped into the main Special Assistance Division lab space. Row after row of raised black lab benches and tables lined the cavernous area. Swarms of men and women in lab coats surrounded different devices in various states of repair or construction. In one corner, ventilated hoods allowed them to work with noxious chemicals or potentially dangerous agents, but the real hard-core hazards of that nature were handled in a different room.

Wonder what Tommy would pay to visit a place like this.

Some devices looked exactly like a layman might expect to find in a place like a CIA lab—sleek, metallic drones or unusual guns. Others were disguised as simple objects, clothes, toiletries, and even pumpkin seeds.

Huh. Glad to see we have a few Surprise Deadly Pumpkin Seeds around if that's what those are. Last time I saw seeds, they were gas bombs.

The disruption of the return of Oriceran and magic might have slowed the advance of human technology but it hadn't halted it, especially in the hidden labs of government intelligence agencies. What humanity lacked in magic, they made up for in technological ingenuity.

The back wall of the room was covered with massive metal bin-filled shelves, many reaching halfway to the ceiling. A computer-controlled arm was available to retrieve the bins far above the height of even the tallest man.

Entire rows of computers lined the far walls of the two remaining sides of the room, but most of the workers used augmented reality goggles and linked AR gloves for their computing needs.

For all the exotic sights in the lab, there was one thing Daniel never saw—Oricerans. No elves, dwarves, gnomes, Kilomeas, or any of the thousands of species from Earth's sister planet. No Oriceran was trusted on the research floor, even if some worked for the Company. It was a Senate directive known to very few. For now, they didn't even trust the magicals who were native to Earth, such as witches and wizards. After all, magicals had participated in the cover-up of magic, which meant they'd kept the country less prepared for potential threats than they should have been.

Daniel was sure that would change in the future. He would make sure it did.

The old government ways of dealing with magic had been focused on total suppression. Without that as a possibility anymore, they needed to adapt and take advantage of any resource they had. They couldn't allow a magical gap with other countries.

An elegantly dressed older woman with silver hair neatly pulled back in a metal clip emerged from a side door and walked toward him.

"Hello, Nessie," he greeted her in an affable tone.

She gave him a tight smile. If she had a problem with the nickname, she hadn't let him know.

"Daniel," the woman replied, her voice smooth. She nodded toward the door she'd just stepped through. "Come with me. I need to give you some information on your Munich assignment."

The agent followed the older woman into her small and spartan office. She pointed to a chair in front of her cherry wood desk, walking around it to sit in her own chair. A large box sat on the edge of her desk.

Nessie folded her hands in front of her. "I trust you're ready for the new assignment?"

"I was ready for this last week. You guys simply keep pushing it back."

"Proper resource distribution is always a consideration in missions of this nature." The woman nodded. "Very well then. The assignment is simple. You'll go to Germany to rescue a dead man from the tomb where he's been resting for one hundred years. Then you'll deliver him to some contacts to be flown to a secure location."

"I'm rescuing a dead man?" He chuckled. "Drinking on the job, Nessie?"

"Very amusing, Daniel. Such a droll sense of humor."

"I'm serious. Dragging around the dead is a bit above my pay grade."

Nessie shrugged, leveling a look at him. "Get the man out of his sarcophagus in Munich. I'll pass along all the particulars to your Company phone for review."

"And who is this man?"

She offered him another thin smile. "You don't need to worry about that right now. Just concentrate on the recovery."

"Of a body? Am I robbing a grave?"

Nessie shook her head. "No. Our information suggests he's a man in need of rescue, not a body, and he's not in a cemetery, but in a sarcophagus being stored with some archaeological and historical artifacts."

Daniel sighed and shrugged. "Not a dead man, but he's in a sarcophagus. He must be flipping out. Who is this man and why don't we send in an entire team?"

"The sarcophagus belongs to a man named Gunter Holst who died in World War II."

"Come on, Nessie, make sense. Did they push poor, dead Gunter out to make way for the guy who's entombed alive?"

"It's a little more complicated than that."

"You're talking in riddles, my favorite. Gives the mission an added level of difficulty. Why do we care about some crusty German from a century ago?"

She shook her head. "We don't. You are correct. We don't believe the man inside is Gunter Holst. Part of your assignment is to recover a body that will appear dead and ascertain his identity. Our information suggests he might be a useful asset in terms of dealing with magical threats."

"Appears dead, got it. That's a new kind of spooky. But you're not even sure who he is? Just that he's important enough that I go rescue him?"

"His identity is unclear at this time." Nessie cleared her throat, giving herself a moment. "We have reason to believe that he's been in that box for a hundred years."

"And not dead and gone." Daniel smiled, looking around the room. "Is this some kind of prank you're pulling off for the Christmas party? Come on. You almost had me."

Nessie released a deep sigh and waited. He spun around, holding up his phone to detect infrared lights that would give away a hidden camera. Nothing but the usual array.

She shook her head. "No, it's not a joke. A human who's been lying in state for over a hundred years—since 1943 to be exact. We've received a tip from a reliable source that suggests it would be to our advantage to recover this man, though."

Daniel let the smile drop. "Nice understatement there, Nessie. Okay, so I need to go rescue a dead man who's not really dead, who's older than shit, who may or may not be there, and who may or may not even be someone worth rescuing."

"Yes, that would be an accurate summary of the situation. Is this a problem?"

He shrugged. "I've dealt with worse missions."

Nessie unfolded her hands. "Excellent. You'll be working with Ronni on this assignment." She shook a finger at him. "Don't mess with her head this time. No more telling her stories about weird artifacts. I see her talking to herself enough as it is, poor thing. She's talented, and I'd hate to have to revoke her security clearance."

Daniel grinned. "You don't even want me to tell her about the Horn of Ragnarok that I had to stop from being sounded to prevent some giant serpent destroying Norway?"

The woman rolled her eyes, but she was still smiling. "I'm far less credulous than Ronni, and I don't have time for jokes. I need to get you signed off on all your devices, so you can catch your flight."

She pushed the box forward.

Nessie grabbed a small gray electronic signing pad with

an attached stylus. "First things first. You'll need to sign for everything."

The agent laughed. "What am I signing for? Half these things break in the middle of missions anyway or don't work."

"Advanced technology often has bugs, and don't ever dismiss the power of the bureaucracy. They merely want to be able to dock your pay for the millions it cost them to make it if you lose them. A nice excuse."

"Even if they don't work?"

Nessie nodded. "At least they'll have a chance to examine why they failed."

Daniel laughed. "You keep telling me that, but the reliability of a lot of these gadgets doesn't seem to improve."

She snorted. "That's only partially our fault. You keep breaking things, too, Daniel."

"I'm not exactly a guy who works in an air-conditioned office. I simply want a few reliable toys."

"What about your car?" Nessie smirked. "You seem to believe it's reliable enough."

"You've got me there." He stood and looked down into the box. "So, what do we have here?" He picked up a few silver disks with small buttons. "Broad-frequency jammers. It also looks like we've got a few single-use EMPs. Lock-pick kits, physical and electronic."

There was nothing surprising about those. Those were standard gear on most missions.

Nessie pointed to the pad. "Sign, please."

She tapped the box. "The tie pin inside is a single-use stun grenade. Just bend it and throw it."

Daniel scribbled down another signature then picked

up a simple golden ring. "Kind of my style, but what does it do?"

"Holographic decoy. It lasts about one minute. Even provides a realistic thermal signature."

The agent whistled. "Nice, very nice."

Nessie nodded. "Try to find an excuse to test it out. We don't have any decent field data on it yet."

He chuckled. "Another Guinea pig run?"

"I can think of a variety of uses for such a device once we perfect it." She shrugged and pulled out some silver glasses. "Standard disguised AR glasses. These will rely on your Company phone to interface with Ronni."

Daniel held them up. "Nice and stylish. Does the Company have a fashion designer on staff?"

Nessie rolled her eyes.

The agent picked up the last item in the box, a small white orb. "What's this?"

"They call it a chameleon ball. Optical camouflage, not total invisibility. You'll have a blurry little outline, and it only lasts a few minutes, but it's still quite good."

He grinned. "I'm not complaining."

Nessie nodded. "Good. Stop by the armory on your way out for your firearm, but you'll still need to sign here for it."

Daniel scribbled down yet another few signatures. "With the exploding rounds?"

"A small number, yes. We don't anticipate you needing many for this job."

The agent narrowed his eyes. "But there's nothing in here for raising the dead."

She leaned back with a faint smile on her face. "You'll have to figure that out."

"Why hasn't anyone tried to rescue him before now?"

"Lack of intel, dear Daniel. He's been a very well-kept secret, till now. Get going. Oh, and try not to break anything."

"You do care."

She shook her head. "I meant the equipment."

CHAPTER FIVE

Daniel strolled down the crowded Munich streets on his way to a local bar. He needed some additional background intelligence before hitting his target location, Leuchtenberg Palais. For all the background information the CIA lacked on the somewhat dead man—or he lacked, at least—he didn't have to worry about tracking the sarcophagus down, but he didn't want to go in blind.

For one thing, his briefing didn't give him a clue about how he might bring a dead man back to life. Splashing a little cash around to the right man or woman might help with that.

He sighed and lifted his phone to his ear. The implanted directional mic in the top of his tie and the tiny receiver in his ear made using a phone unnecessary, but talking to yourself while walking down the street was as odd in Germany as it was the United States.

"I'm closing in on the bar now," Daniel muttered. "Is the link still strong, Ronni?"

The agent looked like another tourist wanting to check out Munich. That didn't stop him surveying the area and looking for anyone whose gaze lingered for a touch too long or who had a suspicious bulge underneath their jacket. So far, nothing.

I should worry less about tails and more about how the hell I'm supposed to wake up a dead guy.

"Just keep talking," Ronni responded through his receiver. "I'm adjusting some things so I can get a nice read on your vitals."

"My vitals?" Daniel chuckled. "Nice. It might not do me any good, but at least you'll know when I'm dead."

She gasped. "What?"

"Never mind. Just a joke."

He wasn't surprised at the modifications. Ronni had a knack for combining tech and small artifacts with low levels of magic to make something new, despite lacking any actual magical ability otherwise. At least, he'd been told she lacked magical abilities.

Maybe that's the true future. Nothing but magic and technology fused. Kind of hard to see how Earth and Oriceran won't end up that way.

"Almost got it set up," she murmured. "There. Good heart rate, by the way. Very healthy."

"Glad to know I won't have a heart attack anytime soon and all that cardio's paying off." Daniel stopped at a street corner and checked over his shoulder before proceeding. "But how do you do all that without any of Nessie's worker bees noticing? She didn't mention anything like this during my briefing."

Ronni sighed. "Well, I'm using subtle subcarrier information from your transmitter anyway, but it's more the receiver on my end that's the hard part."

He proceeded across the street. "Oh, how did you hide it this time?"

"It looks like a little Pikachu. It can also pick up conversations and transmit the information remotely. All sorts of neatness."

"Ronni, the rule breaker. You have something like that on Company grounds?"

She gasped. "It just happened… It already had some of those functions, and I simply needed the core to modify it. I would never use the other stuff…not in the building. You have to believe me."

Nessie's warning bubbled up in Daniel's head.

"I'm only messing with you, Ronni. Don't worry about it."

The woman let out a sigh of relief. "Don't tease me like that."

"Don't make it so much fun, and I won't." He lowered his voice as he continued down the street. "Still don't know how I'm supposed to recover someone who has been lying in state since 1943. None of the background info they provided said anything useful like whether he's a zombie, skeleton—or hell, goo, for that matter." The agent laughed.

"Even the CIA can't know everything," Ronni responded.

"Maybe we should bet on what the possibilities are." Daniel grinned to himself. This might be crossing back over into messing with his backup's head, but not in a way that would upset her.

She took a deep breath and exhaled slowly. It was times

like this that he hated only being able to hear her. It wasn't as much fun to poke someone if you couldn't see their facial reactions.

"Well, we have to start with what we know," she began. "They told you that he's alive, which at least implies some sort of mobility and ability to interact with him without having to bring in some sort of wizard, medium, or necromancer."

Daniel could almost imagine her little face scrunched up in concentration as she tried to apply rational thinking to the bizarre situation. She was probably tugging on her ponytail.

"What are the implications of that?" he prodded.

"At least some sound generation capability, so probably not a skeleton or goo. Even magical beings tend to still rely on some basic biology."

The grin on the agent's face spread wider. Ronni had no idea that it was simply a game to him. It was time to take the joke further. Maybe too far, but he didn't care.

He laughed and crossed another street. Only a few more blocks until the bar. "Aren't you forgetting something?"

"Like what?"

"Something doesn't have to talk to communicate. An animate skeleton could write something. Or maybe we can read its thoughts."

"I don't think it's doing much thinking without a brain." Ronni snorted. "And if the Company were any good at mind reading, we'd need far fewer agents running around doing things. But you do have a good point about the writing. I'd argue the target still needs to be mostly humanoid, or at least have roughly humanoid hands to produce writing intelligible enough for communication."

Humanoid, huh?

Daniel glanced up and down the street. For all the humans wandering the streets or driving a car, he spotted nothing more exotic than the occasional elf or gnome.

Across the street, a man pulled out a thin, black wand and glanced furtively around. The agent slowed and frowned, his free hand drifting toward his jacket. He wouldn't allow himself to be incapacitated by a spell.

The wizard never turned toward him. He waved the wand and muttered something, but the CIA agent was too far away to make it out.

The agent narrowed his eyes then laughed as the man's car floated a few inches off the ground and away from the two vehicles parked in the front and back of it.

"What's so funny?" Ronni probed.

Daniel shook his head. "Just saw a wizard who'd rather use magic than try to drive out of a tight spot. It's not something I would have thought of using magic to do. It's like a new kind of parallel parking. Wonder if that's on his driving test. Maybe it's a good thing I'm not a magical. I might not be creative enough to pull it off."

"That idea kind of makes sense to me."

He frowned. "Then again, with all this routine magic, even the non-flashy stuff means new security precautions everywhere."

"Like at your target?"

"Yeah. Maybe, but it's a good thing I'm not relying on

magic." He blew out a breath. "Just another way my life's complicated."

Ronni laughed in his ear. "Don't worry. You've got me to help with anything too annoying."

"Sometimes, it's simply strange to think about."

"What?"

Daniel slowed his pace as he approached another crossing. "I'm old enough to remember a world where magic was something you only saw in the movies. Sure, I was a kid, but even then, I got that it wasn't supposed to be real, and then it came back to Earth in a big way, and then—"

No. Not everything's got to be about my parents, even if they probably did know before everyone else.

"Daniel?" Ronni asked. "You still there?"

He frowned. "No big deal. It's just that we went from only knowing about one sentient species to now having a connection to a magical world with thousands." He watched two elves enter a shop. "And most of them are easy to handle, but I've seen situations where it's like the Mos Eisley Cantina come to life."

"Where's that?"

"Where's what?"

"The Mos Eisley Cantina."

Daniel frowned. "You seriously don't know about the Mos Eisley Cantina?"

"I didn't work that mission."

The agent scrubbed a hand down his face. "When I get back, we'll have a conversation about classic sci-fi cinema. There are some obvious holes in your education. Or look it up on the net when you have a chance."

His thoughts drifted back to his missing parents, and he shook his head. He needed to get off the topic.

"Since I still have a few more minutes to kill," Daniel began, "why don't you let me know about the top three on the Homeland Security Enhanced Threat list?"

Ronni sighed. "Sir, you know that kind of thing isn't within our scope of duty. Shouldn't you leave that to Paranormal Defense agents?"

Daniel peeked down a nearby narrow alley. An orange tabby cat stared back at him with a studied arrogance.

"Come on, Ronni. Humor me. Maybe I'll decide I'm tired of all this, and I'll need a new career."

"And what will you change your career to?"

"Bounty hunter," Daniel responded.

The density of people, human or otherwise, was picking up as he closed in on the bar. A few drones whirred through the sky. The good thing about having so many machines in the sky was that no one would think twice about spotting another one, which meant he could always have Ronni provide him with aerial recon backup if he needed it.

She chuckled. "You'll become a bounty hunter about the same time I quit the Company to get a job as a singer."

"Like I said, humor me."

The woman let out a defeated sigh. "Okay, coming in at number three is a gnome named Cailarin."

"A gnome? Huh. I don't know. I half-expected an elf for some reason."

"Cailarin wore out his welcome on Oriceran. As far as I can tell, everyone wants to take him out. He was a big player in the Dark Market there."

"The Dark Market? Interesting."

Daniel scratched his cheek, his finger running over the edge of the scar. The CIA's reach to Oriceran was limited, but they'd tried to collect as much information on the Dark Market as possible. It was an open-air venue for the shady trade of Earth technology often mixed with magic. Not only was it on a different planet, but its location had become mobile, and their defensive magic kept even powerful Oriceran authorities from easily tracing them.

"Interesting?" Ronni echoed. "What? Is visiting that place on your bucket list?"

"Only for the purposes of research."

"This guy's big," she explained. "Well, he's a gnome, so he's short, but he's a big deal. He's helped create a new dark web system nicknamed Venger. You not only need specific software but also a minimum of magical ability."

"So, most humans can't use it. Annoying."

"Exactly, and I've read a lot about this. The CIA hasn't had much luck getting magical help. Sure, they can find some contractors or whatever, but none who are both magical and big enough dirtbags to dig into something like that."

Daniel snorted. "Have to appreciate loyalty, even among scum."

"Number two. Oh. Wait."

He frowned, some tension spreading across his neck and back. "What's wrong?"

"Nothing's wrong," Ronni replied. "Just the number two was taken out yesterday by a bounty hunter, a class-six guy from LA."

Relief spread through him. No one liked their backup telling them something was wrong during a mission.

The agent turned a corner onto a side street. He was close to the bar now, and the crowds began to lessen. "Impressive. Not a lot of class-six bounty hunters out there. Okay, so number two is toast. What about number one?"

"Huh. She's new."

"Who?"

"The number one has no name, only an alias, Morgana. The weird thing is they have all sorts of information about her alleged crimes, including some mass murders in some remote villages in a few different countries, but not a lot about her actual capabilities. They don't even know if she's from Earth or Oriceran. They've only found a lot of dead bodies, many with organs missing, and a few fuzzy pictures and a cryptic message scrawled in blood mentioning her name at two of the massacre sites."

Daniel grimaced. "Makes the gnome look like a saint in comparison."

"Yeah. I'll say."

He shook his head and approached the weathered, wooden door leading to his destination.

"I'm at the bar. I'll have a quick chat with Rolf to see what he can tell me."

Ronni sighed. "I can't believe you trust all these shady contacts of yours."

The agent allowed himself a smile. He couldn't do anything about mysterious women killing people in villages, but he could handle the job in front of him.

"Money's more powerful than magic at times."

Sure, he had to keep track of the money he spread around to get better intel off the books and expense it through Nessie in creative ways, but he doubted she didn't know exactly what he was doing. Sometimes, when it came to working for the CIA, everyone needed a little plausible deniability.

Daniel rubbed his hands together. "Okay, Rolf, let's see what you've got for me."

CHAPTER SIX

He skulked along the darkened streets as he made his way to the Leuchtenberg Palais. Midnight had come and gone. Clouds blocked the moon and the stars, even if they didn't do much about the street lamps and the light filtering down from the high rises in the distance. It was a good night for a break-in.

Nice to have some cloudy weather and a little more darkness.

"Do you have a good visual on me, Ronni?" he murmured. "Rolf's little briefing was useful, but he won't exactly cry if I end up shot. He already got his payment."

"Yes," she replied in his earpiece. "Got two drones up with full IR capabilities, one following you and one flying around the site. Nothing suspicious or unusual other than you creeping through the streets at night."

Daniel chuckled, adjusted his tie, and shook his head. "Then this should be easy, especially with the information he gave me on the alarm system. I won't even need you to go full out."

"And you buy everything he told you?"

"I paid for it, so sure."

Ronni sighed. "You know what I mean."

He grinned. "The fact that our allegedly semi-dead man, John Rainer, is a former OSS agent might explain why the CIA's so interested in him, even if they aren't passing that information on to me. If our little proto-CIA agent was doing anti-magic work during the war, that might also explain why they don't have a lot of information on him to pass on. Who knows what kind of magic was used to cover up secrets man wasn't supposed to know, especially during a world war?"

"And it doesn't bother you that your random contact knew exactly who was supposed to be there but the Company didn't?"

"First of all, they might know and simply don't want to tell me. Second, we all have our areas of expertise."

"And you really think, 'Open up the sarcophagus, and John will do the hard part for you' is believable? Not even a fancy incantation or something?"

Daniel looked down the street. "Maybe this is more where wishful thinking comes into play. I'm really hoping I won't have to haul a dead body several blocks back to my car. Even with the light foot traffic this late at night, it'd get a little dicey, and I don't want to beat up a bunch of cops."

He stepped out of a side street in front of his target building, a reinforced concrete-and-brick multilevel structure covered with windows. The modern Leuchtenberg Palais was a re-creation, but that didn't make the museum or the historical artifacts inside fake.

They've got a semi-dead guy inside, too.

The agent took a deep breath. "Okay, ready to get this started. I need you to redirect the camera feeds."

Ronni didn't say anything for several long seconds before expelling a deep breath. "Done, but remember there's a time limit on this."

Daniel smiled and lifted his phone. "Don't worry. I've no intention of overstaying my welcome. We'll go wake the dead and head back to my car. It'll be easy."

A few quick taps and swipes, along with a few addresses and codes courtesy of his informant, gave him access to the main alarm system. Shutting it off would be too obvious. The failsafes would activate and contact security, but no one had thought to add one for maintenance mode.

"Every lock has a key," he muttered to himself and sent the command. "Can you confirm success, Ronni?"

"Yes. Power changes throughout the building. Alarm's disabled and running a diagnostic cycle. Thermal scans have the guards on the opposite side of the building. Better move fast."

The agent reached into his pocket and pulled out the optical camouflage device with his left hand. He ran his fingers over the activation grooves and tapped in the haptic code listed in his briefing documents. A second later, he mostly vanished.

Daniel looked down at his hands. The vague outline was there but almost impossible to see in the dark.

Huh. Maybe the Predator was simply a CIA agent.

"Ronni, do you see me on IR?" he asked.

"Yep."

"Good to know the limitations. Remind me later to point that out to Nessie."

The semi-invisible agent jogged toward a service door in the back. He reached out with a gloved hand and tried the handle. Locked. Not unexpected.

Daniel pulled out a thin metallic card and waved it over the keypad next to the door. The pad beeped, and the door clicked open.

Three steps into the storage room, he winked back into existence.

The agent snorted. "That didn't last long."

"What's wrong?"

He looked down at his hands. "Check the feed from my glasses."

"Those are nice gloves," Ronni commented. "And a little bit of invisibility is still pretty useful."

"Says the woman thousands of miles and many time zones away."

She sighed. "I'd be worthless in the field. I'd trip over my own shoelaces and get you shot."

Sometimes, that girl is no fun to tease.

Daniel cracked the storage room door to the darkened hallway. "Like I said, we all have our areas of expertise. Just let me know about those alarms. That'll be the key to all this."

"Yes, sir."

The agent hurried down several hallways until he reached a stairway. Even though they'd restored the external façade of the palace when they'd rebuilt it, the interior had been redone several times throughout the decades to better match modern layouts. He wasn't sure if that made the job easier or harder.

According to Rolf, the sarcophagus lay hidden in a

basement storage facility. Thus far, his codes and other information had proven accurate, so Daniel had no reason to doubt the man. As long as you coughed up the cash, Rolf was reliable.

Someday, someone's going to pay him a big wad of cash to ask about me. He doesn't know too much, but he knows enough. That'll be an interesting day.

Daniel's footsteps echoed as he headed down the stairs to the basement, ignoring the obvious cameras. Ronni might not be able to take a joke, but she could take care of a few cameras as easily as he'd beat up that thug in the corner grocery.

We all have our roles in protecting the country.

Another electronic lock was at the bottom of the stairwell. With a quick wave of his card, he was through the door.

Lights clicked on in sequence. His stomach tightening, he hissed and jumped back, his hand going to the stun grenade disguised as a tie pin. No reason to kill some poor guard who was merely doing his job.

"You okay?" Ronni asked.

Daniel's gaze cut back and forth. "Just motion-sensitive lights. No big deal. Where are the guards?"

"Still on the other side of the building, and they're stationary," she reported. "Time's ticking. You don't have much time before they do a sweep of the building."

"I know. Don't worry. I've got this, assuming I don't have to fight Mr. Semi-Dead Rainer."

A hint of desperation crept into her voice as she spoke next. "And what if you run out of time? I guess I could kill the lights or something for you."

He grinned. "Don't worry. I can always hide in the sarcophagus."

"Hide with a dead guy?" Her voice shook as she said it.

The agent shook his head. Even if she wasn't there, she'd be able to see the motion through her AR glasses feed. "Nope. Remember, the guy's not supposed to be dead."

Daniel made his way down the end of the hallway. It opened into a large room filled with crates and other items wrapped in plastic or canvas covers. He tapped the side of his glasses for a thermal scan.

"That's weird," Ronni commented.

"What's weird? Just hoping I might get lucky and get a thermal hit off John Rainer, assuming he's semi-alive."

So far, all he saw was a lot of room-temperature objects.

"That's not what I mean," Ronni replied. "I had some weird interference on one of the drone feeds both in the IR and visual bands."

"Not exactly in the middle of the forest here, so not all that surprising."

"Yeah, maybe, but not getting any interference on your comm or your vitals."

Daniel narrowed his eyes, the hairs on the back of his neck standing up. He hoped it was nothing, but he couldn't be sure. "Your little magical boost helps."

He said it as much to convince himself as Ronni.

"Oh, I didn't think of that."

The agent deactivated his thermal scan. He wasn't having much luck. It was time to start pulling canvas covers off objects and hope for the best.

He continued lifting covers and looking under them. An old piano, a billiards table, a cuneiform tablet, but no sarcophagus.

Ronni swallowed. "You okay? Your heart rate is slightly elevated."

"Fine," Daniel replied, keeping his voice cheery. "Merely frustrated."

He saw no reason to panic her because of a distant suspicion, but that didn't mean he couldn't be more alert.

Something's wrong, but what? If the museum guards knew I was here, they would have already set the alarm off, and Ronni would know even if they decided to use a silent alarm.

Daniel tugged at the edge of a cover and smiled, some of his tension melting away. The corner of a stone sarcophagus lay in front of him. He pulled the rest of the cover off.

Bingo.

The large, stone sarcophagus was covered in a thick layer of dust but was otherwise featureless.

"That's boring," Ronni commented. "I expected it to be spookier. You know, have magic symbols on it or hieroglyphics."

"This isn't an ancient sarcophagus housing a pharaoh." Daniel furrowed his brow, wondering if he should try to be quiet when he pushed off the lid. "Where are the guards? And what are the alarm and camera statuses?"

"Guards are still stationary, but it's darn close to their patrol time. Alarms are still disabled. Cameras are still looping."

He shrugged and pushed hard against the lid. "Screw it. Let's just get this over with."

The lid fell off with a resounding and echoing thud.

His target, dressed in a faded black suit, lay inside with his arms crossed over his chest. He looked peaceful for a skeleton.

"Well, damn," the agent muttered. "This just looks like a dead g—"

The skeleton jerked upright. The agent backpedaled, going for his stun clip before dropping his hand.

What am I going to do? Disable a dead guy with some nasty volts? Maybe my explosive rounds?

He began reaching for his gun, but his hand never made it. He watched, wide-eyed, as lungs grew in the rib cage of the skeleton, then a stomach appeared, kidneys, a liver, and a brain. Muscles threaded themselves across the body until a few seconds later, the skeleton in a suit had been replaced by a skinless man in a suit. Daniel swallowed hard, unable to look away.

As he watched, skin spread from the hands and over the body. In the course of fifteen seconds, the skeleton had been replaced by a well-built, square-jawed, blond-haired, blue-eyed man.

The corpse sucked in air. John Rainer had been nothing but bones less than a minute before, and now, the dead man was alive once again.

Damn. Rolf was right. John did do all the hard work.

The CIA agent shook his head. "Well, shit, that's not something you see every day."

Ronni sighed. "Look, that was both the most awesome and most disturbing thing I've seen for a long time. I think next time on a mission, I might not watch your AR feed, but you've got to move. They will start their patrol any minute now."

John jerked his head back and forth, blinking, his face pale. He locked eyes with Daniel. "Where the hell am I?"

"You're John Rainer?"

"Yeah. Who's asking?" The man eyed him with suspicion. "How do I know you're not a Nazi?"

Ronni gasped. "He's got no clue."

Of course not. He's been dead for a long time.

Daniel didn't voice the thought. The last thing he needed to do was confuse an already panicky man.

The other man narrowed his eyes. "You're not a German."

He blew out a breath. "You're in Munich, Agent Rainer, and I'm not a German or Nazi. Fuck Hitler."

John frowned. "Who are you then?"

A little lie will soften the blow.

"I was sent by OSS to recover you. The higher-ups lost track of you. All I know is it might have something to do with magic." Daniel shrugged. "I tracked you here and found you in that sarcophagus where you were...uh, resting."

The man's eyes widened. "So, you're really in the know, huh? Yeah. Okay. That makes this easier. Glad to have someone save my ass. They told me that the elf dame might help me out, but if I got in too deep, then I was on my own."

Elf dame?

Daniel nodded. "Look, I don't have a lot of time to explain, and we need to get going sooner rather than later."

John looked down at the sarcophagus and shook his

head. "Maybe I shouldn't be surprised." He hopped out of his not-so-final resting place and wobbled. "Damn. Sorry, pal, just a little woozy. Damned Nazis."

That's because you've been dead for almost a hundred years.

Daniel pondered his response. "You've been through a lot. I'll explain everything later."

His companion shook his head. "Yeah, sure, pal." He rubbed the bridge of his nose. "If I were at one hundred percent, I'd be able to beat down any of these krauts all the way to the North Pole and wouldn't need help from a skirt, elf or not."

Oh, John, you'll have to spend some time adjusting to the twenty-first century. A lot of stuff has changed.

"Daniel! The guards are on the move, and we've got more showing up," Ronni reported, static eating her voice. "And…I—" The link died completely.

What the hell? Jamming?

"The CIA shouldn't play around with magic if they don't know how to stop it from being disrupted," a husky voice purred from behind him.

He spun and yanked the stun pin off his tie. A leggy elf with long blonde hair stood behind him with her arms crossed. Her black leather outfit clung to her body like a second skin. If his heart hadn't been beating so hard from the surprise, it might have done so from the sexy sight alone.

"Daisy," Daniel muttered. "Why am I not surprised?"

"Daisy?" John shook his head. "Nah, that's Marie."

The CIA agent gritted his teeth, glaring at the woman. "Guess I know which elf babe you were talking about."

She chuckled and shrugged. "You're not still sore about that little thing in Budapest, are you, Daniel?"

"Yeah, I am. And the little thing in Seoul and the little thing in Bogota." He kept the stun pin in his fingers.

Daisy grinned. "You didn't seem to mind that little thing in Paris."

Damn. She's got me there, but I don't have time for this crap.

Daniel shrugged. "Plus, I might pay people with no loyalty for information, but it doesn't mean I trust them simply because they're hot and have a little magic."

She wagged a finger. "I'm loyal enough. Just because I'm an independent contractor doesn't mean I'm disloyal. It merely means my loyalties are subject to revision."

Trust as few as possible and for as little time as possible.

John shook his head. "I don't understand what the hell is going on. I thought you were supposed to help me out, Marie. You working with the Krauts now?"

"Oh, John, I haven't gone by that name in…whew, a good forty years, now." Her smile vanished. "And I never worked for *those* people."

He blinked several times. "Forty years? What are you talking about? I know you elves live a long time, but you told me that was your name when we met a few weeks ago."

Daisy laughed. "Oh, too perfect. You didn't even bother to tell him?"

"Tell me what?"

Daniel took a step forward, ignoring John. "Why are you even here? Other than to screw with me? I thought I made my opinion clear when I left you that message in the bar in London."

The elf sighed. "See, I'm sorry, but I need to recover Johnny Boy there. I was responsible for him, and I kind of lost track of him. Now I'm cleaning up my mess. It's nothing personal."

"Who you working for this time?"

She winked. "No one. Like I said, it's more about cleaning up my mess."

"If this is about the OSS, it doesn't matter. I'm taking him back to the States."

Daisy shook her head. "It's more complicated than that. I'll need him to come with me. Don't make this hard, Daniel."

John looked back and forth between the two. "What the hell is going on?"

The elf ignored the man and snapped her fingers. Glowing symbols appeared atop her leather-covered arms. "Come on, Daniel. Don't do this. I like you. I don't want to have to hurt you."

Daniel snorted. "I think that's my line."

The door burst open and six guards rushed in, all holding contact Tasers.

"Damn it," he muttered. "Of course."

CHAPTER SEVEN

Daniel gritted his teeth. The stun pin might take out one, but that still left a lot of them, and he couldn't kill innocent men because he'd gotten sloppy and let a hot elf surprise him.

Shit. Forgot that Ronni was being jammed. Should have kept track of the time myself.

"Put your hands in the air," one of the guards shouted in German. Even if Daniel didn't already understand the language, the intent would have been obvious.

Daisy let out a long sigh and the symbols faded from her arms. "Unfortunate."

He rolled his eyes and shook his head. "Thanks, Daisy. If you weren't jamming me, I would have known they were coming. Thanks for that, by the way."

John shook his head. "Who are those Krauts? They don't look like Nazis or Wehrmacht."

A slight frown settled on the elf's face as she looked at the guards and then John. All her mirth from before had vanished. "Take care of him, and I'll cover you." She sighed. "But I better not regret this. I already lost him for long enough. And don't get used to me helping you, especially for free."

Daniel shook his head. "I swear I won't let anything happen to him."

The other man just blinked. "I have no idea what the hell is going on."

"On the ground," shouted a guard in German, his face reddening.

Daisy sauntered toward the guards and stretched her laced hands above her head. "Won't even need magic to deal with these."

The men all frowned.

"You will surrender." This time it was in perfect, if accented, English.

She stepped toward the guards with a grin. "You better get going."

Daniel nodded. "I owe you one."

"I'll add it to your tab."

The elf sprinted forward, all but gliding to the side as a guard thrust a contact Taser at her. She slammed a fist into his stomach, and he fell with a grunt.

Before the man had even hit the ground, Daisy spun and smashed an elbow into the next closest man's nose.

"Let's go," Daniel shouted to John and sprinted off.

The other man hurried after him, frowning and glancing over his shoulder.

The CIA agent bent the stun pin and tossed it at a guard on his way out. It bounced harmlessly off him.

Helpful.

Some of the guards tried to take off after the pair, but a few quick kicks from Daisy refocused their attention.

The OSS and CIA agents ran through the hallway.

John frowned. "I still don't get it."

"What's to get? We're escaping from some Germans."

"Do you even know what's going on?"

Daniel laughed. "I was only told to rescue you because you had useful information the Co…that the US government needed."

His companion snorted. "Yeah, that sounds like the brass. Need to know and all that crap. We're over here risking our lives against the Fascists, and they act like we'll lose the war if any of us grunts on the bottom knows any part of the big picture. They already let us know magic is real. Why not tell us the rest?"

"You're preaching to the choir, John."

Daniel saw a chance to get better information on who knew what and when. *Love my country, will defend it all day long, but still, need to know more.*

First, though, he needed to make sure the outside was clear.

The agent nodded. "Yeah. Ronni, can you hear me?"

There was no response over his receiver.

"Ronni? No, pal, the name is John. You already said it. How could you forget?"

The CIA agent chuckled. "I was trying to get hold of someone else. Long story."

John's face scrunched. "This some magic nonsense?"

Daniel chuckled. "Yeah, that's not totally inaccurate."

They hit the stairs and took them two at a time. John wobbled and reached for the banister, slowing them down.

"Sorry," he said, looking confused. "I work out all the time. Not sure what's wrong with me."

Very long nap.

The agent reached the first floor and looked over his shoulder at the other man. "What were you doing when you got…captured?"

The OSS agent still didn't seem to have any clue about what had happened to him. Daniel didn't know the best time to let him know the truth, but he doubted it was as they were fleeing from guards and, most likely, with police closing in.

John frowned. "The last thing I remember is that I was supposed to be looking into those damned Nazis getting all fresh with some evil magic types about making magical rockets. Toys they can fling not only across the channel at the Brits but anywhere. From space even. How weird is that?" He shook his head. "But next thing I know, someone nails me from behind, and then I wake up here." He glanced around. "Surprised not to see more of those bastards around. And what were those krauts even holding, earlier? That more magic?"

Daniel shook his head. "A type of stun device. It's not magical at all."

"They're ahead of us on that kind of thing? Not good. Lucky you saved my butt." He snorted. "I told the brass that I needed more backup than Marie or Daisy or whatever her name is. By the way, pal, what's your name? I've never seen you before, and I thought I knew every one of the guys working this part of Germany."

"You can call me Daniel. I was recruited a little more… recently than you."

The agent watched his companion become steadily more agile as his muscles grew stronger. Whatever physical troubles John had right after his resurrection were disappearing. He finally had no trouble keeping pace.

Their loud footfalls echoed down the hallway as Daniel led the other man toward the storage room.

"Just so you know, Daniel," John began. "If you're worried about leaving a dame behind, Marie may look like Lana Turner, but she fights like Jake LaMotta—but from the sound of it, you already knew that."

He laughed. "Yeah, we've definitely run into each other. I know how much ass she can kick."

The other man grinned.

The CIA agent broke toward the storage room door. Despite the presence of the guards, the alarms hadn't gone off. Ronni still had his back, even if she couldn't communicate with him.

Keep it up. We're almost clear.

"Can..." *crackle* "...me?" Ronni's staticky voice sounded in his ear.

He threw the storage room door open, then the door to the outside. "Yeah, I can hear you, Ronni."

He twisted the ring, and a holographic copy of him appeared ten feet away.

"What the hell?" John shouted.

Daniel grinned. "A little distraction, that's all."

He was fine with the man thinking it was magic for the moment.

Ronni sighed. "I tried to switch frequencies and adjust things, but I couldn't reach you."

He chuckled. "You did fine. It was magical interference."

John glanced his way, shook his head, and muttered underneath his breath.

"Did you get John Ranier out?" she asked.

The CIA agent looked over his shoulder. "Yeah, I definitely did."

They hit the street, and John stopped dead on the sidewalk. He looked right and left as cars and trucks zoomed past. His eyes widened, and he turned slowly, taking in the lights of the buildings around them and off in the distance.

The ring on Daniel's hand sparked and zapped him, and the decoy vanished. He shook his head.

Well, it was cool while it lasted.

John shook his head. "This isn't Munich."

"It most definitely is." The CIA agent put a hand on the other man's shoulder. "Look, I get that you have a lot of questions, but we still need to run unless you want to have to explain yourself to a lot of angry Germans."

"Yeah, pal. Sure, that makes sense."

Daniel looked over his shoulder, then in the sky for any following drones. "Ronni, what's the situation?"

"Looks like you're clear, sir. I've lost access to the cameras. The police are on their way, but they can't get hold of anyone at the museum. Did you take them all out?"

He glanced back as the Leuchtenberg Palais faded into the distance, a bright spot in the darkened area.

The CIA agent chuckled. "No, had a little help, and now I owe someone a favor."

Forty-five minutes later, John stared out the window of the

Jaguar. They were almost at the rendezvous point. The OSS agent hadn't said more than a few words since they'd arrived at Daniel's car.

Maybe it's a bitch to have the Company transport the thing around the world for me, but it's not like I can find a rental car with all these enhancements. I wonder if this car was the thing that finally pushed him over the edge.

The man sighed and shook his head. "Level with me, Daniel."

He glanced at his passenger. "About what?"

"The city, those stun gadgets, your invisible walkie-talkie. Damn, even this car. It looks like something from a Buck Rogers serial." John pointed to the touchscreen display. "And it talks to you."

"That was merely the GPS earlier." Daniel shrugged.

"GPS?" He frowned. "I need the truth, and don't feed me any need-to-know OSS bullshit."

Daniel released a long sigh. "First of all, I don't work for the OSS."

"But you don't work for the Nazis."

The CIA agent shook his head. "No. Even if the Nazis were still around as a major threat, there's no way in hell I would work for them."

John eyed him. "What, you working for the Brits? You don't sound English, but your accent's funny and you talk all fancy."

Daniel chuckled. No one had ever called him fancy before in his entire life.

"I work for the CIA. Central Intelligence Agency. President Truman dissolved the OSS after the war, and the CIA took its place. An important part of the Cold War, too."

"Cold war?"

"Yeah, kind of us and the Soviets staring at each other, waiting for the other side to blink."

John snorted. "Yeah, Reds were better than the Nazis, but not by much." He furrowed his brow. "Cold War? President Truman? I guess I was out for a lot longer than a few days or weeks." He grinned nervously. "But if we could have a Cold War with the Reds, it meant we won the big war at least, right?"

"Yep. And then some. About a year after you were, uh... were put under, the Allies launched a massive operation. With the help of some more OSS trickery we misled the Nazis, and we ended up with a massive amphibious landing on a beach in France. Pushed in from the west while the Soviets pushed in from the east. Less than a year after that, we took Europe back. Four months later, the Japanese surrendered."

His companion nodded slowly, taking it all in.

He figured revealing the existence of city-killing nuclear weapons might be a bit too much for the man to process at the moment. He turned into an alley where a black van waited. Two men stood in front of the vehicle. The CIA agent pulled out his phone and dialed.

One of the men retrieved his phone from his pocket and answered. "A phoenix will rise from the ashes."

Daniel put his phone on mute. "Verify the voice print, Ronni."

"Already did. He's clear."

The CIA agent unmuted his phone. "But the scorpion will always sting."

The man nodded and opened the side door of the van.

Daniel nodded toward him. "They'll take you from here, John."

The OSS agent opened the Jaguar's passenger door and stepped out. He lingered with his hand on the top of the car.

"I thought I was out for at least two years. It's a hard pill to swallow, but at least I didn't have a wife or kid waiting for me. But I'm guessing I was out for a lot longer than that."

Daniel looked down for a moment. John did deserve to know, but someone else could be the one to tell him.

Screw it. If I had been born earlier, I might have been this guy.

He shrugged. "Not two years. About a hundred."

John went pale and whistled, shaking his head. "No," he whispered. "That long, huh?"

The CIA agent stared at him. "You're still standing. I thought you might take that harder."

The other man shook his head. "Look, my head's spinning like a well-oiled top right now, but it wasn't all that long ago. Well, it wasn't that long ago for me, anyway, that running into some elf dame would have messed with my head, too." He shrugged. "Still got cars, Germans, and elves. The world's not so different."

"Lot more magicals out in the open now. These days, everyone knows about magic."

John grinned. "You're telling me the streets are filled with beautiful elf dames?" He whistled. "Do they all wear outfits like Marie—uh, Daisy?"

Daniel shrugged. "Not quite, but there are still a lot of magicals walking around."

The OSS agent stepped away from the door. "Not a bad thing for this Rip Van Winkle to wake up to." He winked and slammed the door shut.

Ronni laughed over her link. "I guess men don't change, no matter what decade they're from."

He grinned. "Good luck, John. You're going to need it."

CHAPTER EIGHT

Smiling, Daniel drove away from the alley. "Thanks for all your help, Ronni."

The woman sighed. "I wasn't much help after I got jammed."

"It all worked out in the end, so don't worry about it. I'm sure you'll be able to make a link that they can't jam with magic so easily, but for now I've delivered the Company goods, so I'll go offline and call it a night. It's been a busy one."

"Okay, sir," Ronni responded. "You've earned it. It's not as late for me here, so I'll stick around for a couple of hours if you need me."

"Thanks. If I don't talk to you before then, I'll see you in Virginia."

Daniel yanked the small receiver out of his ear, and he tapped his tie mic to kill transmission.

A lot of running, but not too much trouble. And I still have time for my little side job for Pops. I hope it involves fewer surprises.

Halfway to the next destination, Daniel pulled his car into an alley and tapped a few commands into the touchpad. A moment later, the car shimmered. Its silver paint job was replaced by a red one and a new license plate, a disguise for the car with the help of a little resonant nanopaint. It was far too costly for any normal person to even think about using it, but the CIA spared no expense. At least, they didn't when someone in the Special Assistance Division got bored and came up with new ideas for gadgets.

Sometimes, the agent half-wondered if the CIA existed more to test out exotic technologies than to collect intelligence. Maybe the whole point was simply to put men in extreme circumstances and see how their gadgets helped.

The complete history of the government's involvement with magic remained murky, even after all the committee meetings and hearings of the last couple of decades. John Rainer proved that the CIA's predecessor had focused on taking care of magic almost a hundred years before. Scraps here and there had mentioned other groups as well, such as the Pinkertons working with the US government on magical defense as early as the 19th century.

John's right. The world keeps spinning, but things don't change that much. Greedy bastards, dangerous countries, and the men and women trying to protect their country.

Daniel reversed, backing the car out of the alley and onto the street. He'd called ahead and his contact was waiting, but the man wouldn't hang around all night. The agent's car zoomed down the night streets of Munich, and his thoughts raced just as fast.

I hope this guy doesn't try to take me for too much money. I hate it when they suddenly decide they're master hagglers.

Magic—and the truth of it—didn't bother him that much. The intelligence game was all about admitting there were surprising or dark truths hidden in the world. In a lot of ways, learning that magic existed in the world helped certain things make more sense. The only problem came down to a simple question: how can a man learn the truth when he doesn't know the right questions to ask?

Daniel shook his head. He might be great at lying to others, but he never lied to himself. That's what made it so easy for him to slip into other identities when he needed to and then back out of them.

What the hell really happened to my parents? Is the truth sitting there in a file on some spy's computer somewhere? Written on some gnome's scroll in Oriceran?

Tomb raiding had always been a dangerous profession, even before magic returned in full force. It hurt that his parents had gone missing, but he couldn't claim to be shocked.

The agent snorted. He knew some of the government's darkest secrets, but he couldn't have simple closure on his parents.

"Just have to dig it up myself," he mumbled.

The minutes passed, and he pulled toward the open loading bay door of a warehouse that had seen better days judging by the rusted metal roof and vines crawling up the side of the building. Inside, a man with a panic-stricken face marched back and forth in front of a black BMW, a cigarette dangling from his lips.

Daniel stopped his car. The man's appearance matched the contact in his grandfather's file, but he couldn't be too careful.

Too bad I don't still have a stun pin or a holographic decoy.

The CIA agent stepped out of his car. "Are you Gunter?" he called out in German.

The man stopped pacing. He dropped his cigarette on the ground and crushed it with his foot. He pointed across the warehouse. A large, steel, cross-eyed elephant sat there.

Okay, that's different. This guy some sort of artist?

Gunter let out a tortured laugh. "You have to help me," he responded in German. "I was told you were coming to pick up the gun."

Daniel held up a hand to try to calm the man. His grandfather's notes didn't say anything about the contact being so skittish. As far as the agent knew, the artifact wasn't stolen, and no one else was supposed to be looking for it—but no elf was supposed to show up on his main job, either.

"Yes, I'm here to pick it up. Just need to know what you want for it. Money would be the easiest. I can do any sort of anonymous money transfer system, conventional or crypto. Simply tell me, and we can get this over in minutes."

His companion's next laugh was almost a giggle. "Money? Money? You think I want fucking money?" The guy started pacing again.

Daniel shrugged. "Okay, we can talk barter. No one told

me ahead of time, so we'll have to arrange another drop, but I'm fine with that."

"No, no, no. You don't get it. You don't get it at all." The wild-eyed man shook his head.

"Then help me understand. What do you want?"

Gunter stopped pacing. "For you to take the fucking thing off my hands and forget I ever existed."

Daniel furrowed his brow. "Excuse me?"

"You heard me. Take it. Bury it. Shoot it off into space or kick it through a portal to Oriceran. Just get it the fuck away from me."

"You want me to take an artifact from you? For free?"

Calling Daniel incredulous would be the understatement of the century.

Gunter bobbed his head and rushed over to his car. He threw open the trunk, revealing what looked like a gigantic shotgun with a black metal stock. Hand cannon might have been a more appropriate description given that the barrel was over two feet in diameter and half an inch thick, but there were no obvious triggers or buttons.

Strange glyphs were inscribed on both sides, but the agent didn't recognize them.

He frowned, looking the weapon over. "This is a gun, right?"

"Yeah, it's a damned gun. What did you think it was, a ladle?"

The CIA agent shrugged. "It's got no trigger. How do you fire it? What's special about it?"

"What's special about it?" Gunter shivered and shook his head. "Just point it at anything."

Daniel hoisted the weapon up with a frown. It was far

lighter than he'd expected given the size of the barrel alone. He swung it away from his companion.

The man winced. "Don't point it at my car, damn it. Aim at something in the warehouse."

The CIA agent kept the weapon moving until he found the rusted remains of a van sitting on the other end of the warehouse. "Now what? Where's the trigger?"

"I think you're the trigger. I don't know." Gunter shrugged. "You wonder what it can do, and shit happens."

Daniel laughed. "Shit happens?"

"Yeah."

"Let's see if it can do a little something to this van then."

Daniel chuckled and lined up his shot, curiosity getting the better of him. Blue and red particles of light appeared on the sides of the weapon, swirling around it. A dissonant hum erupted from the front of the weapon, the harsh sound visible as distorted waves blasted toward the van. The weapon shook violently, and it took all his strength to keep it from bouncing right out of his hands.

The CIA agent gritted his teeth. His eyes widened a second later. The van began to vibrate, the molecules flowing and swirling in a bizarre vortex, but the basic shape maintained. Taken by surprise, his hand slipped. The weapon jerked, jarring the waves.

A wheel was suddenly mounted on the top of the van.

Sweat poured down Daniel's face. He clenched his teeth as the shaking intensified.

"How the fuck do you turn this thing off?" he shouted.

Gunter had retreated behind a concrete pillar, trembling like a leaf in a hurricane and more than ready to pee himself. "Think of something else. Something neutral."

The agent shut his eyes, trying first to clear his mind, but the image of the swirling particles only loomed larger in his thoughts.

Just like that damned meditation class I took. Try not to think of an elephant...fuck, guess that explains why the steel elephant is over there.

No, no, no. Neutral. Neutral. Harmless.

A yellow lightning rodent popped into his mind. A Pikachu.

Damn it, Ronni.

The gun stopped vibrating. Daniel knelt and set it on the ground before daring to open his eyes.

The van was now yellow with two red circles on the front. Large rodent-like metal ears rose from the front of the roof.

Gunter peeked around the pillar. "What the hell were you thinking?"

Daniel shrugged. "Hey, it got the job done." He shook his head and pointed at the weapon. "It's some kind of particle separator, I think. Rearranging matter based on thought—some sort of quantum effect, I'd guess. The boys and girls in S…let's just say people who know more than me would have a better idea, but whatever that thing is, it's way ahead of any technology we have on Earth."

"Yeah, I'm guessing it's from Oriceran. Doesn't that make it magic?"

The CIA agent shrugged and stepped away from the gun. "Have no clue. Where did you even find something like this?"

Gunter took several deep breaths. "I was renovating a building in—I was renovating an abandoned building, and

I found it in some rubble in the basement along with some other weird things. I thought they might be old Bavarian antiques."

Daniel nodded. "Where's the building?"

The other man shook his head. "No. I want nothing more to do with it. You're already here so you can take that, but I won't tell you where to find anything else. I buried the rest of it somewhere safe and far away. I was going to dig it up later, but now I'll let it rot. Maybe I'll go bomb it."

"I don't get it. Why are you so spooked now? I flew halfway across the world expecting to make a deal."

Gunter's hands shook as he marched over to some weathered crates in the corner. He nodded to an area behind them that was blocked from Daniel's view.

The CIA agent walked to the man and stopped. His stomach knotted. Bile rose in the back of his throat.

A body lay on the ground, except every part of what had once been a man had been fused together, and all in the wrong locations. More than a few organs were outside the body, and half the skin was missing or merged with the ground.

Gunter swallowed and crossed himself. "That was my friend. We were only joking around. We'd used it a few times on some cans and building materials before. No big deal. I didn't mean to do it. I just accidentally pointed it at him."

Daniel pulled out his second phone. "This body can't be left here."

"I know, but I can't call the police. They will think I did it on purpose."

"Don't worry, I know people who can handle this sort of thing discreetly." Daniel dialed.

"Purity Solutions," came a chipper female voice over the line.

The CIA agent rattled off a long alphanumeric sequence. "Put me through to Lydia."

"Right away, sir."

The line clicked over. "This is Lydia. How can I help you today, sir?"

"Please trace this phone's location for an emergency clean up. It's a strange one, so there will be a bonus."

"Right away, sir," she responded. "It'd be best if you vacated the location before our local agents arrive. I estimate they will be on site in fifteen minutes."

"Duly noted." Daniel hung up.

Gunter stared down at the mangled body of his friend. "Can you make sure he gets a decent burial?"

He shook his head. "I don't think that's happening. Sorry."

The other man sighed. "I understand." He stared at eyes on the wrong side of his friend's head. "I asked around, and I found out about Rolf. He said you're a good guy. That's why I was willing to meet you to sell it to you. You've seen it, though. You get that this thing is dangerous. Please tell me you'll take care of it."

"I think I'll have to do a little burying of my own soon." The CIA agent blew out a breath and nodded down at the body. "Some things, man's just not ready for."

He spun on his heel to head for his car.

Gunter ran after him. "Wait. Where are you going? You have to take it!"

"Don't worry. I'm taking it, but I'm not touching it directly again. I'll grab an emergency blanket from my trunk."

Daniel continued toward his Jaguar, shaking his head.

Did Pops know the details? There's no way he'd want something this dangerous for the shop. Why didn't he say anything?

"Some side job," he muttered.

CHAPTER NINE

Daniel stifled a yawn as he opened the door to the shop, carrying the gun still wrapped in a blanket he'd gotten from Nessie for occasions like this. It'd been a hectic trip to Germany, so much so that he'd slept in and decided to take a subsonic flight back to get even more relaxation, even though he'd had his car shipped back via supersonic transport. The Company was picking up the bill, and it didn't hurt to make sure the Jaguar hit the US before he did.

Ronni had informed him that the CIA was happy enough with the job. They'd gotten their OSS agent back without any casualties that needed to be explained away. A few reports mentioned a break-in to the museum level of the palace, but the German authorities discussed the bravery of the guards who'd successfully stopped the intruders from taking anything.

Did they even know there was a skeleton in there, or is that news only for public consumption?

The agent took a few steps inside and frowned. John Rainer was a man trapped out of his time, someone the CIA thought worth recovering. Daniel believed in the agency, but he also knew they weren't sentimental. They hadn't spent millions of dollars on gadgets and sent in a highly trained agent to save a dead man if he wouldn't prove very useful in some way.

He was investigating Nazi magic technology, but how important could something from one hundred years ago even be, especially now that magic's back?

Or is it something about his body itself? The guy was just bones, and he came back. But it didn't seem like he knew what the hell was going on, so I doubt he knew about what happened.

Daniel sighed and shook his head. It didn't matter. A man didn't work for the Company without learning to accept that he'd never have the big picture, no matter how frustrating it was. To the agency, compartmentalization of information was a key aspect of protecting the country in case of leaks and counterintelligence. If saving John Rainer helped the CIA, that was enough. Helping the CIA meant helping the nation.

He glanced down at the blanket-wrapped artifact. Worrying about John Rainer seemed pointless in a different way. Whatever the CIA might be keeping from him paled in comparison to the dangerous tool in his hand. He had no doubts that his clumsy, panicked use of the artifact didn't even begin to reveal all its capabilities. For all he knew, the thing could rework an entire building.

And some guy found this lying in a bunch of rubble. I've run into a lot of dangerous artifacts in my job, and I still wonder how long it'll be until someone accidentally digs up a magical nuke and an entire city goes missing. It's hard enough to worry about the actual threats from Oriceran, but random dangerous artifacts make everything almost impossible.

Daniel took a few steps in the dimly lit shop toward the back room. He needed to get the damned thing into the basement vault where it couldn't hurt anyone. Otherwise, Tommy could stumble on the thing and pick it up, not realizing it was still dangerous even without a trigger. Artifacts could be merged into something entirely different and dangerous.

The CIA agent grimaced at the thought and continued through the shop. The bulky weapon brushed against a knickknack, and a candlestick fell to the ground with a clatter.

He clenched his jaw and waited to see if half his shop would turn into some whacked-out Dali painting. The clicks of several old clocks were the only sounds in the shop for a good ten seconds.

Damn. Need to be more careful.

Daniel continued toward the back room's door, then to the door and stairs leading into the basement. At the bottom of the steps, he set the artifact on a table. He stared at it for a long moment before shaking his head.

Need to go wake Pops up.

The door at the top of the basement stairs creaked open, and the sudden illumination blinded him as someone turned on the lights. A few seconds later, his eyes adjusted.

His grandfather made his way down the stairs in his pajamas with a slight frown on his face.

Peter stopped at the base of the stairs and scowled. "You

could have told me you were coming back home so soon. I thought some punk had broken in."

Considering his grandfather wasn't holding a weapon or artifact, it was unclear how he might have dealt with said punk, but the old man was tougher than he looked. Even then, that wasn't a discussion they needed to pursue immediately.

Daniel pointed to the gun. "I don't want to talk about anything else until we discuss this little side job, Pops.'

The old man's face tightened, and he swallowed. "You managed to get it after all. How much did you have to pay? Have to spend a lot?"

The agent laughed. "Free. I think the guy would have even paid me to take it away."

"Huh. Really?"

Daniel's smile vanished. He shook his head. "Did you know?"

Peter sighed and looked away, saying nothing.

"Did you know?" he snapped. "Tell me the truth. You mentioned an unusual weapon, but this thing's a lot more than an unusual weapon."

"Yeah, I knew it was dangerous." His grandfather looked up with a sheepish expression. "I also knew if you went to grab it, there wouldn't be any trouble even if something went wrong." He shrugged. "But I didn't think there would be any trouble."

Daniel sighed and scrubbed a hand over his face. "Look, Pops. I don't care if you want to send me after some dangerous artifacts. It's not like I don't have the experience. I'm even used to not having the big picture when it comes to my day job." He pointed at his grandfather. "But I don't expect family to hold back, especially you."

Peter sighed and nodded. "You're right. I should have been upfront and told you everything. It's the first time I've really had you grab something that dangerous."

"I don't get it. Why didn't you tell me?"

"You're my grandson, and I know we've got a good relationship, but you're also a CIA agent. I thought if you knew how dangerous it was, you might take it to the Company instead of bringing it here."

Daniel took a deep breath and let it out slowly. No reason to make more of a scene.

"Maybe you could have tried trusting me, Pops."

"I know, and you're right. I helped raise you, after all. I know the kind of man you are." Determination broke out over Peter's face as he pointed at the gun. "But I couldn't help it. There are a few things the world should never know about—or at least not know about for as long as humanly possible. Some things tempt people too much, especially governments." He nodded toward the gun. "And that thing is one of them. Given the way you're acting, I guess you saw what it does up close and personal?"

Daniel nodded slowly. "Yeah, I saw what it could do to a lot of objects, including a person. That's not the kind of thing I'll forget anytime soon, and I've seen a lot of horrible things done to bodies in my time with the CIA.

Peter winced. "Damn. I'm sorry, Daniel."

The agent crossed his arms. "We've established that you know a lot more than you've let on. This thing is an extremely powerful artifact that somehow escaped the notice of the CIA, so you'll have to spill everything you know." He took a deep breath. "First off, what the hell is up with this thing? The power is incredible. Even powerful magicals can't do whatever they're thinking. There are a lot more rules and restrictions to normal magic. Is it Oriceran?"

His grandfather shook his head. "Not completely sure. Doubtful."

"Doubtful? What does that mean? You're saying a wizard or witch here made it? Or some sort of Earth-native magical?"

Peter exhaled a long sigh. "I don't know yet. The main thing I know for sure is that it's not Oriceran. The other thing I know—and if you've seen it in action, *you* know too—is that we better get the damned thing locked up and worry about figuring out where it came from later. That thing is dangerous. Hell, it's almost quaint to call it dangerous, but it's late, and this shouldn't be out one second longer than it needs to be."

Daniel frowned. "I want to know everything about it."

The old man shrugged. "I told you what I know. There's not much else I can say other than it's an awful thing that needs to be locked up in case someone's tempted to use it. Let's get it into the vault and pretend it doesn't exist."

The agent blew out a breath and gave him a slight nod. He could imagine what the CIA would do if they had something like the gun. Some temptations would prove too strong, even for the good guys, let alone the ones who operated in the gray areas.

"Can't say I disagree with you, Pops. Doesn't mean I'm not pissed about the stunt you pulled, but let's get this thing packed away."

He moved over to the back wall and put his hand on a spot near the corner. A low hum sounded, and the wall slid down, revealing a sealed metal door with a keypad and DNA scanner. Daniel tapped in a long code, then pressed his thumb on the scanner, waiting for the telltale burn.

The loud thud of several bolts releasing sounded from behind the door. He grabbed the massive wheel on the front and turned it until the door popped open with a hiss.

The interior of a huge, darkened chamber extended twenty yards on both sides. Densely packed shelves, crates, and boxes lay inside, the treasures from both his life and that of his parents and grandparents.

It's not like I've cataloged everything in here. How many other dark magical WMDs might be sitting in here that Pops hasn't told me about?

Daniel picked up the gun with the blanket before he stepped inside and set the artifact on a shelf near the back of the vault. He stepped out of the area and headed toward the stairs.

He looked over his shoulder as he hit the bottom of the stairs. "Next time don't hold out on me."

Peter nodded slowly, a grim expression on his face. "I won't."

An hour later, the vault door swung open and Peter stepped inside. He yanked out a notched rod embedded in the bottom of the barrel. Several etched glyphs stretched around the rod. Something seemed vaguely familiar about them, but he couldn't remember where he might have seen them before.

He exited the vault and walked over to his rapid 3D scanner and printer that sat on a corner table in the basement.

It was time to make a copy of the control rod. Sure, it'd only be the shape of the thing and would lack the bizarre molecular structure he was sure defined the true object, but that didn't matter. All he needed to do was fool Daniel if he ever examined the gun.

"Sorry to do this to you after making that promise, but you're not ready to know everything just yet."

CHAPTER TEN

Peter strolled down the darkened streets with his coat wrapped tightly around him. Even though there wasn't much of a breeze, the night air chilled his old bones.

Talk about being too old for this crap!

There were also not enough street lights around the neighborhood. If it weren't for his grandson, the locals would probably have more trouble with muggings. He wasn't worried about his own safety, but plenty of his neighbors wouldn't be able to defend themselves.

The cops tried their best, but there was never enough money to hire enough police, and bounty hunters didn't care about petty muggings and assaults since there wasn't enough money in it for them.

Freaking bounty hunter scum.

Peter patted his coat pocket. The rod rested inside. His contact had told him that it was effectively the operating system for the weapon. The old man had no reason to doubt him, given that it was exactly where he'd been told he'd find it. Not only that, but the character's reputation made it hard to believe he'd blatantly lie when seeking help, even compensated help.

A few minutes of walking brought the old man to King Street and a waiting taxi driven by Eagle Cabs, a small local firm with only a handful of drivers. Peter nodded, satisfied.

Daniel would be proud of me if he knew all the precautions I was taking.

It was hard, nowadays, to find a cab company or ride-hailing service that didn't take advantage of full GPS tracking or even magical tracking. Most customers preferred to be able to whip out their phones and know exactly where their vehicle and driver were, but he'd specifically selected the dying company for their lack of that specific feature. Peter needed to make sure no one was tracking him until he could hand the rod over to his contact.

He opened the door to the taxi and slipped inside.

The driver looked at him with a frown on his face. "You still going to the address in Georgetown you called in?"

The old man nodded. "Yeah. There's a better tip in it for you if you can get me there fast."

The cabbie grunted and turned. He pulled the cab away from the curb and didn't seem interested in chitchat. That suited his passenger just fine.

I have the operating system to a terrible and dangerous weapon, and I'm driving it around in a random cab. Anyone with a halfway-decent gun or spell could take me out.

Peter managed not to snort at the absurdity of it all. He

didn't want the driver to ask questions. His only desire was to get rid of the damned rod.

The quiet minutes passed with only the hum of the engine breaking the monotony. They hit the Key Bridge into Georgetown. The bright pinpoints of illumination from the dense buildings surrounding the bridge on both sides of the river never let him forget, even late at night, that he was in a major metropolitan area. The lights from the bridge and buildings reflected off the water and shimmered with the flow. The whole scene was beautiful and relaxing in its own way that the trip was almost worth it for the view.

I don't know if I need to get out more, or if I should appreciate that I'm still alive after all these years.

Peter thought that over for the remainder of the trip.

The cab pulled up in front of a small all-night diner with a brick façade, Harry's. He fished out some good old-fashioned cash and handed it to his laconic driver. One more thing that would make it hard to track him.

"Keep the change. Thanks for getting me here so quickly."

The man counted the cash and grunted with satisfaction in response.

Peter stepped out of the car. He stood in front of the building for a minute, half-expecting an assassin to hop out from the shadows and shoot him for the valuable item he carried.

With a weary sigh, he entered the building and headed toward a back booth. A silver-haired elf with more than a few wrinkles sat in the back wearing a dark silk suit. While elegant clothing choices spoke to his style, the fact that he looked visibly old even for an elf suggested he was more ancient than many countries on Earth. After all these years, possibilities like that were still hard for Peter to wrap his mind around.

The elf waited with his hands folded in front of him and his gaze locked on the new arrival.

Peter slipped into a seat across from the other man. "Good evening, Fixer."

His companion's mouth quirked into a smile. "I told you before, I'm not the Fixer anymore. My time has come and gone. I'm simply Turner Underwood now. No real responsibilities to magical beings, and no real resources either."

"You say that, but you're still here, aren't you?"

Turner shrugged. "Yes. Simply because I don't *have* to do something doesn't mean I'm not willing to do it. I have a lot of free time on my hands these days. Might as well fill it with a few projects."

Peter reached into his jacket and pulled out the control rod. He held it in his palm. His companion reached over and picked it up.

The elf examined it slowly from several angles and nodded. "You managed to get it. I'll be honest, I wasn't so sure you'd be able to."

"My grandson is the one who grabbed it, technically." Peter shrugged. "The only reason I don't understand is why he even had to bother."

Turner frowned. "Why? I thought you sent him on the mission. We discussed this when we made our agreement in this matter."

He shook his head. "That's not what I'm getting at. I

don't understand why you didn't merely get it yourself." He frowned. "I didn't see the gun in action, but judging by the way Daniel reacted, it's just as dangerous and deadly as you said, so why waste time hiring a human? Even if you're not the Fixer anymore, you're still a centuries-old Light Elf with powerful magic."

"Human curiosity never ceases to amaze me." Turner chuckled. "That powerful magic is the problem, you see."

"What do you mean?"

The elf waved a hand. "Magical beings have tried to go after that artifact before. The last person who tried—a gnome, if you care to know—set the thing off by touch when he went after it in Russia. It was the last thing he ever did. If it were only him, that would be a mere tragedy, but he proved that the weapon could be a disaster if it were inappropriately used near a major population center." He shook his head. "It's fortunate that people could be fooled and were convinced it was a comet or meteor. That at least kept it from landing in someone else's hands for several decades."

Peter blinked, his stomach tightening. "What are you talking about exactly?"

"Tunguska. Look it up." Turner shrugged, a weary smile on his face. "I do wonder how the gun got all the way from Russia to Germany without any hint of its use, but sometimes mysteries are best left unsolved. The point is that a human with no magical ability was needed. It was the safest option in a decidedly unsafe situation." He held the control rod up. "And without this, the gun's useless, which is all I—and anyone who values limiting unnecessary death—care about."

The old man frowned. "You sure? Not saying we don't intend to keep that thing locked away in the vault, but who knows? It'd be harder to sneak the gun out without alerting Daniel, but I could come up with something. I'd try to melt the thing down, but I'm afraid of what might happen."

"A good first instinct." Turner nodded. "And unnecessary in this case, anyway. The materials and knowledge necessary to create this control rod are, to the best of my knowledge, not available to humans. Let's set that aside. You've done your part and helped make both Earth and Oriceran safer places, so it's my turn to give you your payment."

Peter nodded. "It'd be nice, assuming you weren't pulling my chain."

Not that there was much he could do if Turner was. He'd agreed to the trade because of the former Fixer's reputation, but a small part of him wondered if he'd been used.

The elf snorted. "No, I'm more than prepared to offer you what I promised. I should state upfront that I know more than you, but not everything. Even before my… retirement, it wasn't like I possessed omniscience."

The old man shrugged. "I'll take what you know, then. Any news is better than the almost nothing I have now."

Turner leaned forward. "Very well, then. Your daughter Susan and her husband Brian were investigating previously undiscovered ruins in the jungles of Belize. From what I understand, the ruins were shielded from most technological and magical detection, but a contact had passed knowledge of the site along to them."

Peter nodded slowly. "Not all that different from any other tomb raid."

"Not at first, but this site wasn't totally inactive. That was the source of the complications."

"Other tomb raiders?"

The elf shook his head. "No, nothing like that. From the information I was able to gather, there were apparently some sort of defenses still in place. Not mere traps, but something a little more active. Interestingly enough, the Winters seemed to be aware of this."

The old man furrowed his brow. "They knew they were walking into something dangerous?"

Turner raised an eyebrow. "Didn't they always? It's as you said—not all that different from any other tomb raid."

Peter sighed. "They got taken out by the magical traps?"

It wasn't all that much of a surprise, but that didn't make it hurt any less.

The elf shook his head. "I didn't say that."

"Then what the hell *are* you saying? That's my daughter and son-in-law—my grandson's parents, for crying out loud. I want to know the damned truth. I need to know."

His companion sighed and held up a hand. "Calm down. What I'm saying is they were in fact wounded, but there were more than a few reports of a non-native man and a woman later stumbling into a small village in the area."

Peter's eyes widened, and his heart kicked up. "They're alive?"

"Maybe, or it might have been random tourists." Turner shrugged. "I happened to have come across the information when I was still Fixer, and I was investigating certain...dangerous artifacts."

"Why didn't you go and help them, then?"

"Both humans. My responsibility was to magical beings. Not my jurisdiction." The elf sighed. "Can't save the entire world, even if I wanted to."

Peter narrowed his eyes, but antagonizing the elf wouldn't help. At least he now knew there was a slim possibility his daughter and son-in-law were still alive.

"Can you at least tell me the location of the village? Or the site they were investigating?"

Turner looked down for a moment and shook his head. "That might be difficult."

"Why? If you want to cut another deal I'm willing to do it, even if I have to go grab an artifact myself."

The elf frowned. "It's not difficult because I want more. It's difficult because the village and site don't exist anymore."

"What do you mean, they don't exist anymore? Someone destroyed them?"

He looked at Peter and shrugged. "I honestly wish I knew. It's more that there's no sign they ever were there. No rubble, no crater, no magical residue. They simply don't exist anymore, and as far my magic can tell, they never did. Let me assure you that something like that is incredibly difficult." He frowned. "There's one last thing. One of my contacts provided me a copy of a rubbing from the site—obviously from before it disappeared. There were strange symbols on a wall. They were very similar to what is on the control rod."

The old man stared at his companion, his mouth open

in disbelief. He couldn't begin to understand the implications of what had just been said.

Turner stood and brushed some lint off his shoulder, then slipped the control rod into a jacket pocket. "I'm sorry, Peter, but I really do need to get going. That's the only information of use I can provide you. Thank you for your help in this matter. I hope my information might be some use to you. You might think me callous, but I can assure you that I sympathize with your loss."

With that, the elf headed toward the door, whistling under his breath and never looking back.

No site. No village, and only vague information about two people who might possibly be Daniel's parents. Even if their disappearance hadn't been years ago, there was no one left to interrogate.

Peter slammed his fist on the table and gritted his teeth. He'd come close, but it had been a disappointing tease in the end. He needed to confirm if Susan and Brian were dead for Daniel's sake, but he didn't know how to proceed. Turner didn't exactly stop by every day to offer deals. Now he had the control rod, and with it all of Peter's leverage, and it didn't even seem like the elf had much more to offer.

Maybe there's something else I can squeeze out of him with the right bait. He came upon that information incidentally, but what if he actually went looking and asking around? Even though he's not the Fixer anymore, he still has a lot of contacts from the old days.

No, damn it. I need some other lead I can follow up on. Something that doesn't require me to beg for scraps from Turner.

The old man frowned. Yes, Turner might have the control rod, but he didn't know that Peter had a copy of it.

The gun might be disabled and not work with the copy, but the symbols on the rod had to mean something. The more he thought about them, the more convinced he grew that he'd seen them before. It was only a question of where.

He allowed himself a tight smile. For the first time in a long time, he had a trail to follow.

CHAPTER ELEVEN

The next morning Daniel stepped out of the shop with coffee in hand, thanks to Tommy's efforts. He sipped the bitter brew as he surveyed the neighborhood. With the Munich fun over, he had more time to worry about threats closer to home. While he couldn't let himself be distracted on a CIA job, his mind was now free to wander to dark possibilities.

That thug at the corner store seemed to know I was the guy keeping things in check in this neighborhood, which means whoever sent him here isn't a total idiot and at least knows how to ask around. I doubt his last statement was an idle threat.

That means there should be something or someone out of place. If I can spot them before they cause trouble, maybe I can stop this pest infestation before it starts.

An elderly ebony-skinned woman in a broad-brimmed hat walked slowly up the street from the opposite direction. She raised a bony hand and waved at Daniel.

"Good morning, son." Her smile was almost as broad as her hat.

He smiled. "Good morning, Mrs. Carmichael. Nice day."

"Yes, lovely day indeed. So wonderful to see you. You're always so busy with your trips out of the country for your shop. It feels like it's been ages."

The agent laughed. "I think it's only been a few weeks, but I know what you mean."

"Hush now, you. How is your grandpa doing? He doesn't go anywhere, but somehow I manage to see him less than you." Mrs. Carmichael laughed. "Not that Peter hasn't always been a cranky man."

Daniel chuckled. He couldn't really disagree with her assessment.

"He's doing fine, Mrs. Carmichael."

"So glad you can be there for one another. I barely see my grandsons these days." She sighed. "Tell your grandpa that I said hi. We should have brunch someday when you both aren't busy."

"I'll let him know, ma'am."

She smiled. "Such a good man. Not enough good men left in this neighborhood."

The old woman turned and shuffled away.

Daniel nodded, looking past her at a scowling, muscular man driving past in a beat-up pickup truck. He didn't recognize him, which left a couple of possibilities. He might be a troublemaker or simply some poor man lost in the neighborhood and frustrated by misleading GPS directions.

Not like I can gun down every person I don't recognize in the neighborhood because they look like they might be dicks, but I can't ignore the thugs and pretend they aren't out there waiting for their chance, either.

This is my neighborhood and my neighbors, and I'll protect them.

After another quick sweep of the immediate area and a wave to the old woman, Daniel continued across the street. The light foot and vehicle traffic made it easy to inspect everyone coming and going.

No one looked all that suspicious. A happy couple murmured quietly. A businessman shouted into his phone about stocks. A few bored-looking construction workers drove through in their equipment-laden truck.

Daniel slowed and frowned.

What do we have here?

A florist across the street was inside her shop, a panicked look on her face as she spoke into her phone.

Normal supply problems, or did someone stop by and threaten her? Then again, maybe she's merely having another fight with her dad.

He shook his head. If a group was moving into the neighborhood, there had to be some evidence. The kind of gang that sent a petty thug to a corner grocery store lacked the subtlety to escape his notice. If anything, the lack of subtlety would be the whole point. They would want everyone in the neighborhood to know they were coming in force to intimidate them better. He felt like he was missing something but wasn't sure what.

Maybe that asshole was only a scout. But he knew about me and even my nickname, which means they've already at least checked the area out somewhat.

The problem with being the "mayor" was that although everyone knew they could come to him, it wasn't like he'd cultivated a relationship with every random thug or criminal in the area. He relied on the locals to let him know if there were problems, and a lack of local informants had left him with blind spots.

Do I really want to start treating my neighborhood like I do other places for my day job?

He frowned and shook his head. Instinct had kept him alive on many jobs, either CIA or side jobs, and instinct now tightened his stomach. There was something more going on in the area, even if he couldn't see it.

His agency phone rang and he pulled it out.

"Okay, then."

For now, he didn't have the time to check into the neighborhood situation. They needed him at headquarters. Time to go grab a suit and return a few borrowed things.

The express elevator dinged and opened on Level B10. Daniel stepped off with a briefcase in hand and hurried past the worker bees of the research floor to Nessie's office. Her door was already open.

The director sat behind her desk with her lips pursed and her brow furrowed in concentration as she manipulated a floating holographic display of a schematic with her hands.

"That's new," Daniel commented. "And it's way cooler than my AR glasses."

Nessie pointed to a small silver projector sitting on her

desk. "It's still not sensitive enough to compete with general typing and mouse movement muscle memory. The problem with so many of our researchers is they focus too much on the general idea and not on the practical considerations."

The agent laughed. "You don't want cool. You want useful."

"Exactly. Useful has an impact while cool ends up a footnote, but it's at least a nice prototype." She nodded at the edge of her desk. "Set them there. Your initial report suggested you were unsatisfied with your equipment loadout this time."

He set the briefcase down. "There were a lot of failures this time. Some were during active tactical situations. I can't say I was all that happy about that."

"I recall pointing out that some of these were given to you as field tests. All cutting-edge technologies suffer failures. Think about how dangerous the earliest aircraft were. The occasional risk is necessary."

Daniel laughed. "That doesn't make me feel better."

Nessie waved her hand and the holographic display vanished. "It should, Daniel. You're only trusted with such cutting-edge gear because you have the skills to handle the situation should things fail. I'll have the researchers review all the items, particularly the tie pin stun grenade. That was tested numerous times, so I'm surprised at its complete failure. I also should point out that most of your standard loadout is very reliable. It's human nature to focus overly on failures rather than successes."

"Not saying they aren't, but I don't always need everything in my more standard loadouts." Daniel shrugged.

"And besides, my reports need to be accurate, so the research teams know what they have to work on."

"True enough." She nodded and looked down. "Very well, then. If that's all, I have a few things to attend to. Thank you for your efficiency, as always."

"Have anything you want to share with me about John Rainer?"

Nessie looked up again, an eyebrow arched. "No. Is that all?"

"Yeah, guess so."

He spun on his heel and stepped out of the office. Everyone was keeping information from him lately—the CIA, and even his own grandfather.

Something more is going on with Pops. It wasn't only about him worrying that I'd turn the gun over to the government. He knows more than he's letting on, but why wouldn't he tell me? How the hell can he not trust me at this point?

Daniel shook his head and frowned. With pest control and family problems, his plate was full, even without day job worries.

He walked back to the elevator. The doors slid open, and a frowning, bald, older man stepped out. Timothy Franklin.

The decorated veteran agent nodded to a small room off the main research floor that had only a table and a few chairs. "Walk with me for a second." He headed toward the room without another word.

The younger man followed, not sure if his colleague's frown meant anything. If the man had a spirit animal, it was a grumpy cat, and a person needed to be more careful when the man was smiling or laughing.

Timothy threw the door open and motioned his companion through.

"How are things?" the older man asked.

Daniel shrugged. "Can't complain. Rescued a dead guy recently who regrew his own flesh. That was strange for me, even in this job."

The other agent nodded. "I heard. Good job on that, especially since you had interference. We still don't know who contracted Daisy for that job."

"Does it matter? Next week it'll probably be someone else anyway. Maybe even us."

The other man snorted. "True enough. Merely telling you to watch your back. I've not stayed alive this long without keeping an eye out for trouble and making sure I know where all the bodies are buried in case someone comes after me. That's a skill and an attitude you should cultivate more."

Daniel chuckled. "I haven't had enough time to piss as many people off as you. Not as many humans or magicals want me dead."

"If you keep doing a good job, that'll change. That's what it means to actually accomplish something in this corrupt world, and don't think Oriceran's any better."

"You're such a ray of sunshine, Tim."

The older man tapped his forehead. "Just being realistic." He shrugged. "Anyway, not here to talk about that. I wanted to know how you were feeling after the Munich job. You okay if you're needed for another quick mission? Maybe something in the next day or two?"

"Why? Nessie say something?"

"Nope. I might have something for you, but I'm still

waiting for the last details. If you're not ready to go, I can ask around."

Daniel shook his head. "No, I'm fine. If you need me, I can leave as early as tonight."

It's not like sitting at home brooding about Pops will accomplish much, and I don't have any real leads for the neighborhood situation.

Timothy patted him on the shoulder, although he still didn't smile. "Good to hear, son. Of all the agents I've mentored through the years, you're one of the few who hasn't disappointed me. Keep it up, and maybe I can start believing in human nature again."

"I'll try." He shrugged.

The older agent nodded and stepped out of the room. He disappeared around the corner, leaving Daniel alone with his thoughts—the last place the CIA agent wanted to be.

He took a deep breath and headed toward the elevator. Not everything needed to be stressful. It was time to go chat with Ronni.

Daniel made his way through the cubicle maze on a higher floor and arrived at Ronni's desk. The brown-haired woman looked up, her hair in a ponytail as always, and her facial expression on the verge of panic, also not unusual.

He smiled. "Hey, Ronni. Just wanted to thank you for your help on the last mission."

Her cheeks reddened. "You don't have to do that. I was only doing my job, and I let that elf mess things up. Sorry."

The agent shook his head. "You kept those cameras down and gave me good visual backup." He grinned as he spotted a small Pikachu plushy sitting on the edge of her desk. Daniel picked it up and laughed. "I didn't expect it to actually look like a toy. Maybe I should have a little fun with it."

Ronni's eyes widened and she waved her hands. "No, no, never here. I wouldn't do anything like that. You have to believe me."

"Of course I believe you." He leaned over and picked up a small mirror. "I'm guessing this isn't simply a mirror."

"I'm still working on it." She frowned. "It's supposed to let you see things in different spectra. I'm trying to see if I can make a magic detector, too, but it's not so easy." She shrugged. "I'll keep trying, though. It's merely a matter of tinkering."

"Hey, Daniel," a man called from behind. "I see you're back from your near screwup. Congrats on not dying."

Daniel turned around to find Jack Buckley standing behind him with his arms crossed.

"I had to fly all the way to Germany to not hear your whining, Jack."

The other agent grinned at him. "From what I hear, you needed someone to pull your ass out of the frying pan in Munich."

Ronni grimaced.

Daniel snorted. "Maybe you need to get your ears checked if that's what you're hearing."

"You denying that elf showed up?"

"Nope, just denying I needed her there. She simply helped me recover the target without wasting as much time." He leaned forward and lowered his voice. "Which is more than I can say for what happened to you in Paris."

Jack smirked. "Paris? Whatever. That shit wasn't even that important. Merely a minor bump in the road."

Daniel laughed. "Not that important? Tell that to the owner of that building you blew up."

"It was old anyway."

"I think the term you're looking for is 'historical heritage building.'"

The other agent shrugged. "Hey, not my fault the French can't keep dangerous magicals out of their country. I can't sit there and do price checks when I'm busy saving the world."

"I guess," Daniel responded. "Although I managed not to blow up anything in Munich when I was there, so I'm one up on you there."

"Luck." Jack glanced at his watch. "I've got a briefing." He wandered toward the elevator. "I guarantee you'll blow up a building before the year is out, Daniel. I'd put money on it."

Daniel laughed and shook his head. He looked at Ronni, who stared at him wide-eyed.

"What?" he asked.

"You're okay with that?"

He furrowed his brow. "What do you mean?"

"He was saying all that stuff about you. I guess I'm surprised you're not angrier."

The agent shrugged. "Trash-talking. No big deal. Simply a way for field agents to blow off steam. Jack would have my back without question in a field mission."

Ronni sighed. "I really don't get the attitude. It's weird to go up and purposely insult someone."

"Nothing but a little bro bonding, just poking fun." Daniel chuckled and looked down at his watch. "I better getting going, but I want to do something special for you because of your help on the last mission."

"Special?" she squeaked.

Daniel grinned. "Yeah. How about I owe you lunch?"

She nodded quickly. "Lunch is good. I eat every day."

He laughed. "I'm glad to hear that. Okay, Ronni, talk to you later."

He headed toward the elevator, his earlier worries about his grandfather and the neighborhood now a mere whisper in the back of his mind. Time for a relaxing night.

CHAPTER TWELVE

Daniel clenched his jaw. They were screwed. He'd thought they were prepared to hit the dungeon with the equipment they had, but now they were surrounded and outnumbered. If the party didn't figure out something clever quickly, no one would leave that room alive.

So much for careful planning. Can't believe we walked into such an obvious trap.

Their dungeon master, Connor, sat across the table from him. He pointed down at the table and the figurines representing each player's character. Then he pointed at all the Dark Elf fighters surrounding them and the priestess in the corner.

"Looks like you're screwed, Sergeant," the man stated with a grin. He picked up a Fresca and took a sip. "Really damned screwed."

"Sergeant?" Daniel laughed. "Nobody's called me that in years, including you. I'm simply Daniel now."

Connor shrugged. "Guess I was just in a mood to think about the old days. Whatever happened to once a Marine, always a Marine? Now, you're managing some antique shop for your gramps."

The gathered group of four men and a single woman laughed. They might be his friends, and they all still had security clearances, but that didn't mean they needed to know he worked for the CIA. They could have fun at their government analyst jobs doing their thing without ever suspecting he was still in the intel game these days, albeit in a very different way.

Someday one of these guys will think things through a little too much, and then I'll have trouble, but for now, I'll keep the game going as long as I can. Nice to keep that one touch of normalcy. Well, as normal as D&D gets anyway.

Daniel flipped Connor off. "I don't have to take crap from some ex-chairborne ranger. I know you probably got a lot of medals for risking papercuts back in the day there."

Connor barked a laugh and his fellow Air Force vet, Taylor, joined him.

"Don't be angry because you weren't smart enough to join the Air Force," Taylor chided. "Or keep your clearance and get a sweet government job after you did your years. I don't know why you didn't. If you didn't want to stay in the game the whole time, do your combined twenty years, then retire so you can run the shop."

Their other two friends, Lorelai and Juan, watched with smiles but didn't say anything.

Daniel shrugged. "I did my part for flag and country, and now I like the quiet life where I can call the shots. It's not so bad. I have you guys to come over and remind me of why I like selling antiques and oddities with the occasional touch of magic to random civilians. Not everything in life has to be about saving the world, you know. If you all love it so much, you would have stayed in the service and not run to the civilian side of things."

I say all that, but I can't even imagine what it'd be like if I wasn't working for the CIA on top of running the shop.

This time, Lorelai laughed. The redhead eyed Daniel for a few seconds. "If I never set foot on a ship again, I'll be a happy woman. You're right. We're all civilians now. But some of us are civilians who get paid more than others. You should be happy we all drag our asses over here to play with your boring ass."

Juan picked up his Coke and took a sip. "Man, how long have we been doing this now? I never thought I'd find a good group again, let alone one where I'd be able to play regularly. Gaming with all you guys, though—what are the chances?"

Daniel smiled. "First Connor, now you? Someone been drinking nostalgia juice or something?"

Juan shrugged. "Just time flies, you know? I used to think I would be a lifer in the Army, and then I left after my first enlistment, got married, and now, I got a kid. My plans changed, my life changed. My future changed." He pointed to the figurines. "D&D's like the only thing I have left from the old days. I don't always think a lot about it, but when I do, it does feel like a big deal."

The way everyone's acting, you'd think they were drinking beer or wine and not Coke, Sprite, and Fresca.

Oh, shit. Guess I should have been telling Connor to stay out of Pops' stash.

Lorelai shook her head. "Wow. No one in this room is older than thirty-five, but you're all talking like old farts."

Daniel grinned. When she was right, she was right.

She pointed to her figurine, a blonde elf rogue. "Connor probably messed with Daniel to distract us from the fact he's going for a total party kill. Don't give in to all this nostalgia garbage when we're about to die."

Connor shrugged. "Not my fault you ignored the obvious trap. And it's still Daniel's turn. So, what's your plan?"

He stared down at the table. "If we don't handle that priestess, she'll nail us with a *Hold Person* spell and we'll be shredded before we can move again."

"You can always beg their forgiveness. Maybe they'll only kill some of you. They'll probably need at least one person to spread the story of their epic slaughter. Maybe you should all decide among yourselves who will live and die. Better hurry, though."

Taylor snorted. "You do love hearing yourself talk."

Lorelai rolled her eyes. "You're such a sadistic DM, Connor. Don't get off too much on the Drow killing us."

"Hey, I didn't railroad you. I merely gave you an option. Your greed is what brought you here." Connor gulped down the rest of his Fresca. "And now, you'll all die at the hands of an angry mob of Drow who are pissed about you trespassing. Enough stalling. What's your action, Daniel? You going to volunteer to be the sacrifice?"

He stared at his figurine—Canath, a level-six human wizard.

In real life I'm around magic all the time, but I'm closer to a rogue than a wizard. Funny how that worked out for me. I still collect treasures, just not from dungeons most of the times. Am I still a real-life adventurer?

Daniel's brow furrowed, and he glanced at the distance between the various Dark Elves and the party. Time to apply some of the tactical awareness he'd learned in both the Marine Corps and the CIA.

"The Drow have us surrounded, but they've only got a couple of them in the back."

Taylor frowned. "If we turn and run, they'll be able to stall us while the rest of them cut us to pieces and that priestess disables us. They aren't weak enough that we can charge through them like a couple of goblins."

"Then we need to make sure no one can attack our backs."

Connor smirked. "And how will you do that?"

Daniel cackled. "Screw it. Fireball. I'll center it on the priestess." His current build put a lot of power into that fireball, but it'd be worth it with a good roll. If luck were with him, he could annihilate the enemy force.

Connor pointed at the Canath figurine. "But you're in the blast radius."

"Yeah, but only me. Our fighter, cleric, and rogue are all clear. I merely need to survive." He grinned. "Why do you think I wasted feats on improving this one spell? Sometimes you need to be ready for that Hail Mary play to win."

"You son of a bitch? You planned this?"

"Maybe not this, but a scenario just like it. It's like Juan said. We've played together for years now. It's not like I don't have a feel for your style. I'm not usually into mismatching a character simply to take advantage of something like that, but in this campaign, I decided to do exactly that and see what happened."

Connor blinked and shook his head. "No fucking way."

Juan, Lorelai, and Taylor exchanged surprised glances.

Daniel picked up his six-sided dice and threw them down one at a time, counting the damage. He'd not hit the maximum on all his dice, but luck had favored him, and he had a high count—more than enough to kill the Dark Elves if they didn't successfully defend with the help of a good saving throw by Connor.

The DM picked up his dice and shook his head. "I'll make you roll for your own damage last. That way, you have time to sit there and anticipate how badly you'll fry yourself."

He began to toss dice for the elves. Failure after failure followed.

"Oh, come on!"

The players all laughed, then cheered.

Connor reached over and knocked the figurines for all the Dark Elves over. The DM had tried for a total party kill of the players, but now, only the two Drow in the back had survived.

Let's TPK these enemies.

The DM smirked at Daniel. "Don't get too smug. Too bad it's going to cost you, hero. Roll your own saving throw."

He picked up his die for his saving throw. His character could survive half-damage with a few hit points left from the blast, but if he failed this roll he would end up deep-fried. He threw.

Success.

A chorus of "Ohhhh" went up from the other players.

Daniel grinned. "Guess I live to fight another day. But just barely."

Connor scrubbed a hand over his face. "You've got to be fucking kidding me. Uh, well, you've still got the two Drow in the back. Don't celebrate yet."

He stared at the DM. "Seeing me fry their entire group and their priestess didn't make them reconsider?"

"It's not always that si—"

A woman screamed from the street.

The veterans shot out of their seats, their heart rates kicking up. They rushed to the window and threw back the curtains. It was hard to make out anything in the darkness outside.

Connor frowned. "I can't see anything. What happened to the street lights?"

Daniel frowned. His friend was right. He'd been so focused on the game that he hadn't even noticed how dark it was outside.

He headed for the stairs leading down to the main shop floor. The others followed. He stopped and opened the door, letting them take the lead even though they expected a certain amount of ass-kicking ability from an ex-Marine, even an intelligence specialist. His current capabilities would go a long way to proving he wasn't simply a humble veteran shop owner. He needed to play the situation carefully, but there was no way he would let someone get hurt right outside his house, either.

Good thing Pops isn't around. The last thing I need is for him to do something dangerous trying to be a hero.

They sprinted through the shop floor, only narrowly missing knocking anything to the ground. Connor reached the door first and threw it open. He ran out, followed by Lorelai, Juan, and Taylor. Daniel brought up the rear.

They emerged onto the street, their eyes taking a few seconds to adjust to the deep darkness. A woman struggled in the arms of a wiry, grinning thug. Four others loomed over a cowering older man.

Daniel frowned. It wasn't just any woman. It was Jeanine, the panicked florist he'd seen the other day, and the man was her father.

My instincts weren't off. Pest control will have to come sooner rather than later if it's gotten this bad.

He looked up at the street lights. They weren't broken, so the goons had used some sort of EMP. It was a little sophisticated for street thugs, and more proof that this went beyond random muggings.

The small gang turned their attention to the arriving gamers.

Daniel looked back and forth. Five on five. Equal numbers. The altercation in the grocery the other day suggested the men wouldn't be the greatest fighters in the world, assuming they were with the same group, but the rest of his friends weren't exactly special forces. Connor was lean and fit and the others were in good shape, but they'd spent their time in the service doing intelligence analysis and related jobs, not kicking in doors and taking down terrorists.

Connor pointed at the thug holding the woman. "Get your hands off her, asshole."

The man shoved the woman to the ground with a laugh. One of the others slammed a foot into the old man's stomach and he doubled over in pain.

The first thug flipped Connor off. "You better run back inside if you don't want some of this, bitch. You don't know who you're fucking with."

Connor charged with a yell, and Juan and Taylor rushed forward. Lorelai shrugged and joined the advance.

So much for careful planning. A bunch of gamer intel analysts should know better.

The muscular thug threw a punch, but the former airman blocked it and managed a nice counter-jab. Connor had a good reach on his enemy, even if he lacked the man's size.

Juan took a solid blow to the face and stumbled with a grunt. Blood poured from a cut lip, but he managed a grin. "That all you got? Man, they should have never let you out of mugger school, asshole."

One of the gang members advanced on Connor from the side, his hand slipping inside his jacket to grab a gun.

Shit. The numbers are only even if I'm involved. My friends might be brave, but sometimes, it's about knowing your limits.

Daniel needed to join the fray. Sometimes, a man simply needed to take a risk to protect his friends.

Too bad I don't have a fireball to throw.

He sprinted toward the gun-toting thug, the darkness and chaos making his movement less obvious. His target frowned and turned to face him. The agent feinted to the side, and his enemy took the bait. A quick throat strike sent the man to the ground gasping. Everyone else was too busy with their own opponent to notice. A follow-up kick knocked the thug unconscious.

Juan stumbled back from a few savage blows. The former soldier might be able to take a hit well, but he wasn't giving as good as he got.

I need to give him an opening without being too obvious.

Daniel grabbed a stray rock from the street and waited until Juan's next attack. He hurled the rock at the back of his friend's opponent's head. The man winced and turned his head, which was a mistake. The distraction allowed the former soldier to tackle him to the ground and begin pummeling him.

Connor headbutted his foe.

The thug let out a loud groan and stumbled back clutching his skull, but he shook his head and tried to stay on his feet. Daniel bowled into the man, sending him flying toward his friend. Connor brought his knee up on pure instinct. After a loud crunch, the thug's eyes rolled toward the back of his head and he fell to the ground.

Shit. Nice.

Lorelai had a strong chokehold on her enemy, but Taylor lay flat on his back, groaning. The agent rushed over to the man standing over him.

The thug threw a couple of quick punches, and Daniel didn't block them. A little blood on his face would make for a nice cover. He let out a few exaggerated grunts as the man nailed him on the side of the head and the chest.

"Call the cops," he shouted.

Everyone went reflexively for their phones, taking their attention off him. With the witnesses occupied he ended the fight quickly, dodging the next blow and laying the man out with three savage strikes.

Daniel spun, looking for signs of enemy reinforcements or snipers. No red dots, no glinting in the distance, and no heavy footfalls. There were only five unconscious thugs and a lot of heavy breathing from the gamers.

"Cops are on their way," Connor called, hanging up his phone.

Everyone realized the futility of tying up the lines and excused themselves, hanging up their phones.

Daniel jogged over to Taylor. "You okay?"

The other man sat up and rubbed his eye. "Yeah. Just hard to fight when it's so dark."

Closing sirens sounded in the night.

The florist and her father smiled at the group.

The woman wiped away a tear. "Thank you so much. Those men came out of nowhere and demanded we give them money. The other day, one of my customers called to say they couldn't pick up a big order because they'd been mugged. What are the cops even doing? This used to be a nice neighborhood."

Connor slammed his fist into his palm. "Too bad for these morons there happened to be a party of heroes nearby. That'll teach the muggers. We probably stopped a bunch of attacks for the next few weeks."

The others all nodded and murmured their agreement, but Daniel frowned.

The woman smiled and helped her father up.

"Thank you," the old man muttered. "I don't know what we would have done without you."

There's no way they would plan to take over the neighborhood with only six guys. This was simply more recon. Defense probing. Between this and the grocery store guy knowing who I am, that means there's someone with half a brain behind these guys.

His gaze drifted to the disabled street lights and back to the defeated men. Worn but casual clothing, and no obvious gang colors. If they were led by someone smart, they wouldn't mention anything to the cops. A few months or even years in prison to protect their gang or organization was a badge of honor for men like this.

No. The police would write it off as a group of opportunistic muggers and nothing more.

Damn it. This pest infestation is getting out of control. I need to find the hive and clean it out before they overrun the neighborhood.

"I'm flying," Connor all but shouted. "A freaking real-life rescue. It's been a long time since I've done something that satisfying instead of merely looking at reports all day."

Daniel nodded at one of the downed men. "They interrupted our game, and just at the good point. We done for the night?"

Taylor wiped some blood off his face, but his nose didn't look too bad. "Hell no. After that, I'm more pumped to continue the game."

Juan, Taylor, and Lorelai nodded quickly.

Red and blue lights flashed. The police would be there soon.

Daniel looked down the street. "I'm sure they'll let us go back to the game soon enough."

As two police cars screamed toward them, he considered telling them about the grocery store incident before deciding against it.

I can keep my neighborhood safe, but I might need to bend the rules to do it.

CHAPTER THIRTEEN

The next morning, thoughts of the neighborhood had to be pushed back as Daniel stepped out of the elevator and headed toward Timothy's office. Stopping regular criminals seemed almost a trivial problem in comparison to his worries at the CIA, where every mission had implications for not only the country but the stability of the world.

Jack Buckley all but jumped out from behind a cubicle wall. Daniel clenched his fists and took a battle stance before he even realized what was happening.

The other agent chuckled and rubbed the back of his neck. "Touchy, huh? Not getting enough sleep? Dreaming too much of sexy elves saving your ass?"

"I'd think another field agent would know that it isn't smart to surprise someone." Daniel forced a smile and unclenched his hands. "You never know what can happen when instincts take control."

Buckley grinned and opened his mouth, but then he

closed it and his smile faded. "Yeah, you're right. Sorry." He eyed his companion for a moment, a serious expression on his face. Not his norm.

"It's good to be careful. You never know who is watching, especially here." He turned and walked away.

Daniel watched him until he disappeared around the corner.

What the fuck was that about? It's almost like he was threatening me.

He shook his head. Daniel and Buckley liked to bust each other's balls now and again, but it'd always been a friendly rivalry, even if Daniel tended to score more high-profile assignments. If the other agent was getting jealous, that might end up causing trouble down the line.

He can put on his big-boy underwear and deal with it. Or maybe I'm reading too much into what he said. I'll worry about it later. I'm not here to have a dick-measuring contest with Buckley. I'm here because Tim needs me.

He reached his mentor's door and found it was already open.

Tim looked up from his desk. "Come in and close the door behind you."

Daniel entered with a nod. "Your text said you needed to talk to me. I'm assuming this is about the mission you had for me? No one else has me tasked with anything, so you've got good timing." He closed the door quietly behind him with a click.

The older man shook his head. "This is less a mission and more a request."

"What do you mean by that? Is this the part where you ask me to pick up your dry cleaning?" He chuckled.

Timothy frowned even deeper than normal. He picked up a rubber stress ball from his desk and started squeezing it.

He usually doesn't respond so poorly to jokes. What the hell is going on?

"There's a man in Vancouver, a very wealthy man," Timothy began. "And it's come to my attention that he's keeping a dangerous artifact, a nozzle. Even though he isn't a complete piece of shit, there's no way he should hold on to something like that artifact. It's a danger to him, his city, his country, and the world."

Daniel leaned forward. "Oh? What's so special about this nozzle? What does it do?"

"Right now, nothing. But my sources say it's a piece of something else far more dangerous. This isn't something we can let some arrogant asshole hoard in his penthouse. The security of the country and the world might be at stake because someone wants to have a neat talking piece for his next dinner party." Timothy grimaced. "And this needs to be handled sooner rather than later."

"I don't get it then. Why isn't this simply a mission? From what you've told me, why not ask a couple of agents and supports to go recover the damned thing?"

"There are some things you're not currently aware of and I can't tell you." The older agent gave the stress ball one last squeeze before tossing it onto his desk with a grunt. "For now, you'll have to trust me on this. This is something I need to look into without the Company getting too involved. Even if I were to try to make this a formal mission, resources wouldn't be officially authorized. I need you to do what plenty of CIA agents have done throughout history. I need you to do something a little shady off the books to help protect the peace of your country and the planet."

Daniel arched a brow and took a deep breath. His mentor had a career that spanned years both before and after the full return of magic. The fact that he was still around at all was a miracle in itself and a testimony to Timothy's personal determination and intelligence.

"How off the books?" he asked. "Are we talking no formal support from the CIA at all?"

"For now, I'd recommend you not involve anyone else here." Timothy shrugged. "This is as much for their protection as yours. Once you've recovered the nozzle, I'll take it from there."

The younger agent chuckled. "You want me to go on a blind mission with no material or personnel support, and I shouldn't even breathe a word of it to any of the people I work with?"

His companion nodded. "Yeah. That's about the long and short of it. I had to do that a lot during my career. Sometimes, the right hand shouldn't know what the left hand is doing." He looked down for a moment. "And just so you know, this mission is even more annoying than that."

"How so?"

"This man isn't responsible enough to have this artifact, but he isn't a piece of shit, either. We've no evidence that he's employing any criminal organizations for his immediate security. If a bunch of bodies hit the floor, this'll end up a major international incident."

Daniel nodded. "I have to get in, grab the artifact, not seriously hurt anyone, and get out. Otherwise, the

Company will come down on both of us for an unauthorized mission."

Timothy shrugged. "Yeah, that's the quick version. Like I said, not a mission, but a request. I can't order you to do something so far off the books, but you're also one of the few people I can trust for something like this."

He nodded slowly, his brow furrowed. There were so many things that could go wrong with this Vancouver operation, but his colleague wasn't the kind of man who'd ask for help for something petty and unimportant.

"Okay. If it were anybody else but you, I'd say no way." Daniel stood. "At least I still have the Jaguar and the silence cube. There are a few other things I should be able to scrounge up without hitting Nessie."

Maybe they weren't as up-to-date or impressive as what the CIA might loan him, but they'd work in a pinch.

He chuckled. *Might need those for my future job if the CIA ends up canning me after this.*

Timothy pulled out his phone and tapped away. Daniel's phone buzzed.

"I've sent you the address and the layout of the target's penthouse. You won't even have to look around. The damned thing's on display in the middle of his living room. Talk about arrogant."

"That shouldn't be a problem." He gave the older agent a mock salute. "I'm off to get you an artifact nozzle. At least Vancouver isn't a long flight."

Timothy managed something resembling a smile. It unnerved the younger agent.

"Thanks, Daniel, and be careful."

"I always am. Well, mostly."

Daniel stepped out of the office and closed the door.

Ronni's broken more than a few rules at times. I might be able to persuade her to play the eyes and ears for me off the books, so I'm not working this totally solo.

He shook his head as he headed toward the elevator. No, it wouldn't be fair to put the woman in that position. She was already nervous enough, and she didn't need any more stress.

I'll have to think of it like any other side job I might do for the shop. I can work those by myself, so surely I can steal one little nozzle without help.

Most people misunderstood security. They focused on gadgets or artifacts, but true security was about people, not items. The problem with people was that they were suspicious, and their little brains wanted to pattern-match threats. Something out of place would poke at the back of their mind until they were forced to pay attention.

In most circumstances, this helped them survive threats, but providing a pattern could force a simple pattern-match, and that was easy to use to a man's advantage.

Daniel straightened his tie as he stepped out of his parked car beneath the massive condo tower. He'd waved off the valet in front of the building with a dismissive and arrogant glare earlier. Better to fake being a suspicious rich asshole worried about his precious vehicle than have some poor guy working for tips press the wrong button and discover the Jaguar was far more than merely an expensive car.

They make me practically sign out every paperclip, but they let me keep this car in my own private garage. Funny how bureaucracy works.

He arrived at an elevator and punched the button for the lobby. With his blond wig and blue contacts, he looked like a different man—all the more important on a side job that had him stealing something without permission from the Company. If anything went wrong, it'd help if law enforcement in Canada didn't come straight at him or request his extradition.

His face putty would help thwart facial recognition algorithms later, as well. The CIA had more than a few disguise gadgets that were far more impressive and advanced, but the classics never went out of style and didn't require a million official signatures, merely a visit to a store.

Nice suit. Nice car. Entitled attitude and a permanent scowl. It was a better way to blend into the tower of privilege than a chameleon ball and didn't require any power. Looking like everyone else was simply another way of being invisible.

Always learn from Mother Nature. She knows what she's doing.

The elevator came to a stop, and the doors opened. Daniel sauntered into the lobby with a practiced scowl. A security guard looked his way, then averted his eyes.

Don't want to deal with someone you think is an asshole looking for trouble? Good.

Four security guards stood in the lobby. All wore

holstered pistols. Two also had contact Tasers on their belts, and the other had two stun rods. He wondered why they didn't all carry the same equipment, but that didn't change his fundamental observation.

That's a lot of muscle for the lobby. At least there are no obvious magicals.

The agent headed away from the elevator toward a stairwell, keeping his walk and expression the same.

A guard stepped in front of him right before he arrived at the door to the stairwell.

"Sir, you sure you don't want to take the elevator?"

He snorted. "I just left the elevator, idiot. Obviously, I don't want to take it. My therapist says walking more is good for my blood pressure—or at least it would be if fools didn't mess with me."

The guard gave him a shallow nod and stepped away with a frown.

Daniel threw open the door and stepped into the stairwell. He walked up three flights before opening the door and heading toward the elevator. Walking up dozens of flights of stairs wasn't a good plan. He only wanted to find somewhere with less foot traffic and fewer witnesses.

Glad all these rich people like to mind their own business. Makes this a lot easier.

The target lived in a penthouse. Security drones hovered around the outside upper floors like angry wasps, ready to detect any hostile forces trying to take advantage of the helipad atop the building, so an internal raid was necessary.

The heavy level of security in the lobby and outside seemed a little much, but they also didn't look like anything he couldn't handle if things got a little out of hand. He figured there were probably a few more men available when alarms were tripped, but they likely depended on rapid-response private security.

Damn. It would have been nice to have some help from Ronni. She could probably have had me take the express elevator right to the penthouse. Then this whole thing would have taken five minutes.

Daniel pressed the up button and waited for the elevator to arrive. When the doors finally opened, he smirked to himself. No one was inside. The universe was smiling on him that day.

He entered and pressed the button for the thirty-eighth floor. There wasn't even a button for the penthouse floor. A keycard or some other verification method was likely necessary, but he wasn't worried. He had a plan.

The elevator hummed quietly as it rose up the shaft. The elevator dinged open, and he stepped out past a young woman chatting away on her phone. She shot him a smile. He smiled back before stepping past her with a polite nod and marching toward the entrance to the stairwell.

A quick trip up the final flight of stairs brought him to a locked door.

Daniel pulled a small metallic card from his pocket—or, as Peter called it, an electronic lockpick or cracker. His personal version lacked several capabilities associated with the Company's version, but he wasn't breaking into a military base or secure research facility.

I hope I don't have to go back down to the car to get explosives.

He waved the cracker over a small panel by the door. The panel buzzed. He tried it again.

Come on. Work, damn it.

The panel beeped, and the door clicked open.

"Finally." Daniel pocketed the card and stepped into the hallway leading to the penthouse. A frowning guard jogged his way.

Personal guards up here, too? Damn it.

The agent tried not to frown. He knew the owner of the penthouse wasn't there. The man had been driven away in his limo fifteen minutes before Daniel parked. That was why he had risked the entry.

"Can I help you, sir?" the guard asked.

Daniel heaved a melodramatic sigh. "I'm here to perform a pre-inspection of the backup emergency lines. Your boss sent a complaint to my company about a recent malfunction. Something about an incident."

The guard furrowed his brow, looking him up and down. "I wasn't informed of any inspection or an incident. You're some sort of repairman?"

"No, I'm some sort of manager of technicians." He scoffed. "How new *are* you?"

The guard's face twitched. "Uh, well, I started a couple of weeks ago, but I've been extensively briefed."

Daniel snorted. "Not well enough. Now move aside. I've got a half-dozen sites I need to pre-inspect today."

The guard frowned. "Sir, I can't let you in there without prior authorization."

The agent pulled out his phone. "I hope you enjoyed your job. You're not going to have it long. I'm on a tight schedule, and I don't have time for this crap." He locked eyes with the guard, pouring every ounce of arrogance and confidence he could muster into his gaze.

The man groaned and scrubbed a hand over his face. "Okay, okay. Just come with me." He headed down the hallway.

Daniel reached into his pocket to pull out an EMP emitter and jammer. These were shorter range than what he was used to working with, but they'd do for the immediate situation if necessary.

The other man waved a keycard over the security panel, then pressed his thumb against the silver DNA scanner pad. With a harsh buzz, the door unlocked, and he opened it.

Daniel followed him inside and closed the door behind him. He reached into his pocket and activated the jammer.

That takes care of the reinforcements.

Multiple white leather couches, chairs, and loveseats filled the living room. All surrounded a long glass table. Floor-to-ceiling windows provided a gorgeous view of afternoon Vancouver.

Daniel chuckled as he moved toward the living room. A large glass display case in the center contained the nozzle. It was nice to have a job that didn't involve him having to search every nook and cranny for the artifact.

That arrogance will cost you, pal.

The guard frowned and pulled out his phone. "You do what you need to do, but I still need to call this in. There are procedures, and it's not like you'll pay my rent if I lose my job."

"Yes. You do what you need to do, and I'll do what I need to do." Daniel stepped past the guard, then spun and put his arms around his neck. A little pressure to the arteries and the man was unconscious in seconds. The agent laid him on the ground, then bound his hands with zip-ties. "Now, on to the job."

The nozzle appeared to be made of blue-black metal covered with mottled banding. The agent had no idea what the material was, but all he needed to do was get it to Timothy.

Daniel frowned as he moved closer. Strange glyphs were embossed on the nozzle. Although he couldn't read them, he'd seen a few of them on the Munich reality gun.

What the hell does this thing have to do with that gun? What's going on here?

He shook his head and pulled out his cracker. He looked for an interface panel but couldn't spot anything.

The guard groaned and stirred.

Should have held the choke longer, but he's all tied up, so no problem.

The man glared at Daniel. "Doesn't matter that you got in here. You're not getting out of here, asshole."

The agent chuckled as he continued to examine the case. "I admire your confidence, but I've jammed everything. No one's coming to help you, and I'll be gone before you can call for help."

The guard grinned. "You think you're so smart, don't you?"

"Smarter than the average bear, sure." Daniel frowned.

Loud footfalls sounded from outside.

Damn it. A patrol?

Someone knocked loudly on the door. "You in there, Smith?"

"Intruder!" the guard screamed. He smirked at the agent.

Daniel sighed and shook his head. "Dead man's switch? Nice. Since the subtlety train has left the station, it's time for everyone to jump off."

He grabbed a nearby brass bookend and smashed it against the display case until the glass shattered. He pulled out a handkerchief and sent a silent prayer of thanks that the nozzle was small enough to wrap it in the cloth. There was no way he wanted to touch something that might rearrange his DNA with a strange thought.

The door flew open and several guards rushed in, all holding stun rods.

The man on the floor laughed. "You're dead meat."

Daniel leapt over a couch as he yanked a flashbang out of his pocket and threw it at the guards. They jumped out of the room, convinced it was a normal grenade.

Sorry, SAD. Sometimes the classics are all you need.

The flashbang went off and the guards groaned and flailed around, clutching their eyes. The agent rolled as he hit the ground and bounced back to his feet. He rushed toward the door and jumped over the moaning men to reach the hallway.

The scuff and thump of heavy boots filled the air. He glanced to either side. More guards rushed him from both directions, their stun rods raised in menace.

What the hell? This guy has a small army working for him.

Daniel ran back into the living room and slammed the door shut. He whipped out an EMP emitter and pressed the activation button. He'd need to replace his cracker, but his shielded phone would survive.

The lights died, but sunlight continued to stream in through the windows.

The guards banged on the door, the sophisticated electronic lock now working against them.

The agent grinned at the guard. "A little smarter setup than I anticipated, but not smart enough."

The bound man laughed. "There's no way out, asshole. You let me go right now and surrender, and maybe you'll get out of this by only going to jail."

His colleagues continued to thud against the reinforced door. The dull, hollow echo suggested it was a thin wood veneer over metal.

Paranoid much? What, worried about random people breaking in and stealing your artifacts?

Daniel headed over toward the window and unlatched it. No point in worrying about alarms with all the guards trying to break into the penthouse.

The guard on the floor laughed. "What are you going to do? We're almost four hundred feet up. Decide you'd rather die than go to jail? I hope you enjoy hell, asshole."

"No. I intend to live a long and healthy life. I'm merely going to try out something I found in my vault the other day." Daniel grinned and placed a foot on the window.

"What the fuck?"

Wood and paint flew from the wall as several bullets blasted through. Metal door, but only wooden walls. Someone hadn't been thorough enough.

The outside guards continued to fire, blasting a hole in the wall.

The agent laughed. He could only imagine how their

boss would feel when he came back to find his artifact missing and a new hole in his wall.

"See you around." With that, he saluted and leapt from the window.

He hurtled toward the ground. At that height, he had less than six seconds until a very painful and sudden splat.

Daniel yanked a small white pyramid out of his pocket, squeezed it, and threw it down. Man and pyramid continued careening toward the cement below. The object hit first, inflating in the blink of the eye into a soft cushion several feet deep. His face and body pressed in about a foot when he hit, and it began to dissolve a few seconds later with a hiss and a pungent odor.

I would have preferred a parachute, but that worked.

He chuckled and rolled off before rushing toward the slope leading to the parking garage. Several people stared at him, their jaws slack and their eyes wide.

What? Never saw a man jump thirty-nine stories before?

He vaulted over the parking arm, the stunned attendant saying nothing.

A sprint brought him to the Jaguar, and the key fob had the car running before he arrived. Daniel slipped into the seat, slammed on his seat belt, and reversed with a quick screech of the wheels. He accelerated toward the parking arm then slammed on the brakes, offering the attendant a bright smile. At this point, the security guards were probably still in the elevator. He wasn't sure if his EMP had enough range to disable all the electronics on the floor.

The agent rolled down his window and continue to smile at the parking attendant. "You can't stop me, so I'll escape either way. If I slam through this, it'll be me escaping and property damage on your watch. What'll it be, pal?"

The attendant sighed and pressed a button. The arm rose, and Daniel accelerated out of the garage and around the corner. A few blocks away, he reached into his pocket. The handkerchief-clad nozzle was still snug and safe.

Not my most subtle exit ever, but it worked.

He pulled the nozzle out and set it on the passenger seat, still careful not to touch it with his bare hand.

Definitely some of the same symbols, but what the hell does it mean?

Daniel shook his head and turned down a side street. "You've got a lot of explaining to do, Tim."

CHAPTER FOURTEEN

Daniel stepped off the elevator, a forced smile on his face as he headed toward Ronni's desk. He glanced around. No one was close to her.

Good. This was one time that her low profile would really help him. There was an obvious mystery he needed to solve, and it was time to start utilizing all his resources.

He took another few seconds to search for Buckley. Even if he wasn't near Ronni, the man might march over the minute he saw Daniel. This was one time he didn't need the other agent looking over his shoulder. No sign of him.

You never know who is watching, huh, Buckley?

It sounded like a simple-off-the-cuff comment, but it'd stuck with him since the conversation. He wasn't sure why. Something about the tone of the other agent's voice when he'd said it.

Daniel shook his head. He needed to concentrate on one mystery at a time. *Start with Ronni.*

The woman was frowning at a complicated schematic on her screen and tapping her lips with a pen.

The agent sauntered over to her desk. "Hey, Ronni."

She yelped and all but jumped out her seat. "Don't sneak up on me like that. You'll give me a heart attack."

"I walked straight from the elevator to your desk." He chuckled. "I could whistle on my way next time if you think it'd help. Call ahead of time to schedule an appointment, maybe?"

Ronni sighed and brushed some dark hair out of her eyes. "Sorry, I was really into my work. I get so focused that I block everything out. Did you need something?"

"I wondered if you're interested in a little treasure hunt?" He smiled.

She furrowed her brow. "What do you mean? I haven't heard anything about a mission. They usually brief me long before I talk to an agent."

"This is kind of an unusual situation." Daniel leaned over her desk and smiled. "So, you haven't seen it yet?"

"Seen what?"

"A few minutes ago, I sent you a picture of an item I recently recovered on a job. It has some symbols that I'd like you to look into." He glanced around the room. A few other agents chatted in the corner, but no one looked their way. "This is a special assignment from the top, and we need things to be a bit cleaner than normal during the analysis."

Ronni blinked. "Cleaner?"

"Yes. I don't want any of this information leaking to anyone. Encrypt this so no one but you can follow your progress. Erase the work when you're done, and only tell me directly, face to face, if you find anything." Daniel locked eyes with her. "Understood?"

She sighed. "I guess I can't complain about weird secrecy requirements since I have a job with the CIA."

"Exactly. Chin up." The agent straightened. "I've got to go find Tim. I'll talk to you later. Remember, inform only me of progress."

He stepped away from her desk and headed back toward the elevator. It was time to visit the older man in his office. When he arrived, he lingered in front of the closed door. His stomach was tight.

The symbols shared by the nozzle and the Munich gun had to mean something, and he didn't trust Timothy so completely that he could ignore the fact that he'd just done an off-the-books job for him. There was an answer, and the other agent had it.

What will I do if he blows it off or he claims he doesn't know anything? It's not like I could go over his head about a side job, and there has to be a good explanation.

Daniel lifted his hand and knocked a few times.

"Come in," Timothy called from inside.

The agent closed the door behind him, then pulled out his silence cube, activated it, and placed it on the edge of the desk.

The older man arched a brow. "And I thought *I* was paranoid."

Daniel removed the handkerchief-covered nozzle from his pocket and set it carefully on the desk. "That place was heavily protected. More than I would have expected."

Timothy shrugged. "Rich people get robbed, too, you know. Was it really that much of a surprise?"

"Maybe. It didn't feel right." He pointed at the nozzle. "It doesn't matter. I jumped out of a building to get you this. What is it? I deserve to know."

"Don't worry about it. The important thing is that you got it, and I can make sure it's safely stored away."

"Not good enough, Tim." Daniel reached behind to lock the door. "Not fucking good enough."

His companion narrowed his eyes. "What the fuck is that supposed to mean, Daniel?"

The younger agent clenched his fists. "It means you've been my mentor my entire time at the CIA, and I know that you know a hell of a lot more than I do about the big picture, and probably where all the mysterious bodies are buried, human or magical." Daniel shook his head and dropped into the chair in front of the desk. "I also know that whatever you might have done at times, you're always worried about protecting the country first and foremost."

"Then why are you acting like I pissed in your cornflakes?" Tim threw a hand up in frustration.

Daniel pointed at the nozzle. "I'm tired of dancing around shit. The symbols on that artifact—what are they?"

Timothy's face twitched. "Just symbols. What of it?"

"I've got a hunch they're a lot more than that. I don't think my little trip to Vancouver would have needed to be off the books otherwise. If you ever want me to help you again with this little side project of yours, then you need to level with me now. I'm tired of people not telling me everything, especially when I'm putting my fucking life on the line. If you don't tell me the truth right now, I'll stand up and walk out of here. Maybe I even ask up the chain about this."

The older agent shot out of his chair, his jaw tight. He paced back and forth behind his desk, running a hand over his smooth, shaved head. "Ever think that maybe it's for your own good?"

"A lot of evil's been done after people utter that phrase."

Daniel's agency phone chimed. He pulled it out of his pocket, unsurprised that it was a message from Ronni.

Some weird alerts on this thing. Don't worry. I covered my tracks, but someone's interested in knowing who is checking it out.

A few more seconds before the phone chimed again.

Oh, yeah. Face to face. Sorry. Talk to you soon.

"Something important?" Timothy asked.

Daniel gave him a hungry grin. "I don't know. Maybe. All I know is that I'm getting a little fed up with risking my life for secrets no one will even bother to share with me."

His companion snorted. "You picked the wrong damned career then, son."

He slapped a hand on the desk. "Don't screw with me, Tim. You sent me off the books to go grab that thing, which means you don't want anyone else knowing about it. If I'm risking my life for side jobs, I at least need to know the damned reason." He shook his head. "That nozzle isn't simply a random knickknack some rich guy was collecting, so fucking tell me the truth. Stop insulting me with crap about how it's for my own good versus merely covering your ass."

Timothy blew out a breath. He stopped pacing and sat back down in his chair, then reached into his desk and pulled out a small action figure—a ninja turtle. It'd long since lost its weapon and colored bandana, so Daniel couldn't be sure which one it was.

What the hell? Why is he getting out a toy? Oh, right.

Daniel frowned. "Wait. I've seen that before. It's one of Ronni's, isn't it?"

"Yes. Don't think I don't know about her own little off-the-books experiments." The older agent pointed at the mirrored cube sitting on the edge of his desk. "That's blocking sound, but it's not blocking everything. This will make sure that even if people have visuals, they can't read our lips later. If you're going to be paranoid, might as well be damned thorough about it." He pressed the back of the shell.

Daniel took a deep breath. "Are you ready to finally tell me the truth?"

Timothy shrugged. "Before I do that, I need to make sure you're ready to *hear* the truth—the unsettling truth that might make it hard for you to sleep at night."

"I'm a spy. I'm all about finding out the unsettling truths, so normal people don't have to worry about it."

"Come on. That's bullshit, and you know it. We're here to defend the country. Sometimes, that means finding out the truth, and sometimes, it means burying the truth. We've both done our fair share of that in our time with the Company."

Daniel scoffed. "And is that what you're doing this time, burying the truth?"

The older man slumped back in his chair. "No, but

there are a lot of people out there who want to, and that's the problem. Once I tell you this, there's no going back. If you're worried about doing off-the-books jobs, you can't walk this path. You'll end up like me and have to keep a lot of secrets even from the people who are supposed to have your back. Knowing all that, you still sure you want to know? It's not too late to stand up, walk out, and forget everything you've seen. You did the job for me, and I appreciate it. I won't ask you for anything else. You simply have to leave and forget any of this ever happened."

A memory of the twisted body in Munich floated into Daniel's thoughts. He grimaced.

I have a few of my own secrets, too. If you taught me anything, Tim, it's that you don't always show all your cards, but this time, I at least need to see most *of your hand.*

"I can't walk away, not from this. Every instinct I have tells me that stupid thing on your desk represents something very important. Some things you can't just forget."

Timothy nodded. "Don't I know it. Let me ask you one question. Where do you think the nozzle came from?"

"Not Earth. That's the only thing I'm sure of. I don't care if there are powerful artifacts here. I'm no linguist or archaeologist, but something about those symbols doesn't feel native."

"Yeah. That's because they're alien."

"If they're from Oriceran, can't you just find some contractor to translate the symbols? It's not like you have to let them near the actual nozzle. There might even be some spell they can use."

The older man shook his head. "No, you don't get it.

The artifact is alien, but I'm not talking about Oriceran. And no, I don't know where exactly."

"What? From a galaxy far, far away?" Daniel offered. "Come on. Stop screwing me. Let's go with the real story."

"That is the real story. Extraterrestrials. The real deal, not anything to do with Oricerans." Timothy frowned. "And, just like the Oricerans, they have been here for a long time. Unlike the Oricerans, though, they aren't magical—at least, not like we know magic. But it's like the man said, any sufficiently advanced technology is indistinguishable from magic. This stuff is worse in a sense because we don't have any way of easily detecting it."

Daniel stared at his colleague and tried to process what he was hearing. "You're not shitting me, are you?"

"I wish to God that I was, son, I really do, but that's the plain truth. The other problem is that the Oricerans might have been hiding before, but they kept their numbers low. The truth was the humans in the know could still pick them out. These other aliens, though, do a better job of hiding in plain sight, even from people who are looking for them."

"You're telling me that all these ETs are walking around already?"

Timothy nodded. "Yeah. They are."

"Doing what?"

"Not sure." The older agent pointed to the nozzle. "We've been able to track some of their artifacts, though. That is part of an extremely powerful weapon. I and some other people in the know have tried to track down several alien weapons. This was part of one we had a good line on, and there's another one that we've tried to track recently.

Some evidence suggests it might have ended up in Germany over a hundred years ago, but we've not been able to locate it."

"Lots of guns, huh?" Daniel shrugged. "Maybe the aliens have driven through L.A. too many times."

"Funny. The point is, we don't know where they're from, how many of them are here, or their intentions. The only thing we know is that they're here, and they are potentially armed with technology hundreds of years beyond what we have available, but that's still a lot of unknowns. Your joke goes to a point. On a planet filled with guns, nukes, and now magicals, maybe it isn't crazy to pack an alien blaster or two." Timothy rubbed the back of his neck.

Daniel sighed and nodded. He was again tempted to tell the man about the Munich gun but decided against it. The alien artifact was safe, sitting in the vault where no one but his grandfather and he knew about it. He still needed a lot more answers.

"The way you're talking, this doesn't sound like it's simply your own personal side gig."

Timothy shook his head. "Yeah, I've had to pull in some favors, but this isn't my solo show, and I'm not the only one running a little research project. I have some issues with how some of this is going down in general."

The younger agent frowned. "What are you getting at?"

"There's a hidden group within the CIA. They report directly to the president. Their primary mission is to acquire the knowledge and materials necessary to support the successful integration of the country, and ultimately, the world. To even protect other worlds and dimensions, but they believe that aliens aren't merely watching but that they're already interfering with things. Politics, economics, that sort of thing."

Daniel shrugged. "Maybe this hidden group is right."

Timothy frowned down at the nozzle. "They could be, but it's a lot of assumptions. Think about how damned lucky we've been with Oriceran. Some strange world shows up with magic? Not everybody was comfortable with them, and a lot still aren't. You should see some of the plans I've seen." He sucked in a breath. "There was even a plan considered for a few years to detonate a few nukes on an island to remind the Oricerans what humans could do. More than a few people were advocating a first strike, talking about how they would flood our skies with dragons and take over Earth. There was talk about grabbing every magical native to Earth and trying to convince them to open portals to lob nukes through at Oriceran."

The younger agent scoffed. "They were going to go to war with Oriceran?"

"More higher-ups than you would have expected." He shrugged. "It's a good thing that calmer heads prevailed on both sides. The problem is the hawks are always there, and the worst thing you want to do is hand somebody a nuke equivalent and let him think it's okay to use or even necessary." He nodded at the nozzle. "There are some things our government shouldn't have, like the weapon this belongs to. The hawks want to arm the country to take on the aliens. The same people who wanted to nuke Oriceran are ready to start a war with an enemy they haven't even identified."

Daniel grimaced. A war fought with weapons like the

Munich gun would leave the Earth a twisted wasteland, if it even survived.

Timothy took a deep breath. "And as worried as I am about these aliens, we're not even sure they're enemies. We could start a War of the Worlds if some paranoid idiot overreacts. Fear makes for poor decisions. These aliens might be a threat, or they might merely be tourists. They might also have a whole fleet of planet killers they use on worlds that kill their tourists."

"And what if the aliens are slowly building an invasion force?"

"Then all the more reason to learn more about them." The older man pointed at the nozzle. "For now, though, I don't trust the humans or the aliens. That's why I've put together my own group within the CIA to look into the aliens."

Daniel rubbed his eyes. "And I guess you won't share notes with the team you mentioned."

Timothy shook his head. "Think of this as a part of the whole checks and balances system that makes America so great."

"Some people might say that this isn't checks and balances but more like you've put together a rogue team."

The older agent shrugged. "And the founding fathers would have been hanged as traitors if they lost the revolution. I'm doing what I need to do to protect my country and the planet. If it costs me in the end, then I don't care. I'll die with no regrets."

Daniel took a deep breath. "This is a pretty aggressive and dangerous plan."

His companion shook his head. "Not if we're going to

survive the coming storm without losing a bunch of cities." He rubbed his chin. "Let me ask you one question. Why did you join the CIA?"

"To protect my country and its citizens."

"That's what my group will do. The question is, do you want to grab magical tchotchkes for the rest of your damned life, or do you want to save worlds?"

Daniel glanced over his shoulder to confirm the door was still closed. "Worlds, plural?"

"Yes, worlds. We're connected to Oriceran now. If things go south, they'll be in the line of fire, too. I might not trust all the magicals, but they haven't gone to war with us, and they've been a part of our communities—our lives—for hundreds of generations."

The younger agent furrowed his brow and looked down. Doing a side job without the Company knowing was one thing, but participating in a fully independent rogue team wasn't merely brushing against the line. It was jumping yards past it.

Daniel blew out a breath. "How the hell will this even work? My last side job was harder than it needed to be because I couldn't use most CIA resources. You want me to help investigate aliens and keep the rest of the agency from learning about it using my smartphone?"

Timothy shook his head. "I've known about this alien research for a while and have more than a few files from some other classified government projects. Lots of different people sharing resources, but also keeping it secret. I knew the day would come when I'd need to make more of a move, so I've gathered the funds I need to support the team, and I also already rounded up a few key allies and people. Yeah, we still need to build up the team, but we've got a good start."

"Who else do you have?"

"Among other people, Nessie."

Daniel's eyes widened even as he laughed. "Of course. Why am I not surprised?"

The older man shared a rare smile. "She's seen a lot of the alien gadgets and human research." His smile disappeared. "And this shit is getting out of hand."

"Fine. I need to talk to Nessie before I give you an answer."

Timothy stared at him for a long moment. "Fair enough, but I told you before that once you heard this, there would be no going back."

"What will you do, kill me if I say no?"

His companion snorted. "I didn't mentor a good man for all those years simply to kill him. I'm saying I know you, and I know you won't walk away from this." He waved a hand. "Go talk to Nessie about it if it makes you feel better."

Daniel didn't even bother to knock. He threw the door open, stepped through, and slammed it shut.

Nessie frowned and looked up at him. "I don't believe we had an appointment, Daniel."

He tossed his silence cube on her desk. "I just got done talking to Tim, and he said I should talk to you, Carolyn."

She arched a brow. Apparently, she'd gotten used to the

nickname, so the use of her actual name by an agent proved a surprise.

The woman frowned and glanced down at the silence cube before reaching into a desk drawer and grabbing something. Daniel's stomach tightened.

Be damned embarrassing if I ended up shot to death in CIA headquarters.

When she sat up, she wasn't holding a gun but another ninja turtle.

"What's this about, Agent Winters?" Nessie emphasized his title and name.

"Aliens among us, and not the kind with magic." Daniel shrugged. "Tim sent me to Vancouver to recover the nozzle to some sort of weapon. When I pressed him, he spilled the beans. Then he told me you were on his team and I should talk to you."

Nessie snorted. "I'm surprised to see you acting so stupidly about this."

"Huh?"

"You should have waited to talk to me." She nodded toward the silence cube and the ninja turtle. "After all, you're being watched. Maybe Franklin hasn't impressed upon you how dangerous this might be."

Daniel shrugged. "Watched? By who? The Company? That comes with getting this." He padded the ID badge on his chest.

Nessie shook her head. "Not this type of surveillance. Some of the other people involved in this…matter have suspected Franklin for a while. He's your mentor, so they suspect you as well. They want all this information to stay buried. Some might even want it to be buried for the right reasons, but it doesn't change the fact they're in over their heads." She gestured to herself, then Daniel. "That's what we represent—a rescue effort, a way of stabilizing this situation."

He stared at her, the woman's frown only deepening.

The agent shrugged. "I'm not so sure I buy all this."

She narrowed her eyes. "You think we're making this up?"

"I don't know what to think other than there are artifacts out there with strange symbols that could mean a lot of things."

The woman slowly. "You successfully recovered the nozzle, then?"

If I didn't tell Tim about the Munich gun, there's no reason to tell her. Might as well keep this shit focused.

"Yes. Tim's little Vancouver adventure went well enough, thanks to my quick thinking."

A look of relief spread over her face. "Thank God. That's not something we needed to have still floating around. You wouldn't believe the kind of damage it could do."

Daniel's chuckle was dark. "You might be surprised what I'd believe."

"Your belief doesn't make the danger any less real. The important thing isn't even that Franklin or I believe in it, but that there are various powerful people out there who believe in all this and are very nervous. Nerves make for dangerous mistakes."

The agent rubbed the back of his neck. "I'm merely not convinced you and Tim running some secret shoestring group will be enough to handle all this."

Nessie rattled off an address in DC. "Go there. You'll be convinced then, and once you're given the full briefing, you'll understand exactly what we're up against and why we have to do what we're doing."

"What's there?"

"Just go. You'll see. Consider this a test."

CHAPTER FIFTEEN

He wasn't sure what he'd expected, but it had been something more than a brownstone that looked identical to every other one on the street. Daniel parked his car on the street and frowned. He stepped out, shaking his head.

This is ridiculous. Okay, so I've let them convince me other alien visitors are walking around on Earth, but will I really join some rogue team? If we're discovered, they'll throw us in a very dark hole for a long time, and that's if they don't execute us outright.

The least I can do is check this shit out.

He jogged up the stairs to the front door. There was nothing unusual on the other side of the mostly glass doors, simply a rather nondescript lobby leading to an elevator and a stairwell.

Should I ring the bell? Or maybe the whole thing's a big misdirect. They could have a team waiting to ambush me.

Daniel shook his head. If they wanted him dead, it'd be

far easier to do it somewhere else rather than sending him to some random DC brownstone.

The elevator doors opened, and a man in a dark suit stepped out. The agent snorted. He knew another CIA agent when he saw one. The man didn't seem tense, and his hands hung loosely at his sides—not exactly combat stance.

The stranger walked over to the doors and tapped away at a keypad. The doors clicked open, and he motioned Daniel inside.

"We've been expecting you, Daniel. I'm Malcolm White. Feel free to call me Malcolm. Please come with me. I've been told to show you around a little. I'm kind of responsible for keeping an eye on this place when I'm not doing my normal job for the Company."

He followed the man into the elevator. The guide tapped a code on a keypad near the floor buttons. A small panel slid down, revealing a DNA scanning pad. Malcolm pressed his thumb against the pad and the elevator descended after a few seconds.

He cleared his throat. "No one gets in here who we don't want in here. This is the HQ for our new task force or whatever you want to call it. The facility has several subterranean levels, but the upper levels have conference rooms and living areas for when people need to keep out of sight—that sort of thing. Everything's secure. Only a small number of people in the entire world know about this building. Right now, you can basically count them using two hands."

Tim wasn't wrong when he was talking about the need to build up his personnel, then.

The elevator doors opened into a room dominated by a

huge round table in the center. A large virtual screen covered the back wall. Several workstations with computers and large headphones lined one of the other walls.

The screen currently depicted a flat map of the Earth marked with several small triangles in various locations with small notes next to them. Vancouver, Canada, and Munich, Germany had both been marked, but there were easily a dozen other notations on the map.

"Where's everyone else?" Daniel asked. "I know you said the team's still small, but I'm guessing it's not only you, Tim, and Nessie."

Malcolm shrugged. "Tim wanted to be careful, just in case. Come on, you're a spy. In the spy game, you can never be one hundred percent sure about where someone's loyalties lie."

That trust thing is an industry rule. Try not to.

"You have an entire little mini-CIA here." Daniel walked over to the screen, shaking his head. "All under the noses of the other alien team, and even the agency. Really going out of your way to stack the deck against yourselves, aren't you?"

"Nope. We've got all the resources but not enough manpower. The Fortis team has a decent head start on us, even if they're clueless."

He frowned and turned away from the screen to look at Malcolm. "Fortis team?"

His companion nodded. "They're the CIA team that reports directly to the President on this matter. They've loosely allied with other classified projects funded and run by different departments. Project Nephilim has been investigating alien artifacts for a while, but these days they are mostly errand boys for Fortis. Project Ragnarok is a group that's a little more interested in direct evaluation and reaching and contacting aliens, if only to assess them for threats. They also have a heavy focus on creating countermeasures to potential alien technologies or abilities. Both those projects dump a lot of time and money into research, both government and civilian. A lot of people working on Ragnarok or Nephilim projects don't even realize who is paying them. It's all unconnected research as far as they're concerned."

Daniel nodded and slipped into a chair at the round table. "None of this sounds that bad, but I don't understand why you're running a side operation instead of working with the other guys. Tim alluded to some stuff, but I still don't get it. I can't connect the pieces."

Malcolm sat a few chairs down from him. He reached into his jacket and pulled out a photograph which slid toward the other agent.

He picked up the photograph of what appeared to be a large crater. "What's this?"

"That used to a small town in Colorado." The other man shrugged. "The Fortis guys became convinced there was a dangerous alien in the town, so they sent in a team. People started shooting. We still don't know who shot first, but their bosses got concerned when they saw some of the tech on display from the target—instant matter rearrangement among other things. Civilians started dying. Other civilians started taking pictures. Then someone panicked, and things got really bad."

Daniel frowned. "Meaning what exactly?"

"Officially... Maybe I shouldn't use that word considering how deep into the realms of black ops the Fortis guys operate. Anyway, someone with a lot of influence and authority decided the sacrifice of a few hundred American lives was worth it to keep things under wraps and a single alien under control—one who hadn't even attacked anyone before the team showed up. Also, the Fortis guys decided they needed to send a message with a new type of experimental bomb adapted from alien technology." He sighed. "So, the town's gone. If you look hard enough, you'll find news reports about an industrial accident and a mandatory evacuation followed by another explosion, but there was no evacuation. They took out that alien, all right, along with all those people."

Daniel's jaw tightened. "I hadn't heard about anything like this."

Malcolm nodded. "Exactly. There's news out there, and satellite images only back up their story, but you have to go looking to find even that much. Anyone who starts looking too hard ends up disappearing or is convinced to leave well enough alone after a few threatening phone calls or late-night visits."

The agent drew a deep breath. "And you're sure they had no other choice?"

"Depends on how much you think someone's life is worth. Me? It makes no sense to say they're protecting the Earth from dangerous aliens if it involves killing the very people they're supposed to protect. Things are out of control, and Fortis is all about shooting first and asking questions later. Last time, it was a few hundred people, but if they keep that kind of thing up, we could suffer war-level causalities from friendly fire, and that's before we consider that we might push the aliens into doing something equally stupid. One well-placed bomb can wipe out an entire city of millions of people."

Daniel furrowed his brow. He wasn't naïve enough to believe the government couldn't be ruthless, but annihilating an entire American town was so far over the line that they wouldn't even see it if they looked back with a telescope.

"Sounds like you need more level heads working on this. People who will at least ask a question or two before they start shooting."

Malcolm nodded. "That's who we are. The level heads. We've got the knowledge and the resources. Now we're working on recruitment. While we'll never match Fortis' numbers, we need more than we have now if we're going to find aliens and artifacts before they do."

Daniel raised a hand. "I get it. I do, and I'm in. But who else are you thinking about?"

The other man's expression darkened. "I just received word that the Fortis guys are looking into an analyst and researcher you've worked with in the past, Ronni Welch. Apparently, she was poking around into some of the alien symbols, and they caught wind of it. I'm sorry. At a minimum she's burned, and I don't think it'll end there."

The agent grimaced. "Damn it. That's my fault. I told her to look into the symbols."

"Then she'd be a good start. If the government is willing to kill hundreds of civilians to keep their secrets buried, they won't blink at killing one CIA employee."

"Why didn't you tell me earlier?"

Malcolm narrowed his eyes. "We needed to make sure you were with us and not Fortis."

He shot out of his seat and rushed toward the elevator.

Damn it. I'm sorry, Ronni. I underestimated how deep this conspiracy went.

The analyst walked down the street toward the nearby bus station. Her earbuds blocked out anything but the show she was listening to. It was a nice night, the clear sky providing a view of the few stars not drowned by light pollution.

"That's when I add the cinnabar," a gravelly male voice said in her earphones. "Can't get the color you want without it. You definitely need gloves and a mask for this unless you love heavy metal poisoning. I call this part of the procedure 'shaken, not stirred.'" He chuckled.

The voice belonged to the so-called Big Gnome, Johnson Lat, an internet streaming and podcast star who specialized in making cool devices and concoctions using a combination of magic and technology. He'd become popular in the last year, but he'd also been dogged by accusations that he was a fraud.

His internet name came from the fact that he was unusually large for a gnome and lacked many of their distinguishing facial characteristics. Detractors claimed he was a charlatan, merely a short human pretending to be Oriceran. He'd explained that he was half-human on his dad's side, and even though his human genes were more prominent, that wasn't enough for many of his doubters.

They also contended that all his demonstrations were fakes. Tricks of the camera, especially since magic made it hard to duplicate.

It didn't help that Johnson had started his career as a conspiracy theorist. Among other things, he'd had a short-lived internet show where he stated that attributing all ancient alien theories to the Oricerans was wrong and that they were only one group of aliens among many who had visited the Earth. Ronni couldn't say she believed him, but it was still interesting.

She also didn't care whether he was a half-gnome or a human with unusual abilities. She knew more than most people about the interface between technology and magic and believed in Big Gnome. It helped that he lived in D.C., and she liked the idea of supporting a local guy.

As he continued to rattle on about his latest creation—a self-propelled bird automaton—Ronni's attention drifted away from the podcast and back to earlier in the day.

Her hands started shaking, and she swallowed.

What is up with those symbols? Someone obviously didn't want me looking into them, but it should be okay. I covered my tracks, and Daniel didn't send me any angry texts back.

I need to be more careful in the future.

Ronni shook her head, her brow furrowed in determination. She would solve the mystery. All she needed was the time.

Two large men in suits closed in on either side of her. She frowned. Some people could be so rude.

The men reached for her arms at the same time. There was something terrible and unsettling in their eyes. Her heart rate kicked up.

"Miss Welch, you'll need to come with us," one of them said.

Ronni ducked and rolled backward. At five feet two, she couldn't take on two grown men, but maybe someone nearby would help her.

There was one small problem. No one else was on the street, not a single car.

That's what I get for taking a shortcut.

One of her abductors smirked. "Don't make this hard."

"You go away right now." Ronni hopped to her feet and reached inside her purse. "T-this is your one chance. I-I'll let you go if you run now," she stammered.

The men rolled their eyes and advanced. She yanked a Gumby out of her purse and held it up.

The first man scoffed. "Is that supposed to scare us?"

Ronni yanked the toy hard on both sides. With a hiss, a thick, noxious green gas poured into the face of the first oversized man. He collapsed to the ground, coughing and squeezing his eyes shut.

His accomplice glared at her. "You're dead, bitch."

Another trip into her purse brought up a tiny Barbie shoe. "Back off."

"What are you, a fucking toy store?"

Ronni threw the shoe at his feet and spun. The bright flash lit up the entire area, turning night into day.

The second man fell to knees, holding his eyes. "I'm fucking blind."

She sprinted toward the corner. The headquarters building wasn't that far away. She grabbed her phone to dial the police.

"What the heck?"

No service.

"I can literally see a cell tower right over there!" Ronni shouted. She kept running toward the CIA, huffing and puffing. All those spinning classes were finally paying off. Thank God she wore sensible shoes.

Sweat streamed down her face, and her heart thundered as she approached the front gate. She slowed her pace to a jog as she spotted a couple of agents standing in front of the gate. One held a box.

She ran up to them and leaned over, her hands on her knees as she tried to catch her breath.

The agent dropped the box right in front of her. It contained all her personal effects from her desk, along with her array of little toys.

Huh?

Ronni lifted her head, her stomach churning from fear and exertion. "I… Two men were after me, and I can't call the police. They might be jamming my phone."

The agent who had dropped the box held out his hand, palm up. "I hereby inform you that your security clearance has been revoked and your employment with the Central Intelligence Agency has been terminated, effective immediately. Give me your badge or you will go to jail on suspicion of espionage."

"E-espionage? But, I never—" Tears welled in the corners of her eyes.

"I won't repeat myself, Miss Welch." The agent reached into his jacket, resting his hand on his gun.

Ronni sighed and pulled out her badge and ID card. She handed them over. "I've done nothing wrong."

"I'm sure you believe that." He nodded at the box. "Now

take your crap and get out of our sight before I change my mind."

She wiped her tears on her sleeve and picked up her box. They obviously didn't know what her toys did. There was no way they'd give them back to her otherwise.

Who were those guys earlier? CIA muscle? Contractors? What should I do?

With a sigh, Ronni began walking away from the front gate, this time in the opposite direction. She looked over her shoulder, but the agents had already started back toward the building. There was no sign of the thugs.

She continued walking, putting one foot in front of the other, not even sure where she was going. Another bus stop, maybe. She wasn't sure how many minutes had passed when a black Jaguar screeched to a halt beside her.

Now what? Is some hitman going to gun me down?

Ronni was too depressed to care.

The passenger-side window dropped, and she looked over. Daniel was watching her with visible relief on his face.

"They burned you, it looks like. Sorry I'm late."

She nodded. "Yeah, guess that also explains my phone losing service. Going to need to get a new one." Numbly, she pulled her phone out her pocket and initiated a factory reset.

The agent frowned. "But they didn't hurt you?"

"Some guys tried, but I got away." Ronni sighed. "I don't even know why. Wait. The symbols. I thought I'd covered my tracks, but obviously, I didn't do it well enough."

Daniel sighed and averted his eyes. "Damn it. Get in. This is all my fault."

She opened the back door to deposit her things on the seat before slipping into the passenger side. "No, it's my fault for being sloppy. I should have taken it more seriously. I never thought the CIA would be the ones coming after me, though."

The agent pulled away from the curb. "I'll give you a choice. I can explain the truth, but once I do there might be no going back. Otherwise, you can go on with your life and pretend you never saw those symbols."

"My life's already over, so I might as well dig deeper into the hole."

Ronni remained silent during Daniel's explanation of Tim's new team, the truth of non-Oriceran aliens, and how the government had murdered hundreds of innocent people as a show of strength and to cover up the truth.

Her response was fairly phlegmatic, all things considered.

"I feel like I'm gonna throw up."

He chuckled. "I know what you mean. We have both been involved in some weird stuff, but somehow, this is still almost too weird to believe. Anyway, the way I see it, since you've been burned, you need something to do with your time. The team could use someone with your talents."

Ronni sighed. "You got me into this."

"Accidently, but yeah." Daniel shrugged. "I'm sorry."

She rubbed the back of her neck. "When I first got out of school, my mom told me I should go work for a startup company. She said I could make a bunch of money and then never have to work for the rest of my life, but no, I wanted to serve my country. I guess it's not too late to go make money."

He scoffed. "Do you want to?"

His companion wiped a new tear away. "No, but what choice do I have? I'm lucky they didn't already make me disappear." She wrapped her arms around herself. "They still might if everything you said was true."

The agent shook his head. "No. I'll make some calls and pull some strings. Since they've already burned you, there's no reason to go further, and I'll make it clear that people will be watching. These Fortis assholes want less attention, not more. So, the question to you is simple."

"What's that?"

"Do you want to look for work in some startup, or do you want to save worlds?"

Ronni stared down at her hands. "All I ever wanted to do was help protect people." She closed her eyes, took a deep breath, and nodded. "I'm in."

"Good." Daniel smiled. "I've already done my part of building up the team, though if you know anyone else you could possibly trust, let me know. This will be hard. We're talking about a team of people on the fringe with skills but who still care enough to want to protect their country and planet in a situation most people wouldn't believe, even with Oriceran being a thing."

She nibbled on her lip for a few seconds. "Now that you mention it, I think I might know someone."

CHAPTER SIXTEEN

Ronni inhaled deeply. This could work if she could convince her potential recruit that she wasn't a stalker. She raised her fist, knocked lightly on the door, and waited.

I can't believe this. What am I doing? I'm trying to recruit people for a super-secret task force that even the CIA can't know about.

A few seconds later, the door buzzed, and a familiar voice rang out from a hidden speaker.

"Who are you?" asked Big Gnome. "I don't recognize you, and you don't seem like you're here to sell me anything dressed in an outfit like that."

"My name is Ronni Welch. Um, I'm a big fan of your show, but I'm not here to talk about that. I mean, I know about you from your show, but it's got nothing to do with that, not directly. Well, kind of indirectly." She groaned and rubbed the back of her neck. "It'll make more sense once I start explaining, but it's not really the kind of thing I can talk to you about in a hallway through a speaker."

It'd been a week since she'd been burned. Even though she'd tracked Big Gnome's address down immediately, she had needed to investigate his background further and work up the courage to talk to him. She had also gotten a new and secure phone, courtesy of the team.

On paper, Big Gnome appeared to be a good candidate, and they would monitor his communications for the next few days in case he reacted poorly to her offer. The last thing they needed was for him to call the FBI and leak their offer to Fortis.

"What are you here to talk about?" he asked. "You didn't seem to have a very good idea earlier."

"Sorry, I got a bit flustered." Ronni pursed her lips, lacing her fingers together. "But it's a unique job opportunity, one that no one else can offer you. So please, let me in, and I can talk to you about this fulfilling opportunity to really put your abilities and skills to the test."

Big Gnome didn't respond, and Ronni sighed. Of course, he wouldn't let some random woman he didn't know into his place. She could be a serial killer for all he knew, or some crazy transforming Oriceran monster.

I should have had Daniel talk to him. This was doomed to fail from the beginning.

She turned to leave. The door clicked open, and Big Gnome stepped out in jeans and a t-shirt that read, King of Makers. Even though he was tall for a gnome—or half-gnome, anyway—she still had a couple of inches on him, but his fuller face and normal ears reflected his human side.

He gestured at her to enter with his head. "Take a giant step for mankind, and let's get talking."

Ronni managed a little chuckle. "*Moonraker,* right?"

Big Gnome grinned. "You're already impressing me, Miss…"

"Ronni Welch, but you can call me Ronni."

She stepped inside his living room. There were a couple of recliners, but most of the space was taken up by huge tables covered with tools and small projects in various states of disarray. Some had power tools, and others racks of colorful chemicals.

I bet his lease doesn't want him smelting mercury ore in his apartment, but we could probably learn a lot from each other about making gadgets.

Ronni headed over to one of the recliners to take a seat. It was on the smaller side and comfortable enough for her small frame, but she could see how Daniel might have had a problem.

She rubbed her wrist. "So, do you like to go by Big Gnome, or Johnson, or Lat?"

"Big Gnome. My handle is my life. I sometimes think about changing my legal name to Big Gnome." He shrugged. "Maybe you think that's pretentious, but that's what I like."

"Oh, okay, then, I'll just call you that." Ronni swallowed and took a few deep breaths. "Big Gnome or Mr. Big Gnome?"

"Just Big Gnome." He sat down in the other recliner. "So, you mentioned a unique job opportunity. That's a hell of a hook, and I hope you don't disappoint me."

She nodded quickly. "Yes. I'm very familiar with your

work, and I share a similar interest in tinkering. I thought if you have access to more money and resources, you'd be able to up your game. Really challenge your limits and see what you're capable of."

Big Gnome nodded. "Not disagreeing. I make a decent living making cool things on camera. I've got to deal with haters and drama, but it's not a bad life. To be honest, though, it's not nearly as lucrative as everyone thinks. So, who do you work for—some media company that wants to help fund a bigger show for me?"

"Not exactly." Ronni leaned forward. "You see, it's not only your skills I'm interested in but rather your open mind."

He furrowed his brow. "My open mind?"

She reached into her pocket, pulled out her new phone and brought up a closeup image of the alien symbols from the nozzle. "Ever seen these before?"

Big Gnome leaned forward and stared at the symbols. "Nope. Don't recognize them. The only thing I can tell you is they aren't gnomic, but I'm not an expert on all languages, Earth or Oriceran."

Ronni took several deep breaths in a feeble attempt to calm her pounding heart. "It wouldn't matter even if you were."

"What do you mean?"

"Let me tell you a little story about aliens."

Twenty minutes later, she finished her explanation. "It comes down to a simple question, Mr. Lat—excuse me, Big

Gnome. Do you want to make internet videos only a few people watch, or do you want to save worlds?"

He hopped out of his recliner, frowning, and paced back and forth. He muttered something under his breath. Ronni couldn't pick out any word but "crazy."

Does he even believe me? Sure, I had my picture of the symbols and a few government documents, but it's not like someone couldn't fake those. He probably thinks I'm a conspiracy theorist stalker nut job who has latched onto him because he's semi-famous.

She clenched her hands so her companion couldn't see the trembling.

He stopped and spun to face her. His frown turned to a huge grin. "I knew it."

"Excuse me? Knew what?"

"I knew it," Big Gnome yelled. "Everyone said I was a dumbass, that we didn't need to even talk about aliens anymore because we could explain away everything about aliens, ancient or modern, by merely assuming some Oriceran did it. But believing in actual aliens from space? Well, that's something only idiots and conspiracy theorists believed in. Fools. Intellectual dead-enders." He pointed a thumb at himself. "But it's all damned true, and I was right all along."

Ronni nodded. "Yes, but keep in mind, if you join our group, it's not like you'll be able to talk about it. I already told you what happened and what the Fortis team was willing to do. Your life could be at risk."

He waved a hand dismissively. "Being in on the truth is its own reward and a little danger? That's part of the Big

Gnome brand. I'm totally willing to join your team, but I have an employee I need to bring with me."

She sighed. "I only approached you because I checked out your background, and you looked like someone we could use who could keep his mouth shut. How do I know this employee can keep a secret?"

"Because she's a pixie who has worked for several of my cousins. They're all involved in under-the-table magical stuff. Trust me, any secret organization needs good clerical support, and she's great at that kind of thing. She's got a mouth on her, but she knows how to keep it shut when it counts." Big Gnome shrugged. "She's pretty put out right now that my cousin can't give her enough work. It annoys her and boy, that is not good. She likes to work a lot of jobs, sometimes two or three. Don't know, maybe it's a pixie thing. She'd love to find another job, especially one where she won't have to deal with new clients constantly, and this sounds perfect for her."

"Okay, I guess I should go meet her. What's her name?"

"Madge You'll love her, in a love/hate kind of way."

A short drive later, they pulled up in Big Gnome's Corvette to the front of an office building. She followed him as he stepped into the lobby, nodded to a security guard, and walked over to an elevator.

"I rent some space on the second floor," he explained. "It helps keep the crazies from showing up at my door—except when they do research." He winked at her.

Ronni's cheeks warmed. "We won't be able to talk about

this here. It's not safe. There could be someone spying or something. This is sensitive information. Your place was one thing, but who knows what kind of monitoring they might do in this office building?"

Big Gnome waved a hand and pulled out a pen. "Don't worry. This doesn't last long, but it's something I made and never talked about on my show. It'll keep our conversation private enough."

The elevator dinged, and the doors opened. They walked to the end of the hall where a small sign read, Lat Productions in Comic Sans.

She tried to hide her smirk but failed.

Her companion grinned. "Yeah, I know. Not all that professional, but I don't care. I figured if I have to do the boring parts of running a business, I'd do it my way and not worry if some suit is offended because of my font choice. That's also part of the Big Gnome brand."

They stepped into the office. A massive desk sat in the center, with a few chairs in front of it. A tiny chair only a few inches high stood on the back of the desk with an equally small stand right in front of it. If it were larger, Ronni might consider it a podium, but it seemed like an odd term to use for something more appropriate for a hamster than a person.

She saw something move from the corner of her eye and yelped, backpedaling a few steps.

"Well, that's rude," came a deep voice. The owner was a winged pixie, fluttering at eye level and pear-shaped rather than being some sort of svelte Tinkerbell. She wore a tiny black skirt and a white blouse. The ensemble was completed by cat-eye glasses.

The voice was so gravelly that Ronni found herself looking for a miniature cigarette somewhere. It'd complete the '50s vibe the pixie had going on.

Big Gnome chuckled. "Don't sneak up on people, Madge."

Wait. Do those wings work through normal physical principles, or is there magic? They don't look large enough to support someone that heavy. Wow, the bumble bee theory in a pixie. She shouldn't be able to lift off and fly, but there she is.

She sighed, trying to push the thought out of her head. The heavyset pixie had a voice like a teamster.

"Who is this woman?" The creature flittered around Ronni's head before hovering right in front of her nose. "She doesn't look that smart. You taking in strays now, BG?"

The woman gasped. "Wow. He wasn't lying when he said you have a mouth on you."

"I'm merely someone who really believes in telling it like it is. Lies don't help anyone, honey."

Ronni looked at Big Gnome. He smiled and clicked his pen.

She took a deep breath. Time to get right to it. "I'm recruiting people for a secret semi-rogue task force to investigate non-Oriceran aliens. Your boss says you might be a good asset. Any organization needs clerical support, and he says you know how to keep your mouth shut."

"Will there be snacks?" Madge asked, her voice as gravelly as ever. Not a hint of a smile showed on her face, and her hands settled on her hips as her wings fluttered behind her.

"Snacks?"

The pixie nodded and crossed her arms. "Yeah. Free snacks. I'm small, so it's not like it'll cost you a lot."

Ronni blinked. She wasn't sure what pixies ate.

She shrugged. "I'm sure we can arrange some. You don't have any other questions, even though I just talked about something shocking and weird? Something that challenges everything people believe about history?"

Madge shook her head. "I like to learn on the job. The important thing is the snacks."

"I guess we all have our priorities."

CHAPTER SEVENTEEN

Daniel stepped into the cubicle farm where Ronni had worked until a couple of days prior. He kept reminding himself that she was okay, but he couldn't stop the guilt that stabbed him. If those two men on the street had caught her she might have ended up as another missing person, a victim of a dangerous conspiracy dumped in an unmarked grave.

For the moment, at least, she spent her time at the brownstone, safe from any troublemakers. There wasn't even any evidence they were still interested in her. No one was watching her apartment, and no one had tried to hack her accounts. Maybe Fortis—or whoever had been behind getting her fired—figured they'd made their point, especially since, as far as they knew, she no longer had access to Company resources to pursue an investigation.

If they're going by her psychological profile, they'd have no reason to believe she'd continue to cause trouble. She's not a trou-

blemaker. She would never have even looked into that without me prodding her.

"Looking for Welch?" Agent Buckley asked behind him.

Daniel forced himself to relax and turned to face him. It was the first time he'd been back at headquarters since Ronni was burned, and he didn't want to give anyone reason to suspect him.

"Yeah, I am. Where is she?"

The man shrugged. "Who knows?"

He snorted. "You're real helpful."

The other agent looked around and leaned in. "You didn't hear?"

"Hear what?"

"She's out. Burned." Buckley shrugged again, the gesture eloquent. "They say she was using Company resources to look into things for personal reasons, maybe even trying to make some cash off it. It's hard to believe that little mouse would do something like that, but it's always the quiet ones." He scratched his stubble.

Daniel frowned. "You growing a beard? I haven't seen that much growth on you in a long time."

His companion chuckled. "Nah. Just…I'm not trying to. Been busy and, you know, forget sometimes." His eyes darted back and forth, and he released a nervous chuckle.

"You okay, Buckley?"

He snorted. "Yeah. Why wouldn't I be? That mission to Kiev…damn. Sometimes, I impress even myself, but I'm just tired. Come on, you never get tired after a long mission? Whatever." He smirked, but something about it looked forced. "And I guess I was wrong."

Daniel looked him up and down. The man kept rubbing his fingers together, his arms hanging at his sides.

"Wrong?"

"Yeah. I always figured you were banging Welch."

"Because I paid attention to her when no one else did?"

Buckley nodded. "Yeah. I mean, if she tried she might be hot, but I also thought she might be a hellcat in the sack or something." He shrugged. "It doesn't matter. I guess you weren't doing her if you didn't even know they burned her."

A loud crash sounded from the corner of the room. Agent Buckley ducked and rolled behind a desk.

"Sorry!" a woman called from across the way. "Just knocked some stuff over."

The agent remained crouched by the desk for several seconds, taking deep breaths and his face red.

What the fuck is going on with him?

Daniel was about to ask when Buckley popped up and straightened his tie, an obviously fake smile on his face.

"I've got crap to do. See you around." He blurted the words, spun on his heel, and hurried to the elevator.

Why are you so nervous? Were you checking on me, Buckley? Are you with them? Are you *responsible for burning her?*

He gritted his teeth and took a deep breath. He couldn't trust anyone.

Daniel's hands clenched into fists as he stepped off the elevator. He immediately uncurled his fingers and forced a charming smile on his face as he gave a polite nod to several S.A.D. workers on his way to Nessie's office.

It'd been a couple of days since his run-in with Buckley, and the encounter refused to leave his mind. The other agent was obviously up to something, and Daniel was willing to bet it involved Ronni.

Does he know I'm the one who told her to research the symbols?

He shook his head. Buckley had avoided him since then, which only made him more suspicious. For now, he had to concentrate on not acting suspiciously himself. If he gave the man any reason to come after him, it might unravel everything Timothy was building.

Just another day at work, back at a place where some hidden team who helped blow up a town tried to take out a good and loyal American, and it's my fault.

It took all his concentration to keep smiling as he made his way to Nessie's office and closed the door behind him.

The longer I can last in the agency, the more resources we'll have to look into the aliens. If they're a threat, we can help stop them without any more panicky, ridiculous responses that hurt innocent people. If they aren't, we can stop Fortis and the rest of the government from overreacting and starting a war.

Nessie looked Daniel up and down as he sat. "Are you all right?"

"I've been better. It's been a rough week."

He wanted to have a more open conversation, but they both knew that the excessive use of anti-surveillance devices would raise suspicion. Given that Ronni had already been burned and Buckley might be watching him, they'd need to be even more careful.

If Fortis could prove Timothy and Nessie were involved, things probably wouldn't end the way they had with Ronnie and two thugs on the street.

I won't let any other loyal agents get taken out or burned.

She nodded. "We all were surprised by what happened to Miss Welch, but we have to concentrate on moving forward. It's not unusual in our line of work for these sorts of disappointments to pop up."

Daniel furrowed his brow. He wondered if he should mention Buckley, but he had no real proof the man was anything but an overworked agent. The last thing he wanted to do was point Nessie or Timothy at him and end up making the man's life harder if he wasn't an enemy. It wasn't like they could discuss it there, anyway.

I've barely started my deep cover life buried inside a conspiracy, and I'm already messed up and seeing trouble everywhere. Nice.

"Yeah, it sucks, but that's the job," he responded.

Nessie inclined her head. "We should concentrate on your next mission."

Daniel managed a smirk. The sentence worked on a few different levels. "I've been bored since my last mission was completed anyway."

If anyone were listening, he wanted them to hear the same cocky agent everyone expected. The more he acted like everything was normal, the less suspicious they'd be.

Nessie nodded. "Good, although this next mission might not be as stimulating as you hope."

"Does it involve another dead guy regrowing his own liver?"

She shook her head. "No. It's far more straightforward.

We've received reports that a ring of burglars has terrorized London, and that they might be using a magical artifact. We want you to investigate and recover it before MI5 or MI6 get involved. Every one we control adds to the safety and security of the United States."

Daniel laughed. "I like how many artifacts we steal out from underneath our allies' noses."

"Oriceran changed a lot, and it's not like the British don't do it to us too when they get a chance. At least this doesn't seem to be a weapon."

He shrugged. "I'll get whatever they're using. What goodies will I get this time to catch the bad guys?"

Nessie reached behind the desk and grabbed a small box. "Directional EMP, chameleon ball—"

"Please tell me it lasts longer?"

She nodded. "We've refined it, so we can guarantee five minutes. Although I'm not sure it'll be necessary."

Daniel nodded. "Have a stun pin that works?"

"They're still testing those after your failure and those of a few other agents."

He snapped his fingers. "Damn. What else?"

"In addition, we've got AR glasses for you, a magnetic grapple gun, and jump pads."

"Grapple gun?" The agent furrowed his brow. "And what's a jump pad?"

Nessie smiled. "Additional details will be in your briefing file, but these thieves tend to use advanced mobility techniques, including parkour that may or may not be enhanced by the artifact. You might end up on a rooftop or two, and we'd like you to be able to keep up. The jump pads will be added to the bottom of your shoes and they'll increase your jumping distance, but they have a limited number of uses."

"This ought to be interesting. I'm guessing you don't want me to gun these guys down. Petty thievery doesn't seem like it deserves summary execution." Daniel shrugged.

"A trail of bodies would cause a lot more trouble than the agency would like at the moment. They aren't known for being particularly violent, so you should need minimum force, but I've also come up with another solution."

She reached into the box and picked up a small tray holding a half-dozen silver capsules. "Prototype immobilization capsule. Agents have had trouble trying to use sonic grenades or stun weapons against some magicals who might have resistance to electricity, but most of them aren't much stronger than a normal human. You simply press the top and bottom together and throw them. Upon contact, they blast out a little quick-hardening polymer web around the target. It should wrap around them and harden in seconds. The material weakens with exposure to oxygen, though, so it only will hold them for maybe thirty minutes at most. Use this to take them down, then use something else to keep them down."

Daniel picked up one of the capsules and eyed it with a smile. "I can work with this." He set it back in the tray. "What do we have on the artifact these thieves are supposed to be using?"

"We've not confirmed it, but the rumors suggest it is a glowing medallion. We've received conflicting information on what it might do. Some reports suggest it increases mobility, and others suggest that it allows people to pass through walls. It might even do both. It also remains unclear whether it only works on one person, or if it works on a group of people in a certain radius. We only know the local authorities and bounty hunters haven't been able to track them down. Even when they get close, the thieves get away."

"Not the most detailed background information. Any backup for me this time?"

Nessie shook her head. "The agency doesn't feel that this mission warrants that use of resources at this time."

A hint of irritation colored her voice. He wondered if this meant Fortis had pulled some strings to make his life harder. Ronni wasn't his exclusive backup, but his proximity to her and Timothy would raise suspicion.

"Okay, then. Let's start signing this stuff out. I have to go steal from some thieves."

She pushed the electronic pad forward, and Daniel moved over to sign it. The S.A.D. director leaned forward to whisper in his ear.

"Don't worry, Daniel. You'll get used to being a rogue agent soon enough."

Daniel slammed his car door shut and activated his alarm as he stared at the lit-up London Eye. The giant Ferris wheel made for an impressive sight, perhaps more so at night.

Wonder what it'd be like to go after the thieves on that thing.

He wasn't sure if he'd ever get used to being a rogue

agent, but for now, the London mission let him concentrate on a problem he could handle himself. Ronni, Big Gnome, Madge, Malcolm, and some of the others were still getting settled in, and Timothy was still evaluating the next best move for their team.

Recovering an artifact that helped people steal rather than blow up towns or rearranged their molecules would be a nice breather, almost a vacation compared to what he'd dealt with in recent weeks.

Just a nice mission. Clear targets. No CIA betrayal or secret teams. Little palate cleanser.

Daniel shook his head and headed down the street, glancing at his watch. The lack of backup was annoying, but he could make up for it with the help of a skilled local professional. A few blocks later, he stepped into an alley.

A tall woman in a long coat leaned against the wall. She looked at him from under her brown bangs. "It's been a while, love. Still going by Daniel, right?"

"Just the way things worked out, Serena."

She pushed away from the alley wall. "I trust you've got no problem with the fee we discussed?"

"I only want the artifact. Whatever other loot they're carrying is yours." He shrugged.

Serena grinned. "Then you've got yourself a little backup, cowboy. And lucky for you, I've done all the hard work this time. I know when and where they'll strike tonight."

"Why bother working with me, then?"

"Because it helps to have a nice strapping cowboy helping me, and it doesn't hurt to earn a few points with someone I might need to ask for a favor in the future." She checked the time on her phone. "We've got about an hour to get set up. Just to be very clear on this, I'm not interested in stopping them. I want whatever it is they're going to steal."

The agent nodded. "Duly noted."

Daniel adjusted the magnification on his AR glasses and switched to thermal mode. Eight heat signatures–all human or roughly human, from what he could tell—made their way up the stairs in the building next to them. There might be some elves in the mix, but he doubted it. If they had access to a magical, they wouldn't rely on an artifact.

Something rumbled in the distance.

This is why I hate outdoor jobs. So hard to keep track of what I should be paying attention to.

"They're almost at the roof."

Serena slipped on leather gloves, laced her fingers together, and stretched her arms above her head. "This ought to be bloody fun, love."

He smirked. "You know what? You're right. It probably will be. No mass death or terrorists or strange-ass creatures, merely a few thieves with a trinket. I can't remember the last time I had a mission this straightforward."

She laughed. "You smile all the time, but you don't always enjoy life, cowboy, do you?"

"I've had a shitty week." He narrowed his eyes and continued to track the thermal signatures. "Only a couple more floors."

Serena spread her feet and smiled at the roof access door.

Daniel tapped the side of his glasses, turning off the thermal scan mode. He reached into his pocket and pulled out an immobilization capsule. All he needed to do was find whoever had the artifact. He'd let Serena worry about chasing the others and getting her precious loot.

This is going well. Should be an easy pickup.

The rumble grew in volume.

"Hear that noise?"

She shrugged. "It's London, love. It's a noisy city. Let's concentrate on the task at hand."

The door flew open, and eight men with ski masks rushed out in single file. They stopped and looked at the two of them.

"Who the hell are you?" one of the men asked.

Daniel gritted his teeth. Every one of the men had a medallion. Either they all had artifacts, or they were smart enough to hide it. Two of them wore backpacks.

So much for easy. Do they have loot in the backpacks, or is it one of the medallions?

Serena shot them a smile. "We're here to rob you, love."

They snorted as a group.

The agent raised his hand, ready to throw an immobilization capsule at one of the men with a backpack. Best to play the odds.

A roar preceded the approach of powerful winds, and a dark shadow spread over the roof. Daniel spun around in time to see a VTOL landing craft hovering above the roof. The side doors opened, and six nylon drop lines fell from the craft. A second later, gloved men slid down the lines and hit the roof, all with stun rods in hand.

They weren't in uniform, but they all wore jackets with matching crests.

Of course. Just my fucking luck.

"It's been a while," the leader said with a smile.

Daniel shrugged. "It's been that kind of day."

"Who the hell is he?" Serena barked.

"John Hollingsworth V, current CEO and leader of Hollingsworth Retrieval Specialists."

"What are a bunch of bloody tomb raiders doing here?"

The agent shrugged. "Same thing I am, probably."

Although it doesn't seem worth their time, given the kinds of things they typically go after.

John gave Daniel a lopsided grin. "Stay out of this, Daniel."

"Sorry, I can't do that. I'm here on the job."

The thieves sprinted toward the roof's edges. They broke into four groups of two and headed in different directions.

Serena's head jerked between the two men with backpacks. They weren't in the same group. After a moment, she hurried after one of the men.

The Hollingsworth men rushed after the thieves, with John going after a man without a backpack.

Daniel's stomach knotted, and he rushed after the same man. Always trust a tomb raider to know where the real treasure was. He pulled out a jammer and activated it.

John frowned and looked over his shoulder.

The CIA agent grinned at him. "Having a little trouble with your comm?"

The other man snorted and continued running.

The thieves leapt off the edge of the building, landing with perfect rolls on the next roof. The tomb raider jumped a second later and landed with far less grace.

Daniel followed and blinked, surprised by the extra boost from his jump pads. He cleared the edge of the building easily and landed hard on the nearby roof. Quickly, he stood and rushed after the thieves.

Several men shouted from another rooftop, victims of Serena's fist or a Hollingsworth stun rod. Daniel tossed his immobilization capsule at one of the men. A web of tendrils exploded on contact and wrapped around the thief. He fell to the ground with a yelp.

John rushed past him and threw an elbow. The CIA agent ducked, then replied with an uppercut that narrowly missed his enemy. They exchanged a few quick punches, but neither man could get past each other's blocks.

Daniel jumped back and pulled out another immobilization capsule. John frowned and leapt to the side as his opponent pulled back his arm. The capsule sailed past the tomb raider and narrowly missed a thief.

The burglar jumped off the building's edge to the fire escape stairs. With a quick push off the railing, he was on the ground.

John broke away from Daniel and rushed toward the edge of the roof. He stopped and shook his head. "Damn."

The agent sprinted to the edge and jumped off. He pulled out his grapple gun and fired it at a nearby landing. The line unspooled, and he swung down toward the fleeing thief, feet first. He smacked into the man's head and sent him face-first into the hard pavement.

Daniel released the magnetic lock on the gun and dropped to the ground. He hurried to the stunned man and bound his hands with a zip-tie.

He yanked the medallion off the man's neck and stared at it.

The thief spat out some blood and grinned. "Wrong."

The agent hopped back to his feet and fired his grapple gun at roof he'd just been on. With the help of the powered line retraction, he quickly climbed the building. John was gone, but the other thief lay entangled by the polymer with his medallion still around his throat.

A rumble from the landing craft caught Daniel's attention. It had stopped hovering right over the original building and floated slowly toward him. The doors remained open, and the Hollingsworth men had boarded it again.

What the fuck? When did that happen?

John grinned down from above and nodded toward a man sitting across from him. A glowing medallion hung around his neck.

"You son of a bitch," the agent yelled. "You purposely led me to the wrong guy."

He yanked out his directional EMP device—a long black tube—and pointed it at the vehicle. John narrowed his eyes and twisted a ring on his finger. A pulsating green field surrounded the aircraft.

Daniel activated the EMP, which buzzed and hissed as it discharged. The green field flashed, but the aircraft didn't go down.

Damn it.

The tomb raider waved, and the engines folded down before the vehicle roared away into the London night.

He scrubbed a hand over his face and looked around. A few of the thieves lay on the ground, but Serena was nowhere in sight. He wasn't there to clean up the local petty crime. He had to get the artifact that John Hollingsworth now had.

Ronni gets burned, and now I lose the artifact. What a great fucking week! I could use a drink.

Daniel sighed as he pushed into W&M's. The quiet, upscale English pub was never too packed but also never too empty, with the crowd split mostly between the bar and the leather booths in the back. The light rock wasn't playing too loud, and there were no televisions to distract anyone from their conversations or drinks.

A few people looked at him as he made his way to a booth.

He waited, taking a few deep breaths until the waitress arrived.

"Give me an IPA. I don't really care which."

The waitress chuckled. "That great a night?"

Daniel nodded. "Exactly."

She smiled and headed toward the bar. A minute later, she returned with his drink.

"Thanks." He picked up the glass and took a long pull.

The waitress moved to a different booth. He took the opportunity to set down his silence cube. The quiet chatter and music didn't bother him, but he had one last chance to try to salvage his trip to London. The agency might not be happy with him, but he could at least help Timothy's team.

Daniel had finished half his drink when Daisy stepped into the bar. She headed toward the booth and slipped into the seat across from him.

"Glad you could make it," he mumbled.

She smiled. "I was between jobs and I happened to get your message. How could I pass up a chance to chat with my favorite," her gaze flicked to the cube, " my favorite CIA agent."

He shrugged. "I was here on other business, so I thought we could chat."

"About what? What you owe me for saving your butt in Munich?"

Daniel chuckled. "Maybe. But I was actually thinking about doubling down on owing you."

The elf leaned forward, resting her elbow on the table and her chin in her palm. "I do like people owing me things. Go on."

"You're a lot older than me."

Daisy smirked. "You sure know how to flatter a woman, don't you?"

"And you're from a planet with a lot of different intelligent species. Sure, with the full return of magic, we're finding more than a few hidden creatures on Earth, too, but it's not like Oriceran where you've had thousands and thousands of years to get used to thousands of species."

The elf chuckled. "Humans can barely handle getting along with each other, and they're the same species. I sometimes even find it amazing myself that things like the

Great Treaty lasted as long as they did on Oriceran, but why point any of this out?"

Daniel frowned and leaned forward. "Ever wonder if there's more out there?"

"More?"

"Species?"

She frowned. "On Oriceran?"

The agent shook his head. "No." He pointed up. "From there?"

Her eyes flicked up for a second before moving down. "The ceiling?"

"What if I were to tell you that Earth and Oriceran aren't the only planets with intelligent lifeforms?" Daniel gulped down some more beer. "And not only that, but there's at least one other planet with intelligent beings and advanced technology that makes Earth's technology look like nothing and gives Oriceran magic a run for its money."

Daisy's smile slowly faded. "What are you getting at, Daniel?"

"Let me tell you a little story…"

The elf sat there quietly for several minutes after Daniel finished his explanation. He'd laid out everything Timothy and Nessie had told him, but as before, he'd kept any mention of the Munich gun to himself.

I'm a rogue in my rogue group. Somehow that seems fitting.

She cleared her throat and furrowed her brow. "Why are you telling me all this?"

"Because we need more people, and you're damned

qualified. I've got a pretty good nose for figuring out who might backstab me for bullshit reasons and who won't."

Daisy smirked. "How do you know I won't simply sell you out?"

The agent shrugged. "Where's the profit in it? The truth is, if you contacted the Fortis guys, they'd simply kill me and then they'd kill you. These guys didn't think anything of murdering innocent civilians. They have absolutely no reason to hold back against a mercenary elf."

She frowned. "Okay, fair enough, but that still doesn't answer the most important question."

"And what is that?"

"Why should I join your little escapade?"

A huge grin broke out on his face. "First of all, Tim can pay well. Besides, do you want to work for others for the rest of your very long life, or do you want to use a few of those years or decades to save worlds?"

Daisy ran a hand through her hair and sighed. "What can I say? At the very least, it should be interesting."

CHAPTER EIGHTEEN

Damn it. It shouldn't have gone down this way.

Daniel frowned and looked down at the table. All his friends' D&D figurines lay on their sides. It wasn't clever tactics or ambushes by Connor that had laid the party low but simple bad luck. The dice didn't favor the party of adventurers, and what should have been a straightforward cut through a group of hostile fungus men called Myconids had been a fight for their lives. The enemy's spore attacks had disabled everyone but Daniel's wizard. Judging by the look on Connor's face, even he seemed a little surprised.

His friend stroked his chin. "You do have another fireball left, but no way to blast them without getting most of the party. Last time, you were willing to sacrifice yourself, but what about your friends? You willing to take them out for survival and glory?"

Lorelei rolled her eyes. "We're not dead yet. I'm sure Daniel can pull something out of his ass."

Taylor nodded.

"It is a big ass." Juan grinned.

Daniel snorted.

My parents were tomb raiders, and I've played D&D since I was a kid. My whole life has primed me to be an adventurer. Was that what I wanted from the Marine Corps? The CIA? I told myself I wanted to defend my country, but maybe I merely wanted adventure.

Now, I have the greatest adventure about to start—investigating aliens—but it's not about simply hitting a tomb or a dungeon and looking for treasure, and I have to lie to people who should be my own allies instead of coordinating with them like I would in the game.

He grinned. "I don't have to sacrifice anyone. Everybody else has already done their part by weakening the Myconids. That and collapsing to the ground."

"What are you talking about?" Connor furrowed his brow. "Oh, you're right." He nodded at the table. "No enemies are blocking you this time. You can still save yourself. Always more adventurers out there, and they knew the risks." He picked up a can of Fresca and took a sip.

I should really tell him to stay out of the stash.

Even if Daniel had not been playing a good character, he wouldn't leave his friends behind, even in a game. His high school wrestling coach's mantra screamed in his mind.

Practice like you play!

"I make a break for the exit," Daniel announced.

Connor started laughing. "Seriously?"

Daniel nodded. "Yeah."

Juan, Taylor, and Lorelei all stared at him, but no one said anything. Their eyes held a warring mixture of trust and confusion.

Just trust me, guys.

Connor shook his head. "They're going call you Caneth the Coward back in the Capital. Fortunately for you, everyone else held the Myconids to the front, so none of them are in a good position to attack you. You're clear and can keep running. I'll even let you know…if you run, no one else will attack you all the way back to the entrance."

"Who said anything about running all the way back to the entrance?" Daniel shook his head. "I stop and face them, casting *Mirror Image.*"

The spell would make illusionary copies of his character, making it harder for his enemies to distinguish their actual target.

Juan clapped. "Knew you wouldn't run. Sorry for saying you have a big ass."

Connor gulped down more Fresca. "Okay, you've got the illusion set up. What now, hero? They're advancing on you and will be on you next round. How will you take out a whole group of Myconids without killing all your friends? Or are you merely hoping they can make the saving throws from a fireball?"

Daniel couldn't risk a fireball. Most of the party was low on hit points—their measure of health from previous blows—and they couldn't dodge due to being paralyzed by the fungus men's spores. That didn't mean he lacked a plan.

He looked down as the DM adjusted the enemies figurine's positions. They now stood in a dense wedge formation as they charged his position. He must have been confident his player wouldn't risk a fireball, but his obsession with the spell blinded him to other opportunities.

"I raise my hands," the agent announced with a smirk, "and I cast *Burning Hands.*"

Connor blinked. "Wait, I thought you'd use them all—" He laughed. "I forgot about the swap-out. You still have the one you memorized in the higher slot." He gestured toward the Myconid figurines. "Yeah, they're all in a fifteen-foot cone for sure, and yeah, the party members should be able to avoid the flames since they're all prone. You lucky sonofabitch."

Daniel tossed his dice. This time, fortune favored him. The DM started his own rolls. By the time everything was finished, the damage from the spell had exceeded the remaining hit points for all but one of the enemies.

Taylor laughed. "Hot damn. No pun attended."

"It's like you can read Connor's mind." Lorelai grinned.

"Just lucky." The DM grunted and started removing figurines from the board.

The agent shrugged. "You were the one getting lucky, and it's not luck when I create my own opportunities. Besides, this group of angry fungus men shouldn't have had us all down. But it doesn't matter. The important thing is for the party to stick together. We all take care of our weaknesses."

A thoughtful expression crossed Connor's face. "Like with those muggers."

Juan touched the fading bruises on his face. "Yeah, we took them out as a party. Hell, it's even like D&D, you know. Army, Air Force, Navy, and Marines. Different classes."

Lorelai glanced toward the window. This time, the streets light shone brightly. "We all did similar jobs in the service, though. Not really different classes."

"Hey, don't ruin my analogy."

Everyone laughed.

Daniel smiled, glad that they had each other's back, including his, even if they didn't know his whole story.

Somehow, I don't think it matters. If I called them for help, I know they'd all show up, no questions asked. That's what it means to have friends, and I've got a lot of good friends.

He looked at the laughing and smiling people around the table. His life had been one of increasing sacrifice, but nights like this reminded him what he was fighting for and why he needed to continue.

Maybe in real life, I don't have to blast myself with a fireball to save my friends and the people I care about, but I'd gladly risk my life so they don't have to worry about Fortis or aliens showing up and turning their home into a crater.

"What's up, Daniel?" Juan asked. "You look like you've got something on your mind."

He shook his head. "Nothing. Just really glad I can still play with you guys."

Daniel waved to Lorelei, the last one out, and closed the shop door behind her. The last hour of the game had gone well, with the party carving their way through the dark caverns without much trouble. Good experience, lots of treasure, and no party deaths. A complete reversal of fortune, even if they had to use up all their healing potions and scrolls.

He took a deep breath and released it slowly, fighting a dark cloud that threatened his satisfaction from earlier.

Real life isn't a game. My parents hit a tomb, and they didn't come back. A good roll won't save you when real magic is around, and the only ones who bring people back from the dead are necromancers.

He made his way toward the basement. His grandfather was out that night at a "Blockbuster movies of the 2020s" marathon. Sometimes, the old man simply wanted to have alone time, which his grandson understood.

In the basement, he headed toward a pile of dusty boxes in the corner. He normally ignored them. They contained too many memories, but the game and recent events had pulled those memories out from the dark corners he'd tried to hide them in.

Were his parents dead? Alive? Turned into living stone? There were so many possibilities.

An answer—any answer—would have been enough to eliminate the gnawing pain of not knowing.

What the hell is this about? Is it only about joining Tim's team?

Daniel set a box on a table and began pulling out old photos, maps, books, and journals, the main physical evidence left that his parents had ever existed, a record of their adventures. They weren't as dusty as he'd expected, and there were more than a few fingerprints in the dust.

Did Pops go through these recently? Why? He didn't mention anything to me about it.

He frowned as he stared at a picture of his parents in safari hats, loose pants, and tactical harnesses in front of a stepped pyramid. He assumed Mesoamerican, but he was no expert. When he went after an artifact, he had a whole team feeding him information beforehand. He specialized in the acquisition, not the research.

Daniel set the picture to the side and picked up a small book with yellowed pages, a chronicle of a forgotten and lost archaeological expedition of Egyptian pyramids led by a Sir Michael Garfield. He tossed the book back into the box. Studying archaeology was part of being a tomb raider, but he wasn't a tomb raider. He was a CIA agent who happened to collect artifacts as part of his job, and he was good at it.

That was why his failure in London stung so much. He wasn't used to losing. Not only that, he'd joined Timothy's team and still didn't know all the players involved in the alien mess. Fortis was an obvious threat, but even *they* didn't have a good handle on the identity of the other aliens. For all he knew, they were right, and the aliens were one of the most dangerous threats on the planet.

His thoughts returned to Agent Buckley. The man had grown increasingly disheveled and erratic. Daniel wasn't sure if he was connected to Fortis or if he'd become an addict. Both seemed depressingly plausible. In either case, the best play was to avoid him.

Risking his life and career without knowing the players and the true scope of danger was something he would have derided as idiotic barely a few weeks earlier. A smart agent approached all missions with as much background information as possible. That way, they didn't end up surprised as he'd been in London.

Was I stupid to join Tim? We've got the resources, but our team is the very damned definition of ragtag, and we're supposed to save the world not only from aliens but alien hunters? I need more information, but how will I get it? Even Tim and Nessie barely know what's going on.

The minutes passed as Daniel continued rifling through boxes and skimming old journals, notes, and pictures. Antarctica. Japan. Brazil. Malta. His parents had traveled all over the world during their adventures.

Is this my future? I'll chase these aliens until one day, I disappear, and no one knows what happened to me? Will I be as smart and ready as Ronni when they come for me?

He frowned as he picked up another journal. The handwriting was his father's. Most of it was written in nearly indecipherable shorthand that likely detailed some important information for his parents' adventurers. Their distrust of a lot of modern technology led to a lot of old-school note-keeping, making it more cumbersome to examine.

The truth was that he didn't want to go through it, which only made it worse, and his grandfather had told him there wasn't anything useful in the notes that might have revealed their fate. The only thing Peter knew was that they were looking into something in Central America when they disappeared, but the old man didn't even know which country. They'd kept it from him for some reason.

Daniel turned a few pages.

"What am I doing?" he mumbled. "If Pops couldn't find anything useful in these, what will I find? Why am I even looking at them? Because I got a little sentimental while playing a game?"

He scoffed and turned the page. His jaw tightened, and his stomach knotted.

A careful drawing of a circle covered the page. Symbols surrounded the circle, some strikingly familiar. Some sort of sigil, maybe.

Daniel swallowed and pulled out the new phone he used for work with Tim, technically his third phone. He brought up pictures of the nozzle. Several of the symbols matched.

What the hell? How is this all related?

He scanned the page, looking for more clues, and found a few notes at the bottom written by his father.

Copied from the Codex of the Sky Gods. Why did they burn it? Need to decipher symbols. No relation to any existing language. Oriceran? Still checking.

"Funny you're looking at that," a voice called from behind him.

Daniel dropped the book and spun toward the sound. He raised his fists only to find his grandfather standing behind him.

"Not often I can sneak up on you," Peter commented and scratched his eyebrow. "But you were pretty damned absorbed in that." He pointed at the journal. "Which means you know something. Something more than you've told me, I'm guessing."

The agent narrowed his eyes. "You're keeping something from me, too. You know something about these symbols."

The old man sighed and moved over to a nearby chair

to take a seat. "The *Codex of the Sky Gods* was something your parents sought for years. I didn't think it had anything to do with their disappearance before." He sighed again, a little more heavily this time. "But I saw something recently with those symbols that made me start thinking about it again."

Daniel's gaze darted to the wall concealing the vault. "The gun?"

Peter nodded. "I suspect it's not from either Oriceran or Earth."

He drew in several deep breaths. "What are you saying, Pops?"

His grandfather pointed at the boxes in the corners. "I've gone through those a lot in the last few days. Recently, I learned that when your parents disappeared, they were looking into some ruins in Belize."

Daniel shot up. "What the hell? How did you learn that? Why didn't you tell me?"

"What's most important is that I realized the gun had the same symbols as depicted in the journal, the one from the *Codex of the Sky Gods*. There's another journal in there, and once you decode your mom's and dad's notes, you can see it talks about how they were going on that last job to look into some ruins that might reveal the meaning of the symbols associated with the *Codex*."

"And did they have any idea what they meant?"

The old man shrugged. "From what I can tell, they thought those symbols in that configuration were the key to a gateway that led to another planet, and I'm not talking about Oriceran. I always assumed their notes were talking about Oriceran before, but when I realized they might not be, a lot of things made a lot more sense. It's no wonder I couldn't understand them. The only thing I know for sure is that they were never able to decode the meaning of the symbols fully, but they knew they were vital to understanding how to reach this other planet."

"You're saying they were looking for aliens?" Daniel frowned.

His grandfather nodded. "As crazy it sounds, yeah, that's what I think. I recently had contact with a very powerful and ancient elf. He was the one who sent me the information about the gun."

"Why were you dealing with him?"

Peter looked down. "He was willing to give me information in exchange for a control rod from the gun. He wanted to ensure the weapon was disabled and that no one could use it."

Daniel stared at his grandfather for a long tense moment. "I guess I can't bitch about that. We wanted the same thing, that weapon out of circulation." He shook his head. "I knew you were hiding something about the job."

"I was only trying to protect you. He offered information on your parents, but I didn't want to tell you and get your hopes up. In talking to him, a lot of things didn't make sense, so I started looking through these notes again. That was when I realized what your parents were actually doing the last few years before they disappeared. They were looking into aliens."

"They weren't the only ones."

"What do you mean?"

He pulled out his phone and brought up a picture of the

nozzle. "Time to tell you about a new little side job I started."

His grandfather paced back and forth for a few minutes in silence after Daniel finished explaining everything he'd learned.

"The government's known for a while, then," the old man muttered. "They might even know what happened to your parents." He looked up. "There's one last thing I need to tell you. I didn't know how to tell you, but you deserve to know."

"What?"

Peter looked away. "That old elf I mentioned? He gave me some information about your parents. They…might not be dead."

Daniel's heart thundered as the room spun. He shook his head and took several deep breaths. "What the hell?"

"Those ruins they were looking into were near a village. There was a sighting of an American couple there, but the ruins and the village are gone now. It's like they never existed, and there were no bodies found."

"Bombed?"

Peter shook his head. "Not like that. No craters or damage. It's more like they simply were never there. Is that something Fortis could pull off?"

"Don't know, but that doesn't mean Mom and Dad are alive. It might merely mean they were vaporized with magic or bizarre alien technology."

"Yes, but the chance is there, and now with this new

side job, there might be an opportunity. Would you rather simply be Tim's tool or pick up where your parents left off and save the worlds?"

Daniel chuckled. "What is up with everyone?" He nodded and stared down at the symbols in the journal. "There's no way I can walk away now."

CHAPTER NINETEEN

Daniel stared at the Fresca on his kitchen table. The revelations of the last few weeks had changed everything he thought he knew about his parents and even the world. It wasn't something a man working for an intelligence agency ever expected.

I thought I knew what was going on, but I didn't know shit. Less than shit.

He shook his head. His parents had disappeared looking into the aliens, and Fortis had killed hundreds of people to protect the secrets of aliens. There was a good chance he'd end up vanishing too.

The thought didn't scare him. He'd always known that devoting his life to protecting the country might cost him his life, and he'd made peace with that idea back when he was in the Marine Corps.

Are Mom and Dad still alive? If they survived their tomb raid, why did they never make their way back? At least I have a clue now, but still no answers.

Daniel took another sip of his drink and stood up. He needed to clear his head. A little walk around the neighborhood would help.

"I'm going for a walk, Pops," he called. He threw the door open and strolled out with his hands in his pockets.

He inhaled the crisp night air, offering a nod to the occasional passing neighbor.

All these people are trying to live their everyday lives, not worrying about other countries or even Oriceran much. They shouldn't have to worry about molecular rearranging guns or alien invaders. And if I'm doing my damned job, they never will.

Barely a few blocks away from his shop, he reached the flower shop. Jeanine and her father had done well since the mugging, even if the woman was now a little nervous heading home.

A loud clang echoed in the alley behind the business. Daniel frowned and jogged that way, wishing he had his AR glasses for a thermal scan.

I'm overreacting. Probably only some stupid cat.

"How fucking hard is it?" a man's voice growled. "Just light it up already."

Daniel hurried toward the alley. Three masked men stood near the back door of the flower shop. One of the men held a gas can and was emptying it along the edge of the building. The harsh stench of the gasoline filled the agent's nostrils.

"Hey, assholes," he shouted. "What do you think you're doing?"

The men's heads jerked toward him. They sprinted down the alley, dropping the can. He rushed after them.

The arsonists emerged from the other end of the alley and ran into a waiting black van.

Glad to see they're keeping to the classics.

Daniel reached for his gun, only to realize he'd not brought one with him. He spotted a Prius with the door wide open and threw himself into the driver's seat. Fortunately, the engine was on, and the key fob sat in the console.

He peeled out, catching sight of someone running out of a nearby store and shaking their fist at him.

I'll bring it back later. Glad you felt safe enough to keep an unlocked running car in the neighborhood. Sorry I ruined that.

The van swerved, taking hard corner after hard corner in a feeble attempt to lose their tail. He frowned. The Prius wasn't giving him the power he needed to catch up, and it wouldn't be that long before cops showed up to pull him off the road for grand theft auto.

I don't have time for this.

Daniel rolled down his window and stuck his arm out, keeping his other hand on the wheel as he tried to keep the car lined up with the van. Time to test out last year's birthday present from Tim.

"Launch tracker," he shouted.

A loud pop sounded, and a small black dart shot from the watch, which beeped a second later. A successful hit. He pulled his arm back into the car and turned into a side street. It was time to get the right tools for the job.

Oh, I'll be back soon, assholes.

Fifteen minutes later, Daniel barreled down the road in his Jaguar, this time using a silver color scheme with another fake plate. He glanced down at the tracking display on his console screen.

The van had slowed considerably, and the criminals obviously thought they'd lost their tail. He cruised along on an intercept course with their vehicle. There was no way he would let those bastards get away.

Tired of these pests in my neighborhood. These assholes are really starting to get on my nerves.

The agent narrowed his eyes as the van came into view. He pressed the accelerator, and the Jaguar gained on the target.

His prey sped up. The car change hadn't fooled them. A proximity alarm beeped, and he glanced down at his side cameras. Two other black vans rushed directly toward him.

He slammed the brakes, narrowly avoiding one of them. The vehicles formed a fast convoy, and a window in the back lowered as a barrel came into view.

Daniel snorted. The muzzle flash lit up the night and the bullet bounced off the Jaguar's armored exterior.

He reached over and flipped up a hidden trigger on his gear shift. His thumb moved a tiny directional pad, and blue target crosshairs appeared on his windshield. The Jaguar jerked to the side, and Daniel lined up on the thug with the gun.

The agent pulled the trigger and a blue bolt blasted from the center of the car, the aim true. The man twitched and slumped down in his seat. His gun fell, smacking against the front of Daniel's vehicle. The force smashed the gun into several pieces that rained down in the street behind him.

Screw it. If I'm willing to use the stun rod, might as well use the EMP, but I don't want these new guys. I need the original assholes.

Daniel floored it, weaving between several other honking cars and closing on the vans. He pulled up beside one and pressed a button on his steering wheel to activate spikes. With a jerk of the wheel, his car swerved, and the protruding spikes slashed into the front wheels of the van. The blowing tire sent the vehicle careening into the second one, and both spun out. The first ended its trip by smashing into a light pole, and the other slammed into a parked delivery van.

He smirked at the crumpled remains. Only the arsonists were left. They screamed down the street now, but there was no way they could outrun him in the modified Jaguar.

I'm sure Nessie will have a few things to say to me about using company resources like this but can't say that I care.

The remaining van turned with a screech, leaving a trail of black marks before barreling onto a side street. His turn was smoother, and without the other vans as obstacles, he soon closed to only a few yards behind his target.

He flipped up another panel hiding a button in his wheel. "You assholes won't get away."

The agent pressed the button. A high-pitched whine sounded. An invisible EMP blasted out and fried the electronics in the other vehicle. He yanked the wheel to the side, avoiding the decelerating van, then whipped the Jaguar around and into the side of the other vehicle. It spun out of control and crashed through a post office box and a stop sign before coming to a stop.

Daniel slammed on the brakes and threw his door open. Before exiting, he tapped the touchscreen on his console to activate the broad-spectrum jamming mode. No need for any electronic witnesses.

The van doors slid open, and the three masked arsonists staggered out. Two men held guns, while the third gripped a phone.

He charged the off-balance men and leapt into the air, delivering a powerful kick to one with a gun. The thug's head snapped back and smacked against the van. He slumped down to the ground, losing his weapon.

"Silver Jaguar," yelled his companion with the phone. He rattled off the license plate number.

Too bad that's fake, pal.

The other armed man brought up his gun and pulled the trigger, but Daniel grabbed his arm and pushed it up, sending the bullets into the air. A throat punch and a jab to his solar plexus had the arsonist on his knees a moment later. He finished him off with an elbow strike.

"Give me the fucking phone," he growled at the last man.

The thug tossed him the phone and sprinted in the opposite direction.

Daniel snatched it out of the air and looked down at the display. Unknown number. Whoever was on the other end knew enough to cover their tracks.

He put the phone to his ear. "Whoever you are, you made a mistake."

"Who the fuck is this?" asked a deep voice on the other end.

"Someone who doesn't like you fucking with his neighborhood. Consider this your last warning. Next time, I won't play so nice." The agent hung up and tossed the phone to the ground.

The sound of loud sirens closed in. Daniel jogged back to his car. He sighed as he spotted several dents.

Yeah, Nessie's definitely not going to be happy.

CHAPTER TWENTY

The next morning, he drove the Jaguar—now with a new plate and black in color—into a nondescript garage across town. Smiling Dan's, according to the sign.

Cautiously, he pulled the car fully inside and put it in Park. A man in blue coveralls approached the driver-side door, a thin silver pad in hand. The worker held it out.

Daniel placed his thumb on the surface, and it burned for a second. A metal shutter descended behind the car, locking the agent's vehicle inside the building.

He waited for a moment. Tim had told him to come to the address, but there was always a chance the whole thing was a Fortis trap. Waiting in a bulletproof car until he was sure he was safe wasn't a terrible strategy.

The man watched him with a blank face for about ten seconds before he stepped away and headed around the corner. A moment later, Nessie strode into the main garage, her lips pressed in a thin line.

Daniel chuckled and stepped out of the car.

I think I would have preferred Fortis over her.

The woman frowned as she surveyed the car. "You do realize that bulletproof isn't the same thing as indestructible, don't you, Daniel?"

He nodded. "Yes, but it's nothing bad—just need to buff out a few dents and whatnot."

Nessie snorted. "Every part of this car is an expensive custom construction, and you banged up this beautiful piece of technology chasing petty criminals."

"They might be petty criminals, but it had to be done. I can't sit by and let my neighborhood go to hell, but don't worry. I think the problem's solved after my little display the other night."

"Yes, your crashing of multiple vehicles and a high-speed chase through the middle of a city." She shook her head. "You're lucky there were no serious injuries."

Daniel grinned. "Luck had nothing to do with it."

Several men in coveralls emerged from a nearby hallway carrying large gray pieces of metal in pairs.

Nessie gave the men a curt nod. "Proceed with the repairs while I brief him." She turned to Daniel. "Follow me."

They walked around the corner and down a dark hallway, then arrived at a reinforced door sealed with another DNA lock. She placed her thumb on the scanner pad. Several large echoing thuds followed.

It sounds like this door is as secure as the vault.

The woman pulled the door open, motioning him inside. The vast supply room inside was filled with racks overflowing with a variety of devices and parts, from simple wheels to long silver railguns.

"To be clear," she began, "this facility is known only to our special team. It's something Franklin decided to invest in a while ago. While we lack the full research capability of the agency, we have more than enough resources to repair anything we have. Also, because of our more focused mandate, we have been able to take advantage of a certain amount of reverse engineering to produce more than a few advances that we've decided not to share with anyone else just quite yet."

"Nice. Very nice."

Nessie marched across the room to a rack of hanging suits. Daniel followed her.

She looked over her shoulder. "To be clear, this is part of your orientation for your new role as the operational head of the unit, so make sure you pay attention. I want you to have a general idea of the scope of some of the equipment we have available."

"I'm the operational head?" He laughed. "It would have been nice if Tim mentioned that was coming. I feel like I'm caught up in a raging river, and people are throwing anchors instead of life preservers."

Nessie chuckled. "In this case, we're depending on you to rescue other people who might be drowning. Besides, what did you think would happen? We've built up the support personnel, but our field agents are limited, and you're easily the most experienced. It's only common sense." The corners of her mouth turned up in a small smirk. "You'll find one nice benefit of working for the team compared to the CIA is a reduced amount of bureaucracy."

He eyed her. "No signatures when I take gear out for a mission?"

"Exactly."

Daniel whistled. "You could have recruited me simply by telling me that."

She rolled her eyes. "Why don't I doubt that?" She gestured to the suit rack. "These suits are not only fashionable but are both bullet and knife resistant. A 9mm shot to a protected area will only bruise. Thinner bulletproof vests mean better mobility. We're finalizing a few things on them, but they should be ready in a few weeks."

The agent ran his fingers up the material. To his surprise, it felt very soft.

Nessie walked away from the suits toward a rack with a half-dozen odd-looking silver guns that had only small dots for barrels. She picked up one of the guns and pointed at one of the suits.

"Note that being bullet and knife resistant doesn't translate into general damage resistance." She pulled the trigger. A soft buzz accompanied a bright blue beam. She set the gun back on the rack and marched to the suits.

Daniel's brow lifted, and he returned to the clothes and examined a blackened hole in the breast pocket of one of the suits. He leaned forward and saw the beam had also pierced a metal plate a few feet back, but it hadn't managed to go through the wall.

The woman cleared her throat. "The blast pistols are nice, but they have limited shots. We don't have a good method for mass-producing their power cells, but it might still be to your advantage to use them in a protracted firefight. We have some training environments available for you to practice with the weapons and familiarize yourself with them."

The agent stepped away from her toward a rack covered with small black drones. They were a little bigger than the palm of his hands. "What's so special about these?"

"That's definitely a technology we don't want to get out there. Those drones contain a small amount of explosive in a shaped charge—not enough for serious damage, but more than enough to kill a person if it explodes next to their head. Advanced navigational AI and pattern-matching mean that this little thing could fly through a building to finding a single target and take him out." Her face twitched. "Although it could be useful in certain defensive situations, if it got out into general use, it'd be nothing but an assassination bot." She sucked in a breath. "That said, we both know there are situations where we might need to take out a target we can't otherwise reach, and it might come in useful, however distasteful it is."

He frowned. "What's to stop the Company from developing them itself? Or MI6, MSS, the GRU, or anyone else?"

Nessie picked up one of the drones. "A small amount of magic is necessary for proper algorithm training at the moment, but you're right. The good news is a decent EMP can take them out." She strolled away from the assassination drones to a massive rack containing a variety of jeweled rings and watches.

Daniel laughed. "What? Worried about me properly accessorizing?"

"If you ever leave the CIA, you should consider a career as a comedian."

"Don't tempt me."

His companion rolled her eyes. "These rings and watches all produce low-powered force fields."

"Actual force fields?"

She nodded. "They work against most forms of energy and physical weapons. They were reverse-engineered from alien technology. Ironically, we've had more success getting these smaller-scale versions to work than something larger."

Nessie picked up a ring and slipped it on, then squeezed it. A shimmering blue field surrounded her. She crossed her arms and waited. About thirty seconds later, the force field disappeared.

"As you can see, it doesn't last that long, but it might be useful in situations where you need a more general defense and don't know what the enemy can produce." She pulled the ring off and set it back on the rack. "Currently, the charging takes some time, and it's not something we can accomplish in the field."

Daniel's gaze roamed the myriad of rings and watches. "Anti-magic?"

She shook her head. "Not directly, no. They'll block physical and energy forces created through magic means, but they aren't directly anti-magic." She pointed to a pile of crystals on silver chains sitting in a tub several racks away. "Anti-magic deflectors that we've purchased from magicals. Of course, each is tremendously expensive, and they aren't exactly subtle, so they should be saved for missions in which we believe there is a high probability of direct offensive magic use."

The agent nodded, frowning for a moment. "In London, Hollingsworth had a ring. It blocked my EMP. You think it's similar?"

Nessie shrugged. "Perhaps. We can't be fully certain of

all the technology available, but it may have simply been a magical ring."

"I don't know. That guy has a lot of neat little tricks, even for a tomb raider, and his timing is always annoying. I half-wonder at times if he's working with MI6."

"Perhaps." She grabbed a tiny black box. "Oh, this is nice." She pulled the lid off. A tiny black speck lay inside.

Daniel leaned closer to stare at the speck. "Looks like a seed."

The woman shook her head. "It's a subcutaneous receiver and transmitter that you implant inside your ear. This little toy is a nice fusion of tech and magic. It'll allow you to be in contact with Ronni and the other support team members without additional equipment, and more importantly, it's undetectable using current agency measures. Simply put it in your ear, and it'll do the rest. I must warn you that you will have some discomfort."

She held the box up. The agent pinched the device and pressed it into his ear. After pulling his hands away, he checked his hand and verified the gadget was gone.

"That wasn't so ba—"

Fiery agony erupted in his ear. He groaned and clenched his jaw. The pain spread from his ear to his head, and his vision swam.

Daniel took a deep breath as the pain finally ebbed over several seconds. "That was fun."

Nessie chuckled darkly. "I told you to expect some discomfort. But go ahead and try it out. To activate and deactivate it, squeeze your earlobe."

He squeezed his earlobe. "Ronni, can you hear me?"

"Is that the guy?" a deep, gravelly voice replied. The

sound was odd—not too loud, not too soft, but lacking any sense of distance or direction.

"Who the hell is this?" Daniel snapped.

"And people complain about *my* manners."

"Sorry," Ronni's familiar voice interrupted. "That's Madge. She's a new hire, clerical and backup support. A pixie."

The agent laughed. "A pixie?"

"What's so funny about that, CIA boy?" Madge asked.

"Merely strange to go from working with no magicals to pixies."

"You ain't seen nothing yet," another voice replied—male, although not as deep as Madge's voice.

"That's Big Gnome," Ronni explained, her voice filled with excitement.

Daniel shook his head. "'Big Gnome?' And who is Madge, 'Little Pixie?'"

"Hey, Big Gnome is part of my brand," the gnome replied. "Don't disrespect the brand."

"This is the guy you said might help with tech development and repair?" The agent glanced at Nessie. She ignored him and checked her phone.

"Yes," Ronni said. "He's a wizard at the kind of stuff I've toyed with. Well, not a wizard, a gnome—or technically, a half-gnome, but you get the idea."

Daniel laughed. "This sounds like the beginning of a joke."

"A joke?"

"A gnome, a CIA agent, and a pixie walk into a bar…"

The three on the other side of the comm laughed.

Nessie looked up from her phone. "The repairs are finished."

He nodded. "Okay, Ronni and company, I've got to go. Talk to you later."

"Bye," the three others responded in near unison.

The agent squeezed his earlobe. "They fixed the car that quickly?"

His companion shrugged. "The damage wasn't severe, and they had all necessary parts ready, but don't get used to it." Her phone chimed, and she looked down at it. "Hmm. Good timing."

"Why?"

"You're needed at the Company to fill out some paperwork. Better hurry. Don't want them getting suspicious."

Daniel chuckled and headed for the door. Advanced and unreliable technology, gnomes, and pixies. They were either the best team to save the worlds or utterly doomed.

CHAPTER TWENTY-ONE

Like all agents, Daniel had a desk, even though as a field agent, he didn't spend much time at it. That helped to explain why there were a bare minimum of decorations and a healthy coat of dust on some parts. He also didn't want to give anyone in the Company too much reason to look into his personal life. Appearing to be nothing more than an agency-obsessed field agent would allow him to maintain his compartmentalized life. It was the way he liked it and now, also needed it.

Don't know how long I can keep this up, but I'll do it for as long as I can.

He tapped away at his computer as he worked on expanding some notes about his recent missions. The dark side of his life as a secret agent wasn't the violence; it was the paperwork. Magic and technology always had to take a backseat to the bureaucracy.

Nothing in life can constantly be glamorous and cool.

He chuckled.

"Something funny?"

He turned around. Jack Buckley stood behind him, frowning, an unusual look for the man. He obviously hadn't shaved for days. There weren't any formal appearance regulations for field agents in their division, but he wondered if someone would eventually make a point of it. Or maybe he was purposely growing a beard for a mission in a country where that would be helpful.

Daniel nodded toward his computer. "Thinking about paperwork is all. Nobody considers joining the CIA and then thinks, 'Wow, I'll fill out so many reports.' But here I am."

Buckley's frown faded, and he let out a little snicker, but there was a weary quality to it. "Yeah. True enough. My father told me about that, though, before I joined. Did you know I'm a fourth-generation agent?"

He shook his head. "I didn't. I'm actually surprised you haven't mentioned it before."

The other man shrugged. "I don't like bragging about my accomplishments. Mentioning it makes it seem like I'm trying to take success from those who came before me. That's never been my style."

"I can respect that," Daniel replied.

Buckley leaned forward, resting one hand on the desk. "Also, screwing with other people has never been my style." Sudden hostility flavored his tone.

What the hell is this?

He stared up at him. "Do you have something to say to me? If not, I should get back to my paperwork."

The other man stood and adjusted his tie. "Yeah, I want

to talk to you about something. Why don't we go grab lunch somewhere? Not the cafeteria."

"What's wrong with the cafeteria?"

"I fucking hate the food in the cafeteria," Buckley snapped. He sucked in a breath and scrubbed a hand over his face. "Just need a little variety. Is that so hard to understand? It's not like you eat here all the time."

Daniel nodded slowly, keeping his expression neutral. "And what is it that you want to talk about?"

"We'll discuss that at lunch."

He pushed the looming agent back with his hand and stood. "I'm still deciding if I'll go to lunch with you, especially since you're acting kind of like a dick all of a sudden."

Buckley snorted. "What's the big deal? You too good to eat with me now? You think you're a better agent than me?"

Daniel narrowed his eyes and kept his tone calm. "You've been acting weird. Maybe I just don't trust you."

"Like you didn't trust Welch?" The man smirked, a triumphant gleam in his eyes that only highlighted the bags underneath. He obviously hadn't slept well in days.

"What happened to Ronni had nothing to do with me." The agent frowned. Something was going on, and he needed to find out what it was.

"Yeah, yeah, I know." Buckley shrugged. "After all, you're still here, aren't you, and she's not."

If he's trying to kill me it'd be way too obvious to invite me out, but I also don't trust him.

Daniel shook his head. "Fine. Let's go to lunch, but we're taking my car."

Neither man spoke for several minutes after they got on the road. It was the very definition of tense silence.

The agent glanced Buckley's way. Even though they liked to joke around in the office and had worked together for years, they'd never socialized outside the headquarters. They hadn't even had any occasion to work missions together, but that was more because of their different primary specialties than anything else. He didn't consider the man an enemy, but he was far from a friend. He'd always assumed his companion felt the same way.

This has something to do with Ronni? Maybe he was into her and is jealous of me or some crap like that. Guess I won't know until he tells me.

"What's this all about?" Daniel asked finally.

Buckley shrugged. "Food, last time I checked. Lunch isn't exactly an epic mystery."

"Don't feed me that shit. You obviously wanted me alone and away from headquarters. Well, you've got me. I'm alone and away from headquarters." He changed lanes and accelerated to pass an old truck. "Are you a junkie now, Buckley?"

The other agent laughed. "What? A junkie?"

"I'm wondering if that's why you're getting increasingly erratic, and you look like you haven't slept or shaved in days. If you tell your supervisor right away and get help, it won't affect your security clearance."

Buckley snorted. "I'm sorry I didn't spend enough time this morning shaving to meet your approval, Sergeant. Get over yourself."

Daniel frowned at him.

The other man smirked. "What? That annoys you? I thought it was once a Marine, always a Marine. I wouldn't know. I wasn't in the military. Never appealed to me, the idea of everyone wearing a little uniform, doing what they're told, and all that. Seems like a recipe to make a bunch of sheep." His grin was almost feral.

If you're trying to piss me off, you're doing a good job, Buckley.

"Sheep?" the agent replied. "You think the Marine Corps produces sheep? Maybe you don't get this because you've only been a field agent, but in actual war, it's important to have group discipline. Not every man can think for himself. If he does, he'll get other people killed. It's not fun or exciting, but it's effective."

Buckley snorted and slapped a hand to his chest. "I'll never stop thinking for myself. No wonder the Company kisses your ass so much. You're the perfect little tin soldier for them. Just wind you up and point you at the enemy. Never question, never care why. Just do what you're told."

Daniel took several deep breaths. He wasn't sure why the man was trying to screw with him. They'd always sparred verbally, but that was just cheap fun—a little male bonding, nothing cruel and pointed like the barbs he now delivered.

Jealousy? Was he always this jealous and I didn't know it? Is he mad because he's still convinced I was sleeping with Ronni?

"You think I don't question the CIA?" The agent scoffed. He changed lanes and turned hard into a parking lot at a shawarma place, no longer in the mood for food. He'd merely pulled into the first lot he'd seen, and if he needed to kick the other agent's ass, he didn't want to do it while driving.

His companion shook his head. "When have you ever questioned the agency? I've never heard you say anything."

He laughed. "What about you? You're suddenly a rebel?"

"I'm fucking questioning it now, aren't I?" Manic energy seized the man's face. "Unlike you. You're a damned coward."

"What the hell?" Daniel parked and killed the engine, ready to get out of the car. *Looks like he's determined to fight me.* He didn't want to get any blood on the leather seats. Experience had taught him that it was hard to get out.

"You heard me." Buckley locked eyes with him. "You're a fucking coward."

"What the fuck are you even going on about? Do you know how many times I've risked my life in the Corps and the CIA? I'm not some desk jockey. I've worked more missions than you."

The other agent pointed at him. "It's easy to say you're not a coward when you're in a firefight. That's simply reacting and saving your own ass. Whatever. Get over yourself, Daniel. I've been in plenty of firefights. Real bravery isn't about risking your life. It's about risking your life for others."

Again, Daniel resisted the urge to slug the man in his smug face. "That's what I've done every day of my adult life, asshole. In the military and now the CIA. What do you call that but service to others?"

"Bullshit. You think I don't know what you've done? You traitor piece of shit."

The agent gritted his teeth.

Fuck. Buckley must be with Fortis, after all.

A long, tense moment passed as he considered his next move. He could shoot Buckley and call Purity to help clean up.

Daniel shook his head. He could do that, but there was no way he would.

I'm better than these Fortis fuckers. I won't kill a fellow agent without a damned good reason, and unless I'm one hundred percent sure, there's no other choice.

He took several deep breaths and smiled, giving himself a moment to think. Buckley talked a good game, but he must have nothing.

His strategy now seemed obvious. Fortis couldn't prove Daniel was onto them, but they suspected something, if only because he was Timothy's protégé. This was nothing more than a fishing expedition. Within that context, the provocations made much more sense.

The agent scoffed. He'd almost let the other man push him into doing something very stupid and shortsighted.

You lose, Buckley. Now that I know, I can take control of this conversation.

"What the hell are you talking about, Buckley?" he asked. "How am I a traitor?"

His companion narrowed his eyes. "You think I don't know? You think I didn't see what you're involved in?"

"I have no idea what you know. I don't have any mind magic, so fuck off. I'm tempted to leave your ass here to eat some shawarma and calm the fuck down. I don't know who pissed in your cornflakes, but you need to go scream at them, not me."

Buckley threw the passenger door open and stepped

out. "Fine. I'll make my own way back to the agency, but don't think that this is over. I know what you are, and I'm calling you out. You're going to have to deal with me one way or another, and I think you'll find I'm not as easy to take down as some of the other people you've thrown under the bus to save your own ass." He slammed the door and stormed off.

Daniel watched him with narrowed eyes before pulling out of the parking lot. He gritted his teeth. He needed to figure out what to do, but first, he needed to calm down and talk to Timothy. This wasn't only about him anymore.

Damn it. I'll go back to headquarters and finish my paperwork. But there's no way in hell I can risk meeting with Tim inside the walls of the Company.

Hours later, in a darkened corner booth of a sports bar, Daniel set his silence cube on the corner of the table. Timothy pulled out his ninja turtle and placed it on the seat beside him.

The absurdity of the situation made the agent laugh out loud. Ronni needed to choose more adult disguises for her devices.

The older man shrugged. "Your message said it was important we meet somewhere, but nowhere important, because you were worried about being followed. I've never been to this place before, so if I can never come back, no big deal."

Daniel nodded. "Yeah. I was worried about being followed by an agent who might work for Fortis."

The older man's frown deepened, and he ran a hand over his bald head. "Damn it. They've been sniffing around you for a while, but because of the Ronni clusterfuck, someone has gotten wind of her looking into alien crap. They're trying to connect the two of you. Who is it that you think works for Fortis?"

He took a deep breath. Time to cross the Rubicon. "Jack Buckley."

Timothy's face scrunched up in disbelief. "Jack Buckley is with Fortis? You're sure?"

Daniel started to nod but stopped almost immediately. "No, I'm not sure."

"No? Huh?"

The agent sighed. "He's been acting erratically around me lately and saying some weird things. He's also very angry at me for some reason."

The other agent shrugged. "I hadn't noticed, but I don't spend a lot of time around most of the field agents anymore. I don't talk to his supervisor much either."

"It's not only that," he explained. "He invited me to lunch out of the blue earlier. While we were driving, he got agitated to the point where I had to park. He flat-out accused me of being a coward and a traitor."

"I see. Did he mention anything about the aliens, Ragnarok, Nephilim, or Fortis?"

Daniel frowned and thought back. After a moment, he shook his head. "Actually, no, he didn't mention anything like that. It was more about me being a mindless sheep because of my military background, and that I was a coward and a traitor. From what he said, it has something to do with Ronni."

Timothy scratched his chin. "To be honest, I don't think he's made you. I think he suspects you, but this was merely a fishing expedition."

"That's what I thought as well, but the question is how I should respond? I won't kill a CIA agent just because he's sniffing around me."

"Nor would I want you to." His companion exhaled in a long sigh. "But you need to defend yourself if it comes down to that."

"What are you saying, exactly?"

The older agent stared at him with a somber expression. "I think they only burned Ronni and didn't kill her because they figured it wasn't worth the trouble. She didn't seem like the type to cause further trouble, but you're an experienced and successful field agent. If they decide you're trouble, they won't be satisfied with merely burning you." He sighed again. "What will you do if Buckley shows up at your place and tries to kill you?"

"I'll defend myself, but I won't kill him based on a suspicion. I'm not Fortis. I don't believe in that kind of ruthlessness." Daniel stared at Timothy. "Have you ever killed another CIA agent?"

His mentor looked at him with haunted eyes. "Don't ask questions you don't want the answers to, Daniel."

Their conversation halted as a waitress came by with two plates, an order of wings, and two beers, the best tools for blending in at a sports bar.

The two men chewed on their wings for a few minutes and sipped their beers, eyeing each other in solemn silence until the younger man sighed.

"There's got to be some way I can convince him I'm not involved in any of these alien investigations."

Timothy set a half-eaten wing on his plate. "That's probably the best plan. If he doesn't turn up, for whatever reasons, they'll only look harder. The first thing you have to do is establish what he actually knows and not only what he suspects, which might be hard without you dealing with him outside of headquarters—and if you do that, you might be walking right into a trap."

Daniel nodded. "I know, but what choice do we have at this point?"

"Arrange a meeting and feel him out, but do it with full support from our team. You might be a rogue agent, but you have an entire group backing you."

CHAPTER TWENTY-TWO

The next morning, Daniel sat in the Jaguar. It remained parked in the private garage, and he stared down at the burner phone in his hand. A couple of minutes had passed since he'd grabbed the cell to call Agent Buckley, but he hadn't been able to bring himself to dial.

Once I do this, there may be no going back. If he is Fortis and he tries to kill me, I'll have to defend himself. I'll have to kill a fellow agent. Even if I escape without any trouble, they'll know, and then I'll be useless to Tim's team.

Any hope of the problem simply going away seemed remote. Buckley's behavior made it clear that if it wasn't resolved soon, the other agent might press the issue.

Daniel lifted the phone to dial.

Then again, if he keeps acting as erratically as he has been, then maybe the CIA will put him on leave. But Fortis had enough power to burn Ronni, so they probably have enough authority to keep him on.

The agent sighed and shook his head. Things were far more complicated when he worked against elements of his own government. Resigned to the inevitable, he dialed the number.

The phone rang three times before Buckley picked up.

"Who is this, and how did you get this number?"

"You know who this is," Daniel replied. "I think we need to talk. After that crap the other day, it's obvious we have some things to work through."

The other agent chuckled. "You could say that. We can't really talk at work about our personal problems, though, can we?"

"Yeah. I guess you could say that'd be inappropriate. I'm willing to meet you to talk."

"Oh, I bet you'd love to pick the place." His voice dripped with obvious paranoia.

Daniel snorted. "As opposed to letting you pick? Screw it. How about the place I left you the other day? That was random, and the only two people who know about it are us."

There was a good chance the line was monitored, but this plan assured him that if Buckley wasn't Fortis, at least they'd have no idea where he would be ahead of time.

Buckley laughed. "Okay, fine. We'll start there, but that doesn't mean we'll stay there. Tonight. Seven p.m. If you're not there when I get there, I'm taking off. If you come with anyone else, I'm leaving."

"Fine. Fair enough."

Daniel crossed his arms and leaned against a door, watching Ronni pull open an action figure filled with electronics. Other parts and tiny crystals covered the table in the small room.

He shook his head. "I don't get why you're basically working in a closet, given that there's an actual workshop in this facility."

She furrowed her brow as she ran her finger along some wiring, her bangs falling briefly into her eyes. "The workshop has a weird vibe. It kills my creativity. It's too industrial."

"What are you saying? Your tinker muse doesn't move you there?"

Her eyes widened, then she smiled and nodded. "Exactly." She looked at the action figure again.

The agent shrugged. "Well, I need to make sure I can still communicate with you if Buckley jams me. Is that something you can do?"

Ronni pointed at a My Little Pony figurine on the edge of her desk without looking up from what she was doing. "We can interface with that. I took the last one I was using apart. It won't last long if he does jam you, though. It's one thing to make a device that bypasses the Company, but it's much harder to create something that can beat broad-spectrum jamming."

Daniel nodded. "I've been meaning to ask you. Why are they all toys?"

She shrugged. "Because they're supposed to be disguised."

"Yeah, but until recently you worked for the CIA. That's not a place with a lot of toys."

The woman sighed. "They're also cuter this way."

Daniel chuckled. "Fair enough. Let's do what we need to get this thing interfaced."

The agent pulled into the parking lot. Buckley's red CIA-issue Mustang idled on the opposite side.

"Can you still hear me, Ronni?" Daniel asked.

"Yes. Clear. Not like crystal clear, but you're coming through. I don't think he's jamming. My drone feed is fine."

"Thanks."

He drove the Jaguar across the lot and parked beside the Mustang. In silence, he rolled the window down and waited.

Buckley stared straight ahead, his hands on the wheel and a frown on his face. Daniel was about to honk when the other man turned slowly. He didn't look frantic or angry, only exhausted. He rolled his window down.

"You came?" The other agent sounded surprised.

Daniel nodded. "I'm here. Want to go inside? Not like we can talk in the parking lot."

The man snorted. "There's no way in hell I'm having a conversation here. Now that you're here, you can follow me to where we're really going to talk."

"And if I say no?"

He shrugged. "Then I'll know you're the cowardly traitorous piece of shit I thought you were."

"Oh, good. I was hoping there would be foreplay. You want me to follow you?" The agent reiterated so Ronni could overhear.

"Yeah."

Buckley rolled his window up and pulled out of his spot. He didn't race out of the parking lot, but he didn't linger either.

Daniel reversed and accelerated to follow the other car. Once on the road, he rolled up his window.

"Keep a drone on us, Ronni. I have no idea where he might be taking me."

"This is making me nervous. Maybe you should tell him it's off."

The agent laughed. "This is the fun part. You just be my eye in the sky, and I'll be fine. The stupid move isn't necessarily walking into the trap. It's walking into the trap unprepared. Besides, Buckley may be good, but I'm a far better agent than he is. There's no way he'll get the drop on me."

She sighed. "I'm less worried about him than, say, a truck filled with other armed guys."

"That's why I brought all these wonderful toys with me. Besides, I've been in far worse situations, except then, I was in some foreign backwater with far less backup." Daniel changed lanes to match the movements of the Mustang.

"But…what will you do if he does turn out bad?" Ronni's voice dropped to a near whisper.

His grip tightened around the wheel. "What I need to do to protect our group and the mission. I didn't agree to come along to assassinate Buckley. I'm hoping if we can sit down and talk frankly that I might be able to convince him I'm not involved in any of this. And we're still not sure if this whole thing isn't a giant fishing expedition."

Ronni hissed. "Darn it."

"What's wrong?"

"Nothing, just…not a lot of drone traffic over there, and I'm worried about him spotting it."

Daniel shook his head. "You and Big Gnome need to work on some sort of chameleon field for the drones."

She laughed. "That's way harder than it sounds. It only works so well on humans because they don't move very fast."

"Just saying."

Buckley made several aggressive lane changes. Daniel kept up, but it was almost as if the other man was trying to lose him.

Or at least lose any tails we might have. A paranoid CIA agent is a scary thing indeed.

The agent checked his mirrors and cameras for any suspicious vehicles but didn't see anything noteworthy. Of course, if Buckley were leading him into a trap, the suspicious vehicles would be near the location and not following him on the highway.

Worried about my backup, Buckley? You should be.

He shook his head again and chuckled.

"What's so funny?" Ronni asked.

"It's hard to fight people who know all your procedures and moves. That Mustang is almost as tricked out as my car. He's probably got some drones following me as well."

"But does he have a team like Big Gnome and me backing him up?"

Daniel snorted. "That's the problem with everyone being so afraid of magicals. We're not using all the tools we can for our job, and that puts us at a disadvantage. We should exploit that angle as much as we can. It might be one of the few advantages we have against Fortis."

He smiled to himself as he pulled closer to the Mustang. His heart didn't thump harder and his stomach didn't knot even though he might be heading directly into an enemy ambush.

A mission's a mission, no matter if the other side is CIA or random artifact thieves. I'm damned good at what I do, and I won't lose. Not today.

The surprisingly long drive took them to Wharf Marina. Buckley parked up the street and hopped out, not waiting for Daniel.

In a hurry to get me to your snipers?

The foot traffic was light and the shadows deep despite the many lights both in the boats and along the wharf.

"Daniel, can you hear me?" Ronni asked over the receiver. The line was choked with static.

"Yeah, but barely." He threw his door open and stepped out. "Problem?"

"Jamming. I can't get the drone much closer without losing transmission signal, and this booster only works with your transmitter."

The agent jogged after Buckley. "It's okay. That means it's about to go down, but if he's jamming he's lost any remote support he has, so we're on a level playing field."

"Unless they have an evil version of me."

Daniel snorted. "True enough."

"I—" Static filled the line.

He sighed and shook his head. The fact they'd been able to communicate at all under heavy jamming was impressive, but now he was on his own. It took a minute to catch up with Buckley, who walked directly toward a pier.

The other agent glanced over his shoulder with a slight smirk on his face. For a brief moment, the facial expression reminded Daniel of the old Jack Buckley and not the wild-eyed asshole who had become increasingly unhinged and disheveled in recent days.

Where are they? Waiting in a building? On a boat?

Daniel closed on him. "It was almost like you were trying to lose me."

Buckley shrugged. "The great Daniel Winters should be able to keep up with me. It's not like I was cutting cars off or anything." He kept walking. "Plus, the more we move, the less your friends can help you."

"What are you talking about?"

"You think I'm an idiot?" his companion snorted. "I know there's been a drone following us."

"There's always drones in the sky around here."

"Doesn't matter. I've done what was needed. I'm sure you figured out by now that I'm jamming."

Daniel nodded. "Yeah. That's probably making a lot of other people have a bad day."

The man shrugged and stepped onto a pier lined with small boats on either side. "They'll live. A small price to pay for someone who is defending them all the time from threats they couldn't even begin to imagine."

"That's how you see yourself?"

He glared over his shoulder. "And you don't? Give me a fucking break. That's why I joined. I wanted to be the warrior in the shadows, the man fighting all the terrorists and magicals who were plotting against our country. Like I told you, fourth generation. I grew up with my dad and my grandpa, and while they were never able to tell me the truth of the kinds of things they did, they made it clear that the strong have a duty to protect the weak. We need to be ready to become the wolves able to kill anything that would attack our flock." He shook his head. "And that's what I dedicated my life to."

Buckley stopped in front of a cabin cruiser. Bright blue paint on the side proclaimed it the *Big Bad Wolf.* Without even needing to examine it further, Daniel knew the boat wasn't company issue.

Fortis doesn't want to be too obvious when they try to kill me?

The other agent walked over to the docked boat and climbed aboard. "This is my boat. Used to be my dad's. Not as fancy or nice as newer ones, but tradition means something. Come on. We'll talk on the water."

"Why there?"

"Because it'll be more private. If you don't want to come, fine."

Daniel frowned. Something didn't feel right. Killing him on the water at night would enable Buckley to dispose of the body easier, but it would also mean he wouldn't have any backup in case something went wrong.

Already joined the super-secret club. Too late now. With a shrug, the agent climbed aboard. His companion untied the cabin cruiser before sitting at the wheel and starting the boat. Daniel sat down beside him.

Buckley continued backing the boat into the Washington Channel. "I'm sure you've got a silence cube on you.

Go ahead and use it. I'm already jamming shit, but that'll help with the other crap."

He pulled his silence cube out, activated it, and set it between them. While the cube had stopped most of the noise, a low rumble from the engine still reached him. The quiet combined with the dark water stretching out around them was eerie.

The other man shook his head as he steered the vessel out of its slip. "Got a very simple question for you."

"What's that?"

"What's the most important part of our job?"

Daniel shrugged. "That's easy. Protecting the people of the United States from all enemies, foreign and domestic."

Buckley let out a dark laugh. "Domestic, huh? That's the rub, though, isn't it? Figuring out who is a domestic enemy of the United States. Some people say random protesters are enemies. People from whatever political party you don't like. Wrong religion. Wrong face. Shit, wrong species now."

An image of Tommy flashed in the agent's mind. The boy was an American citizen born and raised, but groups like the Humanity Defense League would say he had no place here, not only in the country but even on the planet.

Nothing was simple anymore. Many species from Oriceran lived a long time. There were elves older than the country. It was hard to trust someone who had such a long view of things that they might not even think it mattered whether his country continued to exist.

Daniel shrugged. "Nothing worth doing is ever easy. I don't have any fast answers, and we both know the CIA has done a lot of shady shit in its history. I've tried not to, but I've pushed the line more than a few times."

When he thought about it, he realized joining Timothy's group didn't even bother him. Whatever conscience-pricking actions he'd taken throughout his career, his heart didn't feel that was one.

Buckley offered a shallow nod. "Yeah, same here. Can't say that I've killed anyone I didn't think was a bad person, but now I sometimes wonder, how did I know?"

Daniel frowned. "What do you mean?"

The boat approached the Potomac River.

"We do missions because the Company assigns them to us," the man replied. "We rely on Company equipment, assets, information, and backup. Sure, we all have our informants and contacts, but that doesn't change the fact that the CIA is filtering everything."

"It's an intelligence agency. That's kind of the point."

Buckley shot him a wild-eyed grin. "Secrets within secrets. It sounds cool, but it's not. I remember this orientation presentation they made us watch when I joined. The whole point was to, and I quote, 'disabuse you newly recruited personnel of the CIA's involvement in outlandish conspiracies.'" He barked out a laugh. "Can you believe the balls on them, to say something like that? We're the damned CIA. We're pretty much the definition of conspiracies, a bunch of shadowy men and women doing their own thing without most people knowing it. It's like people think that simply because of Oriceran, no one should remember how dangerous regular humans can be."

Daniel nodded slowly. He let his hands rest in his lap. He wanted to be able to get to his gun quickly if necessary.

"So? I doubt you joined as a fourth-generation agent without knowing that you'd be a warrior in the shadows."

"I don't mind doing what I do in the dark. What I *do* mind is when the people who are supposed to give me orders lie to me."

The agent furrowed his brow. This was not how he expected the conversation to unfold. "You mean the Company?"

"Yeah, the fucking Company. They let us believe that the only extraterrestrial threat was Oriceran. It's one thing to lie to the rest of the world, but not us, not agents. We need to know the truth."

Here it comes.

Daniel narrowed his eyes. "What are you getting at, Buckley?"

The other man scoffed and stared at him. "Look me in the fucking eyes and tell me you don't know about Ragnarok and Nephilim. That you don't know about Fortis."

He could lie. He'd trained for most of his career to lie, but he was dealing with a fellow agent, a man who knew all his tricks.

How does he want to play this? If I admit to knowing, it might be game over. He might try to kill me, or maybe someone's waiting at another dock to shoot me as soon as he gives them the all clear.

But there's another opportunity here. As long as I don't let them know about Tim or the others, I can infiltrate them. Maybe claim I stumbled onto everything myself.

It wasn't a great plan, but it was the best he could come up with at the moment.

"Yes, I know," he uttered finally.

Buckley let out a triumphant yell and looked forward again. Daniel was grateful for the light traffic on the river, especially given that it was nighttime.

"I fucking knew it," the other man shouted. "There's no way a guy like you couldn't figure it out."

We can interrogate him if this doesn't work out.

The agent drew a deep breath and let it out slowly. He moved his hands away from his lap and slipped one into his pocket. There was a stun pin inside, and Nessie assured him it'd work this time.

"And what about you, Buckley? How did you figure it out?"

The other agent shrugged a shoulder. "Saw something weird a while back. Didn't think much of it, but saw something in a report that reminded me of it, and when I went to check on that report later, it was gone like it never existed. It was a thread on a shirt, you know? I had to keep pulling, and pulling, and pulling. Just like Ronni did. Is that why you and your Fortis buddies burned her? Is that why you killed her?"

If Buckley had said anything else Daniel would have been ready, but the last sentence struck him like a lightning bolt, stunning him. He stared at his companion, blinking. By the time the other agent had pulled out his gun, it was too late for him to yank the stun pin out—or his own weapon.

"Move your fucking hands out of your pockets and put them in front of you," the man ordered. He still looked mostly straight ahead, but Daniel had no doubt that the trained agent's peripheral vision would be good enough to spot him going for a gun. With a sigh, he complied.

The other agent's laugh seemed a little hysterical. "I caught a brief glimpse of it on her screen when I walked by. Symbols I'd seen before. Alien symbols, and not from Oriceran. She got burned, and then two assholes tried to take her out. I was watching her, and I almost had to gun those fuckers down, but that little techie's tougher than she looks." He shook his head. "I didn't know who'd set her up. It was a trap. Cheese for the mouse. But when I saw you pick her up, I checked her apartment and set cameras up to keep an eye on her and provide protection. She suddenly stopped coming home." He shook the gun. "Then it all clicked. Almost no one paid attention to Ronni, but you did. Why was that? Because you knew she was sniffing around all your carefully concealed shit? Your fucking Fortis coverup, so she had to die."

Daniel gritted his teeth. He almost wanted to laugh. This entire time he'd had the situation backward. "You don't understand."

"I don't fucking *need* to understand, you bastard," Buckley yelled. "You think I haven't looked into this shit? You think I don't know how Ronni's not the first? How you murdered other Americans to cover up your alien shit? I'm sure my great-grandpa, grandpa, and dad did shady shit in their time to defend this country, but they never ever would have murdered innocent Americans simply because they stumbled upon the truth. You make me sick. You're a traitor to this country to its people. You wipe your ass with the Constitution."

"You really, *really* don't understand."

Buckley pulled back on the throttle as they approached another dock. "Oh, I'll understand a lot soon enough. You see, you'll disappear soon, too. And we'll spend a lot of time together while you tell me everything you know about Fortis."

CHAPTER TWENTY-THREE

Daniel couldn't help himself. He burst out laughing.

His companion furrowed his brow. "What the hell is so funny?"

"You don't get it. I keep trying to tell you. Ronni's not dead."

"Bullshit. Then where is she?" Buckley zeroed the throttle and the already-slow boat drifted to a near stop, the light waves making it bob up and down.

"Kill your jammer and I'll prove to you that she's still alive." He reached very slowly inside his jacket to pull out his phone, the other agent watching him with his gun ready.

Buckley shook his head. "She's dead. Your two thugs couldn't take her out, so they sent a friendly face to get her."

"She's not dead. We're hiding her from Fortis for a while. We weren't sure if they would come after her."

"We?" the man asked. "Who's we?"

"People with your same problem. We want to make sure the country's safe from aliens, but we don't trust Fortis." He lifted his phone. "I can make a call and clear it up. I was actually communicating with Ronni before you activated the jammer."

The man shrugged. "Whatever. If I go down, you go down." He reached into his pocket with his free hand. Something clicked inside.

"Ronni, can you hear me?" Daniel asked.

"Yes, all the interference is gone."

"Okay, I don't have time to explain. Call me. I need to prove to Buckley that you're alive. He's not with Fortis."

"W-what?"

"Just do it," he snapped.

"Okay, okay." Ronni sighed.

A few seconds later, the phone rang. He held it in his palm and offered it to Buckley.

The other agent snatched it up and swiped to answer, keeping his gun trained at his companion. "Is this Ronni?"

"Yes, this is me," she replied. Daniel could hear her through his ear receiver.

"Fortis didn't kill you?" He seemed relieved and confused at the same time.

Ronni sighed. "I think they were going to try, but I got away and then Daniel recruited me. I don't think I can say much more than that until he gives me the okay."

Buckley chuckled, relief spreading over his face. "Good to hear you're alive, Welch. I know I didn't talk to you a lot, and we didn't work a lot of missions together, but you're okay."

"Oh, yeah, thanks, Jack."

He tossed the phone back.

Daniel ended the call. "You thought I was coming for you?"

The man stared down at the wheel and took shallow breaths. "I don't know. This shit's messing with my head. At first, I thought it wasn't a big deal, simply more CIA secrets. After Welch disappeared, I started wondering when it'd be my turn." He shook his head. "But I'm not alone. You've got a team—a task force or something? Let me in. You know I'm a good field agent, and you need it, especially considering who we're up against. If you really know anything about Fortis, then you know how ruthless those bastards are."

The agent sighed and nodded. "Look, I need to talk with the others. I'm not the one running the show, but I think we have a place for you. That is, assuming you're not still planning to kill me and dump my body in the Potomac."

"I planned to interrogate you first, but yeah." Buckley grinned. A little color had returned to his pale face. "I proved who the top agent was in the end."

"Huh? What are you talking about?"

Buckley smirked. "I got the drop on you, didn't I?"

Daniel shook his head. "Only because you surprised me by accusing me of killing Ronni. Otherwise, I was going to stun you with a pin."

His companion waved a hand dismissively. "Yeah, yeah. Second place always has an excuse. Whatever. Let's get back to shore. You talk to who you need to talk to, then get back to me. I actually thought you were Fortis and coming for me, but since you're not, that probably means they have no clue that I'm onto them. We've got plenty of time now to work this crap out."

The agent stared into the distance at some of the other boats on the river. Another field agent could be very useful for the team. Sure, he was obnoxious at times, but Jack Buckley could get things done. Not only that, he'd independently stumbled on the conspiracy.

He'll be a good asset. A damned good one.

"Let me get you a burner phone. You can use that for setting up our next meet about this...shared interest. We can talk about saving the worlds."

Buckley chuckled and nodded.

Sitting behind his office desk at the brownstone, Timothy squeezed his stress ball. "Buckley isn't one I would have ever pegged to have stumbled onto this mess by himself."

Daniel shrugged. "From what he told me, it was a similar situation to what happened with me. He saw some strange stuff during a mission and later connected it with other loose ends that led him to aliens."

"We do need more field agents. Right now, you're the operational head of barely any actual agents. He's well-trained and brave, but I do worry about how he tried to take you on. We have to tread carefully when dealing with Fortis if we don't want this whole house of cards to come tumbling down."

The agent nodded. "Maybe we could keep him at arm's length until he proves himself, but now that he knows he's not the only one, I don't think he'll act as desperately."

"Maybe." Timothy set his stress ball on the desk. "But you're right. We can give him a chance to prove himself, but for now, I don't want him aware of anyone other than you and Ronni."

"Sounds like a good plan. I'll fill him in and keep the rest in the shadows."

Daniel whistled as he drove an Audi toward the shawarma restaurant. He'd contacted Buckley via the burner the night before, and they'd agree to meet at the same place for lunch. Now that they both knew neither worked for Fortis, it seemed as good as place as any.

Timothy had suggested he avoid taking the Jaguar in case someone was watching Buckley who was familiar with Daniel's usual car. A simple color change wouldn't be enough in that case.

He grinned. He was more excited about having another field agent than he realized. Daisy was a hell of a recruit, but if they intended to take the aliens on and oppose Fortis, they needed a decent-sized team. There were simply too many artifacts and incidents to look into otherwise.

What am I going to do? Create an entire rogue alphabet agency?

The agent chuckled. Maybe in a few years, there would be a new Extraterrestrial Research Agency. For now, he needed to ease Buckley into operations and make sure the man could handle the stress of being a rogue inside the Company.

A short while later, he turned into the parking lot outside the restaurant. Buckley's Mustang was already parked in front. Daniel stepped out of the Audi and adjusted his tie, a smile on his face. He fingered the silence cube in his pocket, enjoying the idea of hiding in plain sight.

He laughed under his breath and stepped into the restaurant. Chatting customers packed the place. *Food must be halfway decent.* A sign told him to seat himself.

Agent Buckley sat in a corner booth, his back to the wall, giving him a good view of the exits. An athletic redhead in oversized sunglasses, a tight dress, and a hat sat at a table next to him.

She smiled at the man as she finished her pita wrap. Her smile was confident as she grabbed her purse, stood, and walked past him. Her high heels proved to be too much trouble and she tripped and fell into him, the smile turning into a look of surprise.

Guess it's Buckley's lucky day. A beautiful woman is literally falling on him.

The woman laughed and said something to him, but Daniel couldn't hear it over the din. The man's eyes widened, and the woman gave him a little wave before making her way out.

Daniel's stomach tightened. He forced his way through the crowd. Buckley stood, swaying and clutching his stomach. He fell to his knees, foaming at the mouth. A woman at a nearby table screamed, and the crowd parted.

"Someone call an ambulance!" a man yelled.

The agent shoved his way through the panicked crowd as Buckley fell onto his back, convulsing and coughing up blood. He knelt beside him and cradled his head.

The man continued to convulse and cough, drool and blood now running freely out of his mouth. "S-she said I-I should have left w-well enough alone." He coughed some more. "All I-I ever wanted to do was p-protect this country." His eyes rolled toward the back of his head, and his head lolled to the side.

Daniel stared down at him. Buckley had stopped breathing. He doubted he could be saved, but there was one thing they could still give him. Justice.

He hissed and hopped to his feet. "He needs CPR!"

A tall woman rushed out of the crowd. "I'm a nurse." She dropped to her knees and began doing chest compressions.

The agent threw open the door and ran into the parking lot, his head on a swivel as he searched for the assassin. A Fiat pulled out of the driveway. He stared at the license plate number, memorizing it.

As he hurried toward the Audi, he grabbed his second phone and dialed Ronni.

"Come on, come on…talk to me."

She answered after the third ring. "What's up?"

"I need to know…" The Fiat shimmered and changed color. When it drove past, he looked at the license plate again. It'd already changed, but he couldn't make it out. "Damn it."

Resonant nanopaint? And they had the balls to use it in public?

He clenched his jaw. An assassin who could kill a man in public and a vehicle with resonant nanopaint. That cinched it. Someone from the CIA had just murdered Agent Buckley—one of their own.

Daniel paced Timothy's office at the brownstone. "They murdered him in fucking broad daylight and in public. I thought these people were all about being secret, but now they've gone and done it. Idiots. Guess it'll make it easier to deal with them.'

The older man sighed. He picked up his stress ball and squeezed it several times. "Nope. I just got off the phone. Even though it's been only a few hours, the official coroner's report is, amazingly, almost finished."

"What?" He stopped pacing and turned to face Timothy.

"According to the report, poor unfortunate Jack Buckley overdosed on a new dangerous synthetic that was mixed with dust." He took a deep breath. "The Company isn't treating it as anything more than that. They are initiating a formal review of his cases. As far as the official word goes, Agent Jack Buckley had become a junkie."

Daniel snorted. "What bullshit! So that's it? They get to kill him and get away with it?"

His companion nodded. "Yes. We can't investigate this or make any noise. If we do, they'll come sniffing our way, and we're not ready to take them head-on just yet."

"I'm not afraid of them."

"It's not about being afraid. It's about accepting short-term sacrifices in a long-term battle."

The younger agent slammed his fist on the desk. "His family has served this country for four generations, and now they'll be told that he was some loose-cannon junkie who died because he couldn't control an addiction?"

Timothy locked eyes with his protégé. "He's not the first person who died because of this alien shit. And he won't be the last. The only thing we can do is move forward and make sure he didn't die in vain. Do you understand, Daniel?"

He dragged in several deep breaths. "I understand."

"Good. The Company has a mission for you, anyway. It'll be good to get you away from headquarters for a couple of days in case Fortis comes sniffing around. You can use the mission to get Buckley off your mind."

Daniel snorted and shook his head. He headed toward the door, then looked over his shoulder. "I'll concentrate on my mission, but don't think I'll simply forget this. He was a good agent, and a patriot."

Timothy nodded, his expression solemn. "I know."

CHAPTER TWENTY-FOUR

Daniel's Jaguar sped along the rural Quebec road en route to what was supposed to be an abandoned Catholic church. The mission was simple enough—check out the site to see if he could gather any information about a portal-opening artifact. The Company had followed several suspicious and gory deaths all over the world in the past few months, all associated with an anti-magic terrorist group, New Veil.

The agent's assignment included investigating a few unusual local reports outside Montreal. Initial intelligence had pointed toward the Netherlands, but they'd gotten a hit the day before from some informants in Montreal. New Veil was not previously known to be active in Canada, and he wasn't supposed to engage any targets.

They hate magic, but they'll still use artifacts. Got to love human consistency. Guess it doesn't matter.

Not that he was surprised. All sorts of terrorists and revolutionaries throughout history had walked far more contradictory paths of horrific violence in the name of peace and putting an end to the bloodshed. Maybe it was human nature to turn into what you hated. Or maybe it was something darker.

Give a person an excuse to kill people and provide a self-righteous explanation, and they'll gladly sign up. I bet the average terrorist doesn't even really give a shit about their cause at the end of the day. Nothing more than people justifying murder.

Is that what the CIA has become? Or only Fortis?

Daniel gritted his teeth. He had to push Buckley's death out of his head like Tim had said, but that didn't change the fact that people working for the US government had murdered a man for investigating a potential threat to the country. If Fortis were really about protecting the US instead of protecting their own interests, they would have recruited the man, not killed him.

Fuck you, Fortis. I might not be in your face right now, but I will not let you get away with what you've done. You've murdered innocent Americans, and you've murdered loyal CIA agents. Tell me how you're different to the supposed threats you're fighting?

He sighed. If he'd been less suspicious, he might have picked up on what was actually bothering Buckley and recruited him to Tim's team. If the other agent had known about everyone else, he wouldn't have brought attention to himself with his dangerous tactics.

Daniel's third phone buzzed with a message, knocking him out of his brooding. He glanced down at the message.

Activate your receiver.

The agent raised an eyebrow and reached up to squeeze his earlobe. He had a lot of things to get used to now.

"What's up?"

"You're not getting shot at, are you?" Timothy asked over the link. "At least not at the moment?"

"Not yet, anyway. I'm still a good forty-five minutes from the site. Why? Does it turn out these terrorists have links to alien crap? At this point, I wouldn't be surprised."

The older man snorted. "That'd be convenient since you're already on your way, but nothing like that. The Company doesn't even think those guys were important enough to give you active support, but I did want to make you aware of something. Something I feel you deserve to know."

Daniel did a quick mirror check, then looked at his side and rear cameras. No one else was on the road with him. After Ronni and Buckley, he was more worried about Fortis killing him than terrorists or foreign intelligence.

Need them to install radar in this thing. Someday a helicopter will surprise me.

"What is it, Tim? Is this about Buckley?"

"No. There's nothing we can do about that, and I stand by what I said. We're not ready to take them on directly, and that's even if it's a good idea. But this isn't about Buckley and what they did to him. It's about you."

"What? Has Fortis made me? They must have seen me with him."

Daniel frowned. He almost hoped they had. Truth be told, he wouldn't go down easily, and he'd make them pay for what they had done.

"No. Not yet. Thank God." The older man took a deep

breath. "I came across some files—or it'd be more accurate to say I borrowed some files from the Company that I'd been trying to get access to for a while. Most of it wasn't anything new. It just talked about the visitors, things like Nephilim and Ragnarok, but—" He sighed.

The agent frowned. "But what? Don't hold back on me now. I'm not merely in too deep. I'm at the bottom of the damned ocean."

"There was a report in there, Daniel. Something I'd never seen before about an investigation into an incident in Belize."

Daniel's heart sped up, and his jaw clenched. "Belize? What about it?"

"There were some unusual energy readings detected from a couple of sites there. The agency sent some men down to check it out. From what they could pick up, some ruins and a village had simply disappeared. It was like they were never there, but when they did follow-up interrogation of other locals, they found out about two Americans who'd been in the area—tomb raiders who were looking into it."

His hands shook, and he tightened them around the wheel.

They fucking knew?

"Who?" he snapped.

"You already know the answer to that from the sound of it."

Daniel snorted. "You're telling me that the CIA knew this entire time what happened to my parents? And they never bothered to fucking mention that in all the years I've worked for them?"

A few beats of silence passed before Timothy answered. "Some people in the CIA might have known. I didn't. But whoever prepared these reports definitely knew they were your parents because there were some additional notes added about you when you joined the CIA. That's not all."

The agent's fingers further tightened around the wheel. "Oh?"

His mentor drew a deep breath. "There are two recorded statements from witnesses that talk about seeing the Americans after the disappearance of the village and the ruins."

"I see." Daniel swallowed. He wasn't sure if it was too good to be true or a cruel and tantalizing promise of something he could never have.

Timothy released a nervous chuckle. "You don't seem at all surprised."

Sorry, Tim. Even after all this, I need to keep a few secrets of my own. I can't trust anyone completely, not even you.

"Nothing surprises me anymore," he replied. "But thanks for telling me, Tim."

"I'm sorry, Daniel. I wish I had known sooner."

His laugh sounded strained, even to his ears. "I don't even know if it would have made any difference. They might be alive, but no one has any idea where they are. For now, I need to get into the headspace for the mission. Talk to you later."

"Yeah. Be careful."

Daniel reached up to squeeze his earlobe, taking a few deep breaths and trying to calm his pounding heart.

Timothy was right. Given that he already knew his parents might have lived, hearing that wasn't a surprise, but the agency had betrayed him. They knew the entire time that his mother and father might still be alive but hadn't seen fit to pass that information onto him, even after he'd joined the CIA.

Why? If anything, it seems like something you'd tell a man. That is, unless you were responsible for those people disappearing.

If Fortis had killed his parents because they'd found evidence of aliens, he'd burn their entire group to the ground, no matter what it took, and dance in the ashes.

Some things a man simply couldn't forgive. Buckley's death was bad enough, but now they'd gone and made it personal.

"You don't fuck with dogs and family."

Daniel parked the car about a half-mile from the abandoned building. Skulking through the woods brought him within sight of the church. He didn't see any cars outside or drones in the sky, but that didn't mean no one was there. There was also the possibility of magical detection, even with an allegedly anti-magic group.

At least I don't have to watch anyone's back but my own out here.

He slipped the AR glasses out of his pocket and put them on. They were stylish enough to be fashionable and functional at the same time. He activated the thermal scan mode. Four humanoids were detected inside, all with normal human temperature ranges.

That was promising. Daniel could probably handle four

people. He was half-worried he'd stumble into dozens of terrorists.

The agent tilted his head. It was hard to tell using only thermal scans, but it was obvious that three of the people moved their arms freely, but the fourth one knelt on the ground with their arms behind their back and their wrists together.

Not suspicious at all. Having a little falling out, are we? Time for a closer look.

He deactivated thermal scanning mode and pulled out his chameleon ball.

This crap better work this time and for more than a minute.

Daniel snorted and activated the gadget. Soon, he winked mostly out of existence, a ghost of twisted light. Noticeable enough close up, but still hard to spot. He sprinted out of the woods toward the church. If the terrorists were having a disagreement it might be a good time to grab the artifact, assuming they had it with them.

Cracked and rotted wood covered the structure, along with the overgrown weeds. A tree had been felled by a storm and smashed through a window. The stained glass that had once stood above the altar was gone, leaving the interior completely exposed to the elements, along with the many holes in the roof. It was no longer a holy place but a shrine to decay and abandonment.

He peered through a muddy side window. Three men surrounded a kneeling, handcuffed man. The prisoner stared at the ground, his face pale and his expression haunted. The men wore casual outfits like anyone he might see on the street—not that he expected them to wear official terrorist uniforms, no matter how convenient it might be.

What the hell is going on?

The agent moved to the side and deactivated the chameleon ball since he had no idea how it might interfere with the other toys he wanted to use. He needed to remember to ask Nessie about that.

Daniel reached into his pocket and pulled out a thick black listening glove and a normal earbud. He put both on and waited for them to sync.

This glove didn't work so well last time I needed it. Let's see how it does now.

He pressed his fingers against the wall and slowed his breathing.

"We have to do this for the cause," a quiet voice stated through his earbud. "I know it might be hard to appreciate that such sacrifices are necessary, but you have to think of the enormity of what we can save."

The kneeling man shook his head. "You're insane. I never agreed to this. That woman only said I should stop by to talk to someone about signing a provincial anti-magic petition, something about getting a law passed to restrict public magic use. You know, to protect the children."

"Yes, we will protect the children. We will use the tools of these new invaders to do just that. It's merely that we have to refine the tools first for them to be effective, and that requires tests, particularly on living subjects."

"Can't you use animals or something?" the other man whimpered. "Come on. I just bought a new car the other day. I've barely driven it."

"No. We need to see its effects on all manner of thinking beings. We're sorry, but know that what you sacrifice today is in service to a humanity free from the oppression of magic. You don't die a victim, but a martyr to the greatest cause our world has ever known."

"This is bullshit," the kneeling man yelled, his eyes pleading. "You have to let me go. Please, I'm begging you. I won't tell anyone. I'll forget completely about you and pretend this was all a bad dream."

Daniel hissed as the earbud screeched in his ear. He yanked it out and shook his head, trying to ignore the buzzing. He looked up as he realized there was a bigger problem.

A swirling vortex floated in the center of the church. The three terrorists held small glowing leaves in the air. Tendrils of energy connected the leaves to the center of the portal.

The agent took a deep breath. His orders were to observe and not engage. It took him about two seconds to disregard them.

Shit. Screw collecting intel. They've got the damned thing right there. Well, things. I won't let them kill someone and run off.

Daniel sprinted around the corner to the front door. He kicked the rotting wood off its hinges and charged in with his gun out.

The terrorists snapped their heads his direction.

"Thank God." The kneeling man's eyes widened.

"I'm already in a really pissy mood," the agent shouted. "Drop the artifacts, put your hands above your heads, and get on the ground if you want to live. This doesn't have to get bloody, but don't try my patience."

One of the terrorists snorted. "You have a gun."

"Yeah, it's got bullets, too. They hurt when they hit you."

The other man sighed. "My point is you're not a filthy magic user."

Daniel smirked. "Says the asshole generating a magical portal."

The man shook his head. "Members of the New Veil pollute themselves to save the rest of us. Some groups obsess over the nonhumans, but the New Veil isn't speciesist. We'd accept any who came over from Oriceran if they forswore the abomination of the natural order that is magic. Are you so sure, my brother, that you are pointing your weapon at the right people? Magic subverts the natural order and makes a mockery of the expected."

"You've been killing people to test an artifact. Fuck you."

"A better future always involves difficulties. You're law enforcement of some type, yes? Are you saying you've never killed someone in the line of duty? To protect and preserve the peace?"

The CIA agent shook his head. "I don't have time for your bullshit." His gaze dropped to the man in handcuffs. "I've seen pictures, you know, of people cut in half or worse. What? You don't know how to use it right, so you're merely dumping bodies into the portal until you figure it out? You're twisted sons of bitches."

"All wars require sacrifices, and this is a war for all existence." The terrorist shook his head. "Would you wait until nothing makes sense? Until we live in a pseudo-virtual world and not reality? That is the real insanity, not what we do."

Daniel gave him a hungry grin. "Last chance, asshole. Deactivate the artifact and surrender. The only reason I haven't shot you already is that I'm sure a couple of nice friends of mine have a few questions for you and all your little terrorist buddies."

The victim watched, trembling in silence.

The group exchanged glances and nodded.

That's either very good or very bad.

All three men turned in unison. The portal soared through the church, slicing through the dusty pews on a direct path to Daniel.

Okay, very bad. A portal that can move.

He jumped to the side, the deadly magic missing him by a few inches, and fired at the first terrorist. Several birds in the rafters launched into flight and headed for the holes in the roof, the earlier destruction of the door apparently not frightening enough. The bullet vanished, then emerged from the gateway to strike the wall right behind him.

"Oh, that's just fucking perfect," the agent moaned. "Betting you assholes already knew about that."

Two quick shots at the other two terrorists ended with a bullet flying out of the magic aperture and missing Daniel's head by inches.

Yeah, this is suboptimal. Not fun.

His enemies continued to turn, guiding their deadly magic. The portal missed him again and cut into a wall near the front of the building. After a few seconds, it backed up but took a few seconds to get up to speed. The agent's constant movement saved him again as the swirling vortex of death zoomed by him.

These guys should stop worrying about teleporting with the thing and just use it to cut buildings up.

Sweat poured down their faces as they continued to move their arms and carve through the interior of the church with their magic. Daniel dodged and jumped out of the way. The portal's movements were slowing, and the men's breathing grew more ragged.

The agent holstered his pistol and concentrated on jumping, leaping, and vaulting between pews to avoid being chopped into pieces.

I need to figure out a solution. A grenade will only come out the other end. An EMP wouldn't do anything against a magical artifact. Damn. What can I do? If I try to hit them, it'll just— Wait a second. Maybe...just maybe...

He spun and fired several times into the vortex as it flew right at him. Then, he dropped to the ground, hissing at the searing pain as the portal sliced through his suit and into his shoulder. Daniel crawled forward, keeping his back low as the vortex hung over him.

His heart thundered and his shoulder throbbed as he jumped to his feet and spun toward the terrorists. They all lay on the ground, bleeding from multiple chest wounds. Shaking, they kept a grip on the glowing leaves, but the portal had stopped moving.

"Here's a little experiment for you, assholes."

He aimed at the gateway and emptied his clip. The terrorists jerked with the impacts, their hands opening and the leaves sliding out. The portal vanished.

Daniel ejected his magazine and slipped it into his

pocket. No reason to leave the locals any additional evidence linking the deaths to him. The shell casings were generic enough that it wouldn't matter as long as they didn't have his gun. He reloaded his pistol and holstered it before pulling out a small static-free bag. Time to worry about his original mission.

I can't imagine they'll bitch that much that I collected the artifact. Well, artifacts.

The handcuffed man looked with wide eyes from the dead men to Daniel. "Thank you for saving me, but who the hell are you?"

"Think of me as a very pissed off Mountie." The agent grabbed the leaves and slipped them into the bag. He slid the bag in his pocket and pulled out a small autoinjector.

"What's that?"

He smiled. "Just a little something to calm you down. You've been through a traumatic experience. I'll contact the local authorities to come and pick you up, and I don't think it'd be nice to make you sit here with a bunch of dead guys."

The man blinked. "Why not take me with you?"

"Oh, that would bring up more questions, ones I don't want to answer. Like who I am."

The prisoner furrowed his brow. "I thought you said you were with the RCMP."

Daniel shook his head. "Okay, yeah, go with that when they ask you." He pulled the cap off the autoinjector. "The other thing about this drug is that it destroys the last few hours of memories. The locals won't be able to question you about the New Veil guys, but it doesn't really matter since I killed them and took their artifacts. Or maybe you'll only remember being asked about signing their petition." He frowned. "It's almost a shame. Don't want you to get mixed up with them again, but then again, being found by the cops around a bunch of New Veil guys will probably get the message across."

He placed the injector against the man's neck.

"Great. Of course." The man groaned. "It's been a real shitty week."

The agent shrugged. "At least you won't remember the last few hours."

"Doesn't help that much, but thanks anyway."

Daniel pressed the activation button and a needle shot out with a click. The man winced and took several deep breaths, not saying anything. Thirty seconds later, his eyes rolled toward the back of his head, and he fell to the ground unconscious, drool leaking from his mouth.

The agent patted the pocket containing the bag. "Okay, so I went a little above and beyond the call, but at least I got the artifact, and there are three fewer crazy terrorists in the world."

Calmly, he retrieved another autoinjector containing an analgesic and stuck it directly into his wounded shoulder.

"Damn, that was close."

The agent was halfway back to the airport when his personal phone rang. He pulled it out, surprised, and winced from the shoulder wound. It was rare that anyone called him on the phone except his grandfather, and the man had taken a short trip to Savannah to look into buying some items for the shop.

Peter was supposed to be retired, but it seemed he would never be able to hand over the reins to Daniel totally. Not a bad thing, considering how often the younger man had to be out of town.

There was also the small possibility the old man was lying to him and the trip was about some strange alien discovery, but at this point, it didn't make much sense for his grandfather to hold back.

The call wasn't from Thomas, though, but Charlie. Daniel recognized the number. It was from the burner phone he'd given him.

"Charlie?" Daniel answered.

"I know you're out of town on a buying trip, but you have to come back right away. I saw some people breaking into your shop. I tried to call the cops, but it went somewhere else, I think."

Daniel frowned. "What?"

"Yeah, I dialed 9-1-1. They asked me to report my emergency. I said Rooney's Antiquities was getting broken into, and they told me if I didn't want to end up with my throat slit, I'd better mind my own damned business." The store owner sighed. "Shit. This is my fault."

"How the hell is this your fault?"

"That guy you beat up the other day in my store. He probably did it. Him and some buddies."

Daniel had his doubts about whether that kind of scumbag or his crew would be able to intercept a cell phone call, but he also had to admit it wasn't impossible.

"Don't worry about it. You called me, and I'll be back in

town in a few hours. On my way to the airport now, and it turns out I only had to go to Canada instead of the Netherlands. Don't go anywhere near the shop and don't call anybody else. Okay?"

"Okay. I'm sorry, Daniel."

The agent chuckled. "The only people who should be sorry are the ones who broke into my store."

CHAPTER TWENTY-FIVE

With a heavy sigh, Daniel shook his head. He'd circled the building, and although everything else looked untouched, the back door of the shop was wide open.

The break-in lacked subtlety. Someone had shot through the lock. He slipped his gloves on, pulled the door open, and stepped inside.

If those muggers noticed where we came from, they might have been able to call somebody from jail. Revenge for getting involved in this business, maybe.

A few dirty footprints marred the floor, but there wasn't any damage and no additional signs of gunshots.

It didn't make sense. If someone had broken into the shop for revenge they would have trashed everything in sight, especially if they had a gun. If the break-in wasn't for revenge, then the next most likely motivation was robbery. A shop like his had more than a few valuable items, even if many people in the neighborhood didn't realize that.

He opened the door to a storage room near the back and peeked inside. Nothing was missing or out of order. He frowned. Everything felt wrong.

If they'd shot the lock someone would have heard, unless they had weapons they could use that no one could hear. A commercial silencer would still be pretty loud. Plus, the alarm would have gone off. Even if they had black market jammers, it wouldn't be enough to beat some of the physical lines powered by the battery backups.

This wasn't some random punks from the neighborhood. Whoever did this was a professional with expensive gear.

Daniel's stomach tightened as he walked to the main shop floor. A hint of suspicion about the culprits was forming in his mind, and he didn't like where it led him.

Most people would have been happy with what he spotted on the main shop floor. All the objects and minor artifacts were still there. Nothing lay on the ground. No shelves were damaged or knocked over. Someone had gone to the trouble of breaking into his home in a very obvious manner, then did absolutely no damage and stole nothing from his shop.

Maybe they were looking for something—something they knew would be hidden.

He hurried up to the apartment and checked all the rooms quickly. His grandfather's room was untouched. Not only was there no obvious damage or trespassing, but the apartment door had been locked.

Damn it. They couldn't have found it, could they?

One final but serious possibility remained.

His heart pounding, Daniel rushed into the basement and over to the wall concealing the vault. He placed his hand near the hidden trigger and waited for the hum and the wall to slide down. Quickly, he entered the code and pressed his thumb against the DNA scanner, his heart pounding the entire time. After a turn of the wheel, he pulled the door open and flipped the lights on inside. His shoulder sent out a sharp jolt of pain, making him grimace.

If they got the gun, we're fucked. They'll be coming back for us too, now they know the kind of things we're hiding in here.

"What the hell?" The agent looked back and forth among the racks. Not a single speck of dust seemed to be out of place. The Munich gun still lay exactly where he'd placed it, along with several of the more dangerous artifacts that they couldn't exactly stick upstairs for casual sale.

He stepped out of the vault, closed it, and entered a few commands into the keypad to bring a false wall into place.

With a frown, Daniel walked up the basement stairs. Someone had managed to enter his shop without tripping the alarm. They had taken nothing and disturbed nothing—a break-in with no damage and a robbery with no theft. Nothing about the situation made any sense.

The pests he'd run into lacked that kind of restraint, which suggested one strong possibility. The CIA— either the main Company or Fortis.

Why would the Company come here? Were they looking for something? Were they looking for alien tech but didn't find the vault?

Daniel stopped at the top of the basement stairs and shook his head. If revenge or robbery weren't the motives, one other possibility remained—intimidation. Maybe it was a warning to keep his nose out of alien business.

He snorted, half-convinced that explained everything.

You assholes should have put more effort into reading my psychological profile. I don't take kindly to threats.

Tommy whistled as he strolled down the street. His dad had laid off him for the last few days about being a musician, and even school hadn't been all that bad. It was like his luck had turned around all at once. Life was actually approaching bearable, and it'd been a long time since he'd felt that way.

His mom might still be MIA, but he could deal with things as long as his dad wasn't a total dick and he had someone like Daniel in his corner. The man helped remind the half-elf that things wouldn't always be rough, if he could only stick it out.

Too bad he's not my dad. Can choose your friends, but not your family. How fair is that?

The boy sighed and shook his head.

"Yo, kid," a deep voice called from behind him.

The teen turned. Four rough-looking men stood there, decked out in tacky shirts and gold chains. He didn't recognize them from around the neighborhood.

Thought so, universe. Can't have Tommy happy for a few minutes without messing with him. Totally fair. Yeah.

"What's up, dude?" he asked, keeping his tone polite. No reason to piss the men off. The sneers on their faces told him they were looking for trouble. He'd probably just been the first unlucky bastard to run into them.

One of the men stepped forward. "You're Tommy, right?"

"Who's asking?" He frowned.

Who the hell are these guys?

The stranger chuckled. "*I'm* asking, you little half-Ori bitch. Are you Tommy?" He punctuated each syllable of the last sentence by punching his palm.

The boy sighed. If they wanted to find someone with Oriceran blood to beat up, there were plenty of neighborhoods where fullbloods were a lot more common. Maybe they'd asked if there were any Oricerans in the neighborhood, and someone pointed them his way.

Screw this. I'm out of here.

Tommy turned and started walking away. Sometimes he could end these types of encounters simply by not giving the bastards the fear they wanted. He'd been bullied his entire life in school. These men were merely the latest, albeit a little larger than his normal bullies.

The thugs rushed to surround him on all sides.

He looked between them. "Come on!"

The man who had spoken before raised a finger and wagged it. "Who said you could leave, Tommy? I don't think I did, and I haven't heard shit out of any of these guys that sounded like they did, either."

"Look, dude. I don't have shit on me. If this is about money, there are way richer people than me. Even the bums around here are richer than me. I'm nothing. I'm not worth it."

"Good that you know your place, bitch." The thug laughed. He leaned forward and gave the boy a feral grin.

"But, you know, I promised my boys a little something, so it's not like I can let you go. Some things are more important than money. Like pride. Not that a bitch like you has any."

Tommy reached into his pocket and pulled out his wallet. He yanked out the small amount of cash and handed it over. "You guys look pretty tough. Why aren't you mugging some business jerk? They'd at least have an expensive watch or something."

The man slapped the wallet and money out of the boy's hand. "I ain't said nothing about wanting cash, you little half-Ori bitch. Now I'm insulted. I just told you how this was about pride. Now I feel like maybe you're trying to pick a fight with me."

"I'm sorry, sir."

Maybe appealing again to their sense of superiority would work.

The aggressor's lips curled back into a sneer. "If you're so sorry, then maybe you should get down and lick my boots to prove it."

The half-elf blinked and stared at the man. "What the hell is wrong with you, dude? Lick your shoes?"

"You hear that, guys? This little half-Ori bitch thinks he's better than me." The thug shook out his hands. "I've been really nice here, and you had to go and insult me. Like I said, a matter of pride. If I walk away now, then I'll be the bitch, not you, and I can't have that."

Should I yell for someone? Damn it. No one's around. I just have to get away, but how? Wait. That might work.

Swallowing, the boy reached into his pocket to pull out the web cube. The thug sucker punched him in the stomach.

Tommy fell to his knees, gasping and holding his stomach. It was hard not to throw up.

"Leave me alone," he wheezed.

The man slammed a fist into his face. The half-elf sprawled to the ground, his face throbbing.

His attacker laughed. "You trying to stab me, bitch? Is that what you think you can do? This ain't your planet, bitch. Humans rule here. You should be glad we didn't drop nukes on your asses the minute you showed up with your hocus-pocus bullshit."

The teen wiped blood off his mouth. "I was born on Earth, in this city, in this neighborhood. I deserve to be here as much as you."

"Now you're talking back." The man kicked him hard in the side. "This ain't fucking Oriceran. You don't run shit here, elf boy."

"Screw you."

"Why don't you show us some magic, elf boy? Ain't you gonna curse us?" The man kicked Tommy again.

The boy gritted his teeth. The last thing he wanted to do was give them the satisfaction of hearing him cry out. He closed his eyes.

They took turns kicking and punching him, laughing the entire time. He curled into a ball. His jaw clenched as pain spiked through every part of his body. He wasn't sure how long they continued attacking him, but it felt like an eternity before the blows finally stopped.

His body and limbs throbbed, but he dared to open his eyes. The main thug crouched right in front of him, his gun pointed at Tommy's head.

"So, I'm thinking, maybe some of those crazies got it

right. You know Humanity Defense League, New Veil—all them fuckers. They say they're all violent and shit, but being violent don't mean you're wrong." The man shrugged and tapped his gun against his knee. "We don't need no more people on this planet, and you fuckers come here and flash your little magical dicks around like you own us. I don't get it." He looked at his friends. "Do any of you get it?"

They all grinned and shrugged.

"See, they don't get it. Why should we have to give everything up because magic came back? What kind of bullshit is that? Can you tell me that, elf boy?"

Tommy shook his head, tears streaming from his eyes. "I want to study robots, not magic." He managed to pull out the web cube, his hand shaking. "Technology. That's as human as possible."

The man stood with a grin and kicked the cube out of Tommy's hand, then marched over to the cube and stomped it with a boot until nothing remained but a black pile of broken plastic, metal, and goo.

"My webs," the teen whimpered. "You broke it. You—"

He pointed the gun at the boy again. "I could fucking waste your ass right here, and nobody could do nothing about it. That's real power. You understand that? Not some fake bullshit."

What would Daniel do?

The boy's eyes widened, but he didn't look away. If he was going to die here, he wanted the assholes to see him defying them to the end.

His tormentor laughed. "Oh, yeah. I like that look." He kept the gun pointed at his victim's head for several long seconds before tucking it into his waistband. "Nah. You feel free to tell everyone in this neighborhood how we beat your ass down and how they shouldn't fuck with us. We're moving in now, and anyone who gets in our way is gonna fucking die. Make sure that bitch who everyone calls the mayor hears it, too."

He spat on Tommy's face and turned to walk away. The other men fell in behind him, chuckling and high-fiving each other.

"You might want to get scarce soon, half-Ori," the man shouted as he walked away. "Next time, maybe my finger slips on the trigger."

Peter frowned and crossed his arms. He'd returned early from his trip. "You're overthinking it. Maybe it was some local punks who got scared, or they broke in and realized they were in the wrong shop."

Daniel shook his head. "Come on! Local punks who knew enough to get around the alarm and intercept a phone call? If they had those kinds of skills, they wouldn't be doing random break-ins. It must be the Company. Maybe they don't have direct evidence on me like they did Ronni or Buckley."

"You going to give up now? Those spooks spooked you, did they?"

Daniel frowned. "What if they decide to come after you like they did Buckley?"

His grandfather snorted. "Then I'll make sure I take at least a couple of those bastards with me. I raised you. I'm an old man, and if it's my time, it's my time. Don't worry about me. You worry about doing the right thing and take care of that shoulder. Yes, I noticed. You're not an action figure, you know. Go out and save the world without losing your integrity. That's the way your parents raised you, and that's the way I raised you." He crossed his arms. "I'd rather die than run off with my tail between my legs because they broke into the shop. The question is, what about you?"

The agent nodded. "You're right. I'm less scared than pissed off. First the assholes lie to me about my parents, and now they're fucking around in my shop like they own the place."

The old man grinned. "Good. Don't ever forget who you are, Daniel. Even if you weren't in the CIA, you'd be special. Those idiots should have picked a different man to mess with."

I'm tired of them. Ronni. My parents. Buckley. They can't simply push around anyone they want to. No. Pops is right. I already drew the line, and they stepped over it.

As the front door moved, Daniel snatched up his silence cube and slipped it into his pocket. No CIA agent, thug, or terrorist stepped through the door, only a young half-elf, much like he did most mornings.

The agent looked up, expecting to see Tommy with his coffee like every other morning, His breath caught when he saw that the boy's battered face was covered in bruises, and he was limping. One of his arms was pinned to his side, and the half-elf kept it bent. It looked broken.

"What the hell happened to you?"

The teen held up the Green Lantern mug. "What are

you talking about, dude? Nothing happened to me. I was a little late. So sue me."

Daniel sucked in a deep breath, trying to quell the rage that was threatening to spiral out of control.

Did his father do this to him? If so, we'll have a very short and painful conversation.

"I don't care that you're late. I care what you look like. Something obviously happened. You're beaten to hell." Daniel grabbed the mug and set it on the counter, then walked over to Tommy and grabbed his bent arm. "Straighten it."

The boy shrugged. "I can do it." He gritted his teeth as he straightened his arm, his entire body shaking. "S-see. F-fine."

"And I repeat, what the hell happened to you? Who did this to you? *Tell me right now.*" He glared past the boy at the door as if he could teleport the culprits to him by sheer force of will.

Peter shook his head. "Maybe you shouldn't get involved, Daniel. Call the police and let them handle it. You have a lot of other problems to worry about right now."

His grandson shook his head, and the old man looked down, pressing his lips together. The legal system wasn't bad, but it was damned slow, and it wasn't like every cop cared what happened to Oricerans or half-Oricerans.

No. Daniel protected the country, but he also protected the neighborhood. He wouldn't let people beat a boy black and blue on his watch.

Tommy sighed. "Look, it's embarrassing. I fell on the stairs playing with the cube, you know. Not a big deal. You're wrong. No one kicked my ass. I kicked my own ass."

The agent took a deep breath and managed to keep his face from contorting in rage. "Just answer me one question, Tommy. Did your father do this to you?"

"Dad? What? No!" Disbelief mixed with anger in the boy's eyes. "He's annoying as hell, but he's never hit me."

Daniel nodded slowly. The half-elf lacked the experience to lie convincingly.

"You didn't fall. Trust me, I've seen enough people beaten up to recognize it." He gestured toward the bruises on the boy's face. "You can even see some of the tread pattern from the shoes in the bruising. Who did this, Tommy? Tell me. You know I can handle myself around tough guys. You've seen it."

The teen swallowed. "Y-you shouldn't mess with these guys, Daniel. This wasn't just some asshole who wanted my wallet. These guys are seriously bad news. New gang, I think. I'm just going to stay out of their way. I think you should, too, or they might bust up your shop…or they might kill you." He shuddered.

The damned pests again. I've given them two warnings. That's more than some people get. Time to find the nest and fumigate.

Daniel nodded quickly at the boy. "Yeah, you're probably right." He pulled out several large bills and handed them over. "You should go see the doctor, though. Make sure nothing's broken."

Tommy blinked at the money. "You sure you want to give this to me? This is a lot of money."

"Yeah. Like I said, go to the doctor. You won't be able to be a hero if you were crippled as a kid."

The teen managed a laugh. “I could make power armor or an exoskeleton.”

“Touché, but get to the doctor already, Tony Stark.”

The half-elf smiled brightly, then winced. “Thanks, dude. I think I’ll head home now.”

“You want me to walk with you?”

He shook his head and motioned toward Daniel’s suit. “You’re all dressed up. Doesn’t that mean you have to go meet someone about buying something for the shop?” He held up the money. “You’re already helping me out.”

Peter released a long sigh. “He’s right. I’ll help him get home, Daniel. You better get going to your meeting.” He gave his grandson a long meaningful look.

Is that you telling me to stay out of trouble? Come on, Pops, you know that won’t happen. You’re one of the people who taught me to stand up for the little guy.

Peter placed his arm gingerly around Tommy’s shoulder. “You want a Fresca?” The boy tried to smile and shook his head. They stepped out the door and Daniel’s calm mask disappeared, replaced by anger.

“Guess it’s time to teach a few assholes a very, very painful lesson.”

CHAPTER TWENTY-SIX

Thirty minutes later he sat in the private garage housing his Jaguar, a burner phone to his ear. No reason to give the Company or anyone else any links between him and the crime scene he was about to create.

The man on the other end laughed. "Old Town gangs? Since when did you care about petty shit like that, Daniel? What? Did you get fired, and now you've taken up bounty hunting or some shit?"

Daniel chuckled. "No, I'm still gainfully employed. I'm merely a man of varied interests. Now, can you just answer the damned question? I already gave you a nice little deposit upfront based on your reputation alone. I'd hate to be disappointed and have to leave a negative review on your little site on the dark web. I can see it now. One out of five stars—talks a big game but can't deliver anything you wouldn't hear from a corner grocer as you buy your bananas."

The man snorted. "That shit hurts, you know. People

take reviews seriously when it comes to less-than-above-board jobs." He took a deep breath and exhaled slowly. "Calm down. I know what you need. I'm merely surprised, is all. These guys are all human. No Oris, or artifacts, or any shit like that."

"Good. Then they'll be easy to handle."

"I wouldn't say that. They call themselves the Steel Wolves. Used to be a decent-sized gang in Baltimore, but they started some shit with an Ori gang, and it didn't end well. Lost most of their guys and kind of disappeared until rumors of them hitting the DC area started popping up. Why do you care? Did they see some shit they shouldn't see? Stumble on an artifact or something? Not that I care what you do to them. I'm curious, is all."

Daniel grunted. "You don't need to know."

The man laughed. "How did I know you were going to say that? You spooks are all the same."

"Yeah, we are, but you said most of their gang was wiped out already?"

"Yeah, a little over thirty guys survived, I heard. It was a bloodbath. They learned firsthand how a good gun don't always work against magic. Some people are still adjusting to the brave new world, even if it isn't that brave anymore."

Only thirty guys to begin with, and several of them are in jail or the hospital already. I like my odds here.

"How do they plan to take over a new neighborhood with only thirty guys?" Daniel wondered. "Especially given the street situation around here."

His source laughed. "Well, word on the street is there's not much of a gang presence in the neighborhood they're looking at. The street abhors a vacuum as much as nature, you know. They've been asking around about this local hero everyone calls the mayor. A vigilante or some shit. I think they figure if they kick the ass of the local hero, everyone else will know to stay out of their way."

The agent smirked. Apparently, his informant didn't know everything.

"Okay. Do these Steel Wolves have a local base or something like that?"

"Yeah, they've got a house they're renting in DC until they take over their new neighborhood." The informant rattled off the address. "If you're planning to go talk to these guys, bring lots of cash. You won't be able to appeal to their better natures. They are pretty vicious, and into the full package of rape, murder, and assault. The only reason they got away with shit for as long as they did was that they bribed a lot of local cops. But from what I've heard, people were actually grateful that the other gang all but wasted their asses. Threw 'em a block party, I hear."

Daniel chuckled with dark humor. "Okay, I think I've got what I need. I'll send the rest of the payment in a few minutes."

"Thanks. I always like making easy money."

The agent stared out his window with a frown. His initial suspicions about the pests had been confirmed. They were thugs without deep ties to any stronger organizations. The fact that they thought his neighborhood was ripe for invasion because of the lack of other gangs proved how shortsighted they were, and now they would pay for that mistake.

You should have done a little more recon, assholes, before you decided to start kicking people around.

The memory of Tommy's battered face lingered in his mind. Daniel realized the boy was lucky to be alive. The gang might not be so nice the next time they ran into the half-elf.

I tried to be nice about this. I really did try, but they had to break my rules repeatedly. When you break the rules, you have to be punished. That's simply the way things are.

Daniel started his car. He had a meeting to attend at the CIA, but his afternoon was clear. There was plenty of time for a little meet and greet with the Steel Wolves. Maybe he'd pick a few toys up before that. Nessie probably wouldn't mind a loan. He could chalk it up to field testing.

Sloppy. That was all the agent could think as he watched the Steel Wolves' hideout. Everything about them from their exterior security to their cars was sloppy. Even if he didn't live in Old Town he doubted they could take it over, but that didn't mean they couldn't hurt a lot of innocent people in the process.

You were arrogant before, and you lost most of your gang. You were arrogant again, and now you'll lose the rest.

He'd had the house under surveillance for several hours when a thug came over to his currently white Jaguar and knocked on his window. Daniel had expected this for a while. It wasn't like he was hiding, and his fancy car didn't exactly blend in with the local vehicles.

Calmly, he rolled down the window. "Can I help you?"

The man's gaze roamed the car. "Yeah, nice car. Haven't seen you around here before, but you're waiting out here.

Why were you waiting, bitch? You a cop? Because we ain't done nothing illegal, and you can't prove shit." He grinned. "And I wouldn't try to arrest nobody by yourself if you know what's good for you."

These guys are bold. Stupid, but bold.

"No. Not a cop, so no arrests." Daniel shrugged. "And I'm not waiting out here. I'm counting."

The thug frowned. "Counting?"

The agent turned off the thermal scanning mode of his borrowed AR glasses. He'd confirmed over two dozen men inside. That had to be the bulk of the gang, given their prior losses.

He shrugged. "Yeah, I wanted to see how many of you guys were in there before I decided how I would approach you. Your whole gang in there?"

The man frowned. "Who the fuck are you, bitch?"

Daniel almost snorted. If he had good tactical awareness, he would have approached the vehicle with his weapon already out. If he had piss-poor skills, he would have pulled it by this point. Instead, he blustered. Arrogance was a weak weapon in a firefight. Being cocky didn't save you from a bullet.

I should take you out right now to make a point, but I've got a plan. You're stupid, and I'll use that.

He shrugged. "I'm the man who has a proposition and a lot of money to offer the Steel Wolves. I've heard you get things done, and I need men like that. Tough men who know their way around. The people I work for sometimes need street operatives to handle certain matters of violence, and...shall we say...independent pharmaceutical distribution, we'll call it."

"Huh? Independent what?"

Daniel rolled his eyes. "Drug dealing."

It took all his self-control not to add the word idiot to the end of the sentence.

"Oh, yeah. Need some street slingers? We're down with that." The man's eyes gleamed with greed. "Nice fucking car, nice suit, in the know. You're connected?"

He nodded. This was almost too easy.

They say you can't con an honest man. If he wants to think I'm Mafia, that'll make this even easier.

The thug gestured toward the house. "Yeah, the whole gang's in there. We got a few guys in the slam, but don't worry. They know how to keep their mouths shut. If you need them to do anything for you while they're in there, we can arrange that, too."

Daniel stepped out of the car and slipped on some gloves. No point leaving fingerprints to complicate his life later. "Loyalty's a good quality in any organization. I'm glad to see you already have that. I knew I made a good choice in approaching you."

"Yeah, no bitches or snitches in the Steel Wolves." He slammed a fist into his palm. "You give us a little of your sweet Mafia cash, and we'll do whatever you need. We're pushing into Old Town Alexandria right now. Nice neighborhood, just aching for a little more presence, you know? We could do good things there with dealing if you're supplying us. Or if you need us to lean on people as part of collecting protection money, we can do that, too."

The agent forced a smile. "Glad to hear you're so industrious."

His companion bobbed his head. "Yeah, yeah, we're fucking geniuses, you know?"

The man opened the door and stepped inside. Daniel followed him and reached into his pocket to activate a broad-spectrum frequency jammer. He didn't want anyone calling for help when the pain began.

A dozen men sat in the living room around two tables. They were drinking beer and playing cards. Light chatter filled the room, and most people barely spared a glance Daniel's way.

The thug from the grocery store sat at one of the tables. He looked up, and his eyes widened. Panic crossed his face.

"That's the guy from the store!" he shouted.

Silence swept the room, and everyone looked at the front door.

The agent sighed. So much for this being a complete surprise. It didn't matter. He still wanted to give them one last chance.

"Who's in charge of the Steel Wolves?" he asked.

A wiry man with scars covering his face stood from one of the tables. "I'm T.E. I run things. Now, who the fuck are you, and why shouldn't I cap your ass?" His deep voice didn't fit his small stature.

Daniel held up a finger. "Shaking down a grocery store." Another finger went up. "Mugging a store owner and his daughter." Another finger. "Attempted arson." A fourth finger. "And beating the shit out of a random teenager. The last was just petty bullshit." He shook his head. "It's hard to overlook that, you know?"

T.E. shrugged and looked around. "This bitch doesn't seem to like what we've done. What do you say to that, boys? Maybe we all get on our hands and knees and beg his forgiveness."

The assembled gang members laughed and hooted.

The agent shook his head. "Just wanted to check. Hey, is your entire gang here? From what I could tell they were, but I wanted to make sure."

"Why? You scared, bitch?" T.E. smirked. "Yeah. I was talking with my boys earlier about what we would do if we got our hands on the asshole who has been fucking with our guys, and I'm guessing that's you, Mr. Slick Suit. Let me guess—you're the asshole they call the mayor."

"Some people call me that, sure."

The thug who brought Daniel in closed and locked the door.

T.E. nodded and rubbed his chin. "What, you think you're some sort of superhero? That you can sweep in and save the day from the big bad wolves wandering in to eat the sheep? Real life don't work like that, bitch."

Daniel narrowed his eyes, remembering Buckley's boat and his speech about becoming a wolf.

"No. You've got it all wrong, T.E."

"How's that?"

He allowed himself a feral grin. "You're not the big bad wolf. I am."

The gang leader shook his head and laughed. "You probably thought you could come in here and challenge me one-on-one or some bullshit like you've seen in a movie, but it ain't gonna go down like that." He gestured around. "Gangs are strong because we work together."

The agent chuckled. "Now, that's not very fair."

"Too fucking bad for you." T.E. pointed at Daniel. "This

fucker has the balls to walk right in here after everything he's done. I admire that, but the Steel Wolves can't have some fucker thinking he can hurt our guys and get away with it, can we? If we don't make an example, people will say we're pussies. What do you say to that, boys? Should we let him go?"

"Fuck that," the men shouted in unison.

Daniel took a few deep breaths, and his heart rate kicked up, not from fear but from anticipation.

No one can say I didn't try to be reasonable, and you really, really should have left Tommy alone.

T.E. pointed to the thug near the door. "Jay, grab him. We're gonna make this last nice and long. He'll be begging us to put a bullet in his head by the time we're done."

Jay reached for Daniel. The agent grabbed his arm and pinned it behind his back in one fluid motion.

"Too damned slow." He spat the words. "Your gang is sloppy and filled with idiots with no discipline. No wonder so many of you died in Baltimore."

The group glared at him.

T.E. shook his head. "You ain't getting out of here alive, bitch. We're gonna carve you up like a Thanksgiving turkey."

"Funny," Daniel replied. "I was about to say the same thing to you. Okay, maybe not that exact simile." He snapped Jay's neck and let the body drop to the ground.

Let's do this shit.

The gang members' confusion and rage took a few too many seconds to kick in. The agent already had a flashbang hurtling toward the center of the room by the time they went for their guns.

Seconds later, blinded men jerked their arms around, their guns in hand but their blurry vision denying them a clear shot.

Heavy footsteps sounded upstairs.

Daniel whipped out his pistol, ignored the throbbing ache from his shoulder, and methodically put a single round into the chest of man after man until he ran out. Their cries and the thuds of their bodies as they hit the ground formed a song of death, but he didn't let it distract him.

He rushed forward and snatched a gun from a blinded man, shot him with his own weapon, then used his body as a shield and put rounds into the gang members coming down the stairs. Their bodies rolled down to form a pile of dead men.

The agent dropped the body and reloaded his own gun then stepped over the tangle of limbs and bodies and stalked slowly upstairs. Calm and quiet, he stopped before he reached the top and listened for a moment. His count told him he hadn't killed everyone yet, and he could hear heavy breathing right around the corner.

Finally, someone with a little tactical discipline.

Daniel pulled a sonic grenade out and bounced it off the top of the wall after priming it.

"What the fuck?" someone to the right yelled as a high-pitched whine sounded. Several men thudded to the floor.

He immediately crested the stairs. Several men lay groaning on the floor. He fired two bullets into each man before ejecting his magazine and reloading.

The agent performed a quick mental count. Between the men he'd killed coming up the stairs, on the top floor, and in the living room, there should have been only a couple of gang members left. It was time for a little hunting.

Daniel made his way down the hall to two closed doors and reactivated his thermal scan. He looked around, including down, trying to distinguish any new thermal signatures. Killing a man might only take seconds, but it took the dead body a while to cool down.

One man crouched in a room at the end of the hall, and there was another in the room just to his left.

He aimed through the door to his left and squeezed off several shots. The man jerked with each hit before collapsing. The agent turned off the thermal scan and kicked the door open to check on the body. Lifeless eyes stared at the ceiling.

Daniel shook his head. "I gave you assholes so many warnings, but you didn't fucking listen. It's like you wanted me to come and do this."

The thud of boots on wood caught his attention and he jumped into the hall with his gun raised, only to be bowled into by a charging thug. His gun flew out of his hand and hit the stairs, bouncing toward the first floor.

He landed hard on his back. The man on top of him got in a few good punches.

"You're fucking dead, you sonofabitch," the criminal roared. "Without your gun, you're just a fucker waiting to die."

More powerful blows hammered down on Daniel, his head bouncing with each one.

The agent flicked his wrist and slapped the back of his

watch against the ground. A needle popped out. He stabbed it into the thug's neck.

"I'm never unarmed," he explained carelessly.

The man hissed and rolled off Daniel. He rubbed the wound and pulled a gun from his waistband. A few seconds later, the gun dropped from his hands. His eyes moved, but the rest of his body was rigid.

Daniel stood and looked down at his suit with a sigh. "Bloodstains are very hard to get out, you know." He marched over to the downed man and picked up the gun. "Single-use paralytic agent. The injector's not always reliable." He shrugged and shot the man between the eyes, then dropped the weapon on top of the body.

That should be all the ones I saw, and even if they still have guys left, they're done as a gang.

Shit. I'll need some good makeup to cover the bruises.

He headed down the stairs, plucked his gun up, and made his way over to the body of the first thug he'd encountered, the man from the grocery store.

The criminal wasn't dead. He coughed up blood as he stared up at Daniel with terror in his eyes.

The agent sighed and shook his head. "Okay, I didn't think I needed to spell it out, but here goes. No dogs, no family, no kids." He put three rounds into the man to finish him off.

His job complete, he holstered his gun and ran a hand through his hair before grabbing his second phone. It was time to call Lydia at Purity Solutions for a little cleanup.

Going all-out against criminal trash didn't risk his cover, especially since there was no one left alive to tie him to their disappearance. Lydia's team would take care of all the physical evidence.

Daniel chuckled.

All these contacts I've cultivated will come in handy, especially now that I'm trying to get my new life to work.

I'm like a damned Russian doll. I've got my identity working with Tim inside another identity working for the Company inside another identity working the shop and constantly changing last names.

No problem. I should be able to make this work.

He headed toward the door and looked over his shoulder one last time at the slaughtered gang.

I really did try to warn you. It's like my friend Akito used to tell me: even Buddha gets mad after the third time.

CHAPTER TWENTY-SEVEN

Daniel adjusted his tie as he waited for Tommy. The sun was just fighting its way over the horizon, and he wasn't sure if the teen would get there on time. Juggling his schedule was one of the many unsurprising problems that came with the new job working for Tim.

Wonder how long I'll be able to keep this up, especially if the Company's already got their eye on me? Will I end up like Buckley?

He shook his head. His grandfather had been right. He couldn't let the CIA in general or Fortis in particular scare him. He'd faced danger to protect others his entire life. Multiplying the number of enemies did nothing to change that.

A few seconds later, the front door opened and Tommy stepped in with the oversized mug. His face was still battered and bruised, but a lot of the swelling had gone down.

Don't worry, Tommy. I made sure those bastards paid.

The boy set the mug on the counter. "I can't believe you asked me to wake up before the sun was even up. That's cruel and unusual punishment."

Daniel yawned. "Well, I need my fuel for the day or it's hard to get going." He picked up the coffee and gulped down some Stumptown goodness. "You feeling okay?"

"Yeah, I'm fine, dude. The doc checked me out. Said nothing was broken. Gave me some pain pills for the next few days." The half-elf glanced over his shoulder as if expecting a spy or a thug. "Then the cops showed up last night to ask me about them. I didn't call them, so I don't know why they came. Maybe the hospital did, or my dad." He shrugged. "You know what, though? The cops told me not to worry about the guys coming back."

The agent resisted a smirk. "Oh, did they now?"

"Yeah. They said they were pretty sure the guys who did it are from some gang called the Steel Wolves, but word is they apparently left town in a hurry the other day. From what the cops said, they had some trouble with some guys in Baltimore, and they might have come looking for them. They're probably halfway to Mexico by now."

Daniel snickered. "Couldn't have happened to a bigger group of assholes." He held up the mug. "Thanks for bringing my coffee, and thanks for not complaining." He pulled out twice the normal amount and handed the bills to the teen. "I've got to get going. Why don't you study here for a while and lock up when you're done?"

"What about your grandpa?"

"He's out of town."

Tommy surveyed the shop with a surprised expression. "You trust me to lock this place up?"

Daniel lifted the mug. "I trust you with my coffee. That should tell you a lot."

The elevator in the brownstone headquarters opened to the operations center. He took a few steps in before raising an eyebrow.

The same large round table was there, along with the massive screen in the back, but now several floating holographic displays ringed the table.

Ronni and Big Gnome tapped away at virtual keyboards in the air. Both looked over and waved at him. The overweight pixie zipped back and forth, chattering on a ridiculously small phone. It was as adorable as it was weird.

"Good morning," Ronni said with far too much cheer for so early in the morning.

Daniel walked to the table and set his mug down. "Malcolm didn't show me this the other day." He gestured to the holographic displays.

Big Gnome snorted. "That's because it wasn't here the other day." He grinned at Ronni, and she smiled back.

Daniel sighed. "Maybe I don't have enough coffee in me yet, but would someone like to clue me in? I'm supposed to be the operational head of our little group, after all."

The woman smiled and shrugged. "We were both working on a similar project. We thought it might be cooler if we had these holographic displays. The agency's experimented with some, but they have so many approval procedures for anything but field gear that it'll be years before they implement a system like this. We don't have to worry about the bureaucracy here, though, so we went ahead and did it."

"Wait a second. You thought it'd be cooler?" He arched an eyebrow.

"More effective, too." She shrugged again, the gesture eloquent.

Big Gnome's fingers stabbed into the light. "Still not sold on the virtual keyboards. Need to do something about the lack of haptic feedback. It's too weird otherwise."

Ronni snapped to attention. "Maybe some gloves with pushback?"

He nodded. "Maybe." He looked at Daniel. "But this isn't even the coolest part."

The agent chuckled. "Okay, what's the coolest part?"

Big Gnome entered a few quick commands and gestured grandly to the center of the table. "This is."

A three-dimensional rotating wireframe holographic display of the Earth appeared and floated above the table. Flashing dots were spread all over it.

Daniel arched an eyebrow. "Are we supposed to look for a weakness in the Death Star using this?"

His companions exchanged confused looks.

"Never mind. Philistines." He rubbed his chin. "I'm guessing these dots mark possible alien activity or artifacts?"

Ronni nodded. "Exactly."

"Looks like our operations are up and running."

The two techies exchanged huge grins.

Daniel watched the spinning globe, almost transfixed by the hypnotic quality of the display.

The *Codex of the Sky Gods.* That was what his parents had been seeking, a source of information that would lead them to a gateway to another world, and now he had his own source of information that might lead him not only to get that gateway but to his own codex.

I'll protect my neighborhood, country, and planet from all enemies foreign and domestic. Human or magical. Terrestrial or extraterrestrial.

The Daniel Codex was operational.

The End

Daniel's adventure continues in Artifact of the Sky Gods.

What's funnier than a swearing, troublemaking troll?

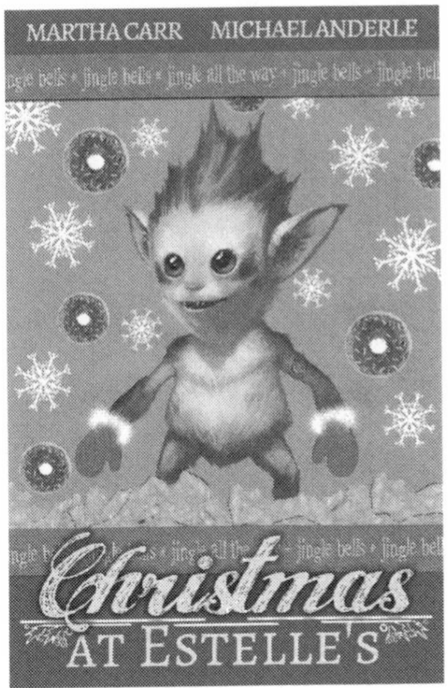

A swearing, troublemaking troll at *Christmas*.

Sign-up and keep up to date with all things Oriceran and receive a free copy of Christmas at Estelle's, a short story starring YTT. (Other people are in it, too.)

GET IT NOW!

AUTHOR NOTES - MARTHA CARR

SEPTEMBER 20, 2018

I'm sitting in a hotel room in New York City, finally taking a vacation after two years of this wonderful, wild ride. Just a weekend away, but it'll be a good one. Broadway show, seeing old friends (I used to live here) and shopping, of course. I need a break from unpacking and opening the door to someone to fix something. New house, first world problem, I know. I'm writing this looking out over W 57th Street and leaving soon to walk up Broadway past Lincoln Center. Life is good.

The Offspring is back in Austin launching his career as a music manager and things are going well. But there are times I feel like I'm watching a younger version of myself and one question keeps rolling around in my head.

What would I have wanted to know back then that would have helped? I've written about this before but new insights keep running into me. Followed by the thought that I could stand to take a lot of this good advice even now.

Biggest one is to understand that when you're starting out, you will probably be the only one who believes you can do it. You're not wrong. When I started writing my desire was stronger than my abilities. Turns out if you pair desire with willingness to learn and change, you can go pretty damn far. But, hearing everyone tell me to become a real estate agent, or Starbucks put a ding in my enthusiasm. Were they right?

Depends on how you look at the world. It took me years to become financially stable and included a corporate job along the way. Some might say I chose the harder path. I'd say I chose the only one that mattered. Back in 1990 when I was supposed to be terminal and dying I had this constant peace about how far I'd made it in life. It was okay, even though I didn't own much because I could look back at all the adventures, the words that changed people's lives, the books I wrote and I knew I was on my path. That turned out to be enough. I got that we never get to the end of the path so being on it is what counts. Remember that part.

The next part is to slow down and enjoy the ride. I didn't do enough of that all the time – worried too much about where things were going. That's the consequence of listening to all the people who have a better idea for your life and tell you in great detail. But there was the time I was signing books in Cooper Vineyard in Virginia on a beautiful day sipping chocolate wine. That was a good day.

The last one for now is that the first advice I got turned out to be true. The writers (or music agents) who succeed are the ones who hang in there and are willing to grow. Very simple and right on the money. But, if you do your best to have a good time on the journey when you get to the financial reward, which might hit when you're in your late 50's like it did for me and is still sweet, you'll still stop and appreciate all the small moments because by now, I've learned how much they matter.

Enjoy the start of this new series. It's one of my favorites right up there with Leira and that troll and we'll see what comes next. More adventures to follow.

AUTHOR NOTES - MICHAEL ANDERLE

OCTOBER 29, 2018

THANK YOU for not only reading this story, but these author notes as well .

(I think I've been good with always opening with 'thank you'... If not, I need to edit the other author notes!)

RANDOM (*sometimes*) THOUGHTS?

Since this is a book 01, I will give a very short overview of who I am in case this is the first series you've read that I have been a part of.

In November 2015, I released my first book, Death Becomes Her, and from there the Kurtherian Gambit series (and The Kurtherian Universe) was born and my life was changed in a good way forever.

Fast forward a few months (about 12) and many released stories, and I was listening to a writing podcast where those speaking were discussing what happens when your successful series ends.

What do you do *then*?

Well, that concern was stuck in my mind and I figured I would get a small series started with another Universe, so I would have something to go play in when The Kurtherian Gambit was finished.

(Joke was on me, the series and the universe is still running while all of these other stories are going strong, too.)

So, I wrote the beginning of what became The Unbelievable Mr. Brownstone. Having the idea for Oriceran and how Earth and this other Universe would behave, I reached out to another author I knew by the name of Martha Carr.

Where I was thinking a series, she heard 'universe' and *life got interesting.*

Again. (Check out the Leira Chronicles to read our first series together.)

After we closed on our Shay stories, Martha and I discussed what was next and together, we wanted to discover what was going on in the government related to aliens. Non-Oriceran aliens, specifically.

Thus, the Daniel Codex was born. I hope that you enjoy this series and our new characters!

HOW TO MARKET FOR BOOKS YOU LOVE

We are able to support our efforts with you reading our books and we appreciate you doing this!

If you enjoyed this or ANY book by any author, especially Indie published, we always appreciate if you make the time to review a book, as it lets other readers who might be on the fence to take a chance on it as well.

AROUND THE WORLD IN 80 DAYS

Tonight, I'm writing this from a Hampton Inn in West Covina, California. I'm visiting with my younger brother who is in town so we can go see Stryper (http://www.stryper.com) at the Whisky a Go Go on Halloween Night.

I have been a fan of Stryper since I was in High School (yes, that's dating me) and he and I have seen them a couple of times together. When we learned that they were on another tour, my wife looked into where they were playing. Now, I've KNOWN about the Whisky for many years, but I've never been in LA when someone was playing I wanted to see.

With Stryper playing there on Halloween night, I thought how cool would it be to cross off my desire to see a concert there with that night and this band?

Call up my younger brother and plans were set.

FAN PRICING

If you would like to find out what LMBPN is doing, and the books we are publishing, just sign up at http://lmbpn.com/email/ . When you sign up, we notify you of books coming out for the week, any new posts of interest in the books and pop culture arena and the fan pricing on Saturday.

Ad Aeternitatem,
Michael Anderle

OTHER SERIES IN THE ORICERAN UNIVERSE:

Other series in the Oriceran Universe:

THE DANIEL CODEX SERIES

I FEAR NO EVIL

THE UNBELIEVABLE MR. BROWNSTONE

SCHOOL OF NECESSARY MAGIC

THE LEIRA CHRONICLES

REWRITING JUSTICE

THE KACY CHRONICLES

MIDWEST MAGIC CHRONICLES

SOUL STONE MAGE

THE FAIRHAVEN CHRONICLES

OTHER BOOKS BY JUDITH BERENS

OTHER BOOKS BY MARTHA CARR

BOOKS BY MICHAEL ANDERLE

For a complete list of books by Michael Anderle, please visit

www.lmbpn.com/ma-books/

All LMBPN Audiobooks are Available at Audible.com and iTunes. For a complete list of audiobooks visit:

www.lmbpn.com/audible

CONNECT WITH THE AUTHORS

Martha Carr Social

Website: http://www.marthacarr.com

Facebook:
https://www.facebook.com/groups/MarthaCarrFans/

Michael Anderle Social

Website: http://lmbpn.com

Email List: http://lmbpn.com/email/

Facebook:
www.facebook.com/TheKurtherianGambitBooks

Made in the USA
Las Vegas, NV
06 December 2021